OUT *of* REACH

OUT *of* REACH

A Novel

ELIZABETH COOKE
WRITING AS ELIZABETH McGREGOR

Cover design by Kat JK Lee

ISBN: 978-1-5040-1948-4

Distributed in 2015 by Open Road Distribution
345 Hudson Street
New York, NY 10014
www.openroadmedia.com

OUT *of* REACH

PROLOGUE

*T*HE HOUSE HAS A HUNDRED THOUSAND ROOMS.

Every one empty.

She climbs wearily, up the steepening stairs, the widening treads, in the growing darkness. He is only eight weeks old, and he is somewhere high above her, out of reach. He is crying.

'Wait,' she whispers. 'Wait . . .'

This nightmare is familiar, closer to her than any friend. She knows it intimately, without dread, stepping seamlessly into its endless repetition.

Kate reaches the top at last, the breath burning in her throat. Ahead of her, the corridor reels as far as the eye can see. Dark now, even the doors have become blurred, their locks invisible.

She sees him everywhere. In the street, in houses, in landscapes, in crowds . . . even in complete isolation. Even when there is no one there, he still haunts her.

Ten years ago, she told her waking self that the search was over and that her son was dead.

But asleep . . . asleep, it is a different matter.

Asleep, each night, she searches, with blind fingertips, the endless echoing house that holds him.

ONE

$\mathscr{H}$E WENT UPSTAIRS AND LOCKED THE DOOR.

Stopping for a moment in the half-light, he looked around him, to savour his possessions.

In the attic room, sealed off from the rest of the house, the type-writers were ranged in strict rows. Exactly six inches separated each one. They were labelled with their date, manufacturer, original cost, and the amount they had cost him to buy. The date of the auction. The name of the auctioneer.

How many bid against him.

He closed his eyes, aware already of the letter he was going to write. It lived, fully formed in his head. Had done for almost a month, now. He knew the shape of every word. He knew its impact.

He remembered vividly buying the first machine, the Mignon. He walked to it now, and ran his finger along the top. It had been in a junk shop, buried in a tea chest with plates and saucepans, only the white lettered metal backplate showing. He had been young. It had cost fifty pence.

The Mignon stood in the centre of the lowest shelf; around it, others in their pristine ranks. A Corona folding, 1912. Then an Underwood. And a Sholes and Glidden, one of the earliest made. The Sholes had a decorated flap—pink roses on a brown background, and, at the side, a cameo portrait of some eighteenth-century figure in a swathed pink satin cloak. He had stood all day in an auction to get that one. It had cost him seven thousand pounds.

Some difference between fifty pence and seven thousand pounds...

The rain drummed softly on the window overhead as he sat down. It was late afternoon, and hunger made him light-headed; left a dry, stale taste in his mouth.

Looking with longing at the Mignon, he nevertheless took down a later instrument: a mass-produced Olympia. There were many like these left, even in this age of the soulless electronic keyboard.

The letters took minutes to type, even the short ones. It was not just the savouring of the words, it was the very action of the keys. He liked to hear them as they struck the sheet. A metallic sound, as irreversible as a gunshot when you pulled a trigger.

He slotted a piece of white copy paper into the roller feed.

He fingered the key, the letter I, and pressed the shift.

I KNOW...

Gunshot on the page, tearing through her, stopping her dead in her tracks.

He had to stop a second, wait for his fingers to steady. The rain hammered harder on the glass above him.

Then, he continued.

I KNOW WHERE HE IS.

TWO

*K*ATE STOOD BY THE UPSTAIRS WINDOW, watching the lane.

It was eight a.m., and the dry summer had given way to a damp autumn; the trees in the little Dorset village were turning colour. Mist hung at shoulder height, streamed across the midway point of the lane and into the fields on either side. She waited, watching that midway point, waiting for George Dale to pass through it on his way back from the village.

She looked down again at the bracelet in the palm of her hand.

It was beautiful. An Art Deco angularity. She turned from the window momentarily, looked at her room.

It was spare, and spartan in the extreme. She had made the bed, straightened and tidied and cleaned, as always, as every morning. She never slept later than six. A single bed was against the wall, a table in the centre of the room. Two chairs. A dark red rug. The telephone sat on a pile of directories, on the thin cream carpet, the coil of the lead carefully stowed behind the books, the phone positioned dead centre.

The bracelet was warm now in her grasp. She extended her hand, and held it up, at waist height, considering, biting her lip unconsciously.

She had found it as she opened the small door to her porchway at seven that morning. Lying on the mat next to the paper there had been a small, midnight-blue box, tied with a satin ribbon. There had been no card or note. Just the bracelet inside, carefully wrapped in white tissue paper.

She looked up again, thinking she saw movement under the trees.

Her flat was set on the first floor of a horseshoe of nineteenth-century buildings. When George Dale had moved here twenty years ago, he had modernised the place. He lived in the thatched house; the warehouse and the stables became the Gallery and his workshop. Kate lived in the set of rooms over, facing the house across a drive of raked gravel.

It was an odd place—misshapen, and almost pleasant in its weathered ugliness, Virginia creeper smothering the stone. The roof of the house was now linked to the second storey of the old warehouse, and the shoulder of the warehouse to the right-angled edge of the stables.

She had been right about the movement. Here came George now down the lane. His golden retriever, China, padded ahead of him, nosing the high grass of the verges.

Kate turned away, picked up her bag and file, and the gift box, into which she slipped the bracelet. Glancing up as she headed for the door, she saw herself briefly in the only mirror. Pale, with cropped blonde hair, her face without make-up, she looked young. Certainly younger than she was today, her thirtieth birthday.

A stairway led to the ground floor. Here, in the porch where she had found the box, was the door to the antiques workshops where George stored much of his furniture for the Gallery.

She opened the door to the yard.

China saw her first: she came bounding across, writhing peculiarly as her tail wagged.

'Hello,' Kate murmured, reaching down to pat her. 'Good dog. Good girl.'

George brought up the rear.

He was about sixty; well-dressed, smooth-looking. He had an air of well-fed contentment. This morning he wore a tweed jacket, flannels, a yellow waistcoat, a yellow-and-brown cravat under a white shirt. His face was rosy, almost cherubic. His hair was very curly and rather long, grey with a considerable amount of white. George always looked immaculate, as if he had been scrubbed and polished.

'Kate!' he said, smiling.

She walked towards him.

'Happy birthday,' he said. 'Over the hill now, eh?'

She stopped, so that he would not try to kiss her. Occasionally, if in a very good mood, George would kiss and cuddle her, if he could get his hands on her. She did not suppose it was particularly personal: he was the kind of man who had to paw everyone, in a friendly manner, rather like someone squeezing stuffed toys in shops, or fingering a fabric before they bought it. He weighed people with his touch, felt their flexibility.

Kate held out the box. 'Did you leave this?'

He laughed, placing one hand on his chest. 'Me?'

'Come on, George.'

'What might it be?'

She sighed. 'You know very well,' she said.

China snuffled at Kate's side. George smiled broadly. 'What is it? Let me see.'

She opened it.

'Oh . . .' he said, touching the gold links. 'Do you know what that stone is called? It's chrysoprase, a kind of green quartz. Pretty thing. Got an admirer? Why don't you put it on?'

She laughed in exasperation. 'Because you know very well that I don't wear jewellery. Even if I did, I haven't anything that this would go with. And—'

'Well, buy yourself something. It's your birthday.'

'George—'

He stepped towards her, beaming. 'Tell you what,' he said. 'You go and buy yourself a lovely little dress. What about a green one? Or a yellow one? Go with your bracelet. Not all that dreary black you young girls like. Then, when you've got your finery, I'll take you out to dinner.'

She shook her head. 'George, *please* . . .'

He looked utterly blasé. 'Lovely gold, that is,' he told her. 'About 1930, I should say. Craftsmanship. Very nice. You ought to be grateful to whoever it was.'

She blushed. 'I *am* grateful.'

'Well, then. Now how about dinner?'

She looked levelly at him, wryly smiling despite herself. 'You shouldn't have sent it, George.'

He had turned for the door, swinging his keys on one finger. 'Who said *I* sent it? You might have a dozen men for all I know. Come along, Chi. Breakfast.'

He opened and closed the Gallery door in one swift, dismissive movement. Kate looked in frustration at it a moment, then walked to her car, head down.

George stopped in the centre of the shop, watching the point where Kate's car had disappeared for almost a minute after she had gone.

As he looked, the cheerful expression slid from his face. It was replaced with vacancy. He stood unblinkingly in the twilight of the unlit space, his eyes fixed on the bend beneath the trees, and on their overlaced brown and green canopy.

In the half-light, the glass of the cabinets around him gleamed. In each section of the shop—each floor divided into roughly five sections—there was an arrangement like any domestic room: couches surrounded by desks; chairs, lamps, toys, paintings, china, carpets. His kingdom stretched behind him into the luxurious dark; a closely woven landscape of riches. In the corners of sofas lay fans and patterned quilts; on the shelves were spelter and bronze. Music boxes, mantel clocks; writing slopes. George Dale only bought the best. He had an eye, a feeling for only perfect quality.

Next to him now was a mahogany davenport, the sloping fall-top open to show the drawers within. Its surface was as smooth as a horse chestnut, and alive with the same glorious colour. Beyond that, on the chair, sat a Victorian doll, her face white against the moquette.

Unconsciously, he had rested his hand on the chair at his side, picking at the carving. At last, after more than five minutes, his gaze registered the actual glass of the window ahead of him.

He moved towards it, until he was standing in the bay. Fifty feet away, the external light flickered against his name on the signboard in the yard. *George Dale . . . Fine Antiques*. White lettering on red.

In the corner of the window at his side, a crane fly hung in a web.

He looked at it dispassionately: the fragile thorax drying in its prison. It must have been there since the hot weather, those last dying, burned-down days in August. He touched the empty shell of the insect, prying at it with his fingernail, shaking the web until the spider came out from the crack in the frame.

'Caught you, did she?' he said. He regarded the construction of the crane fly closely. Each segmented leg of the fly was as thin as hair; each whorl of tissue was lovely, perfect in structure. Every opaque cell, every overlapping connection, was a triumph of nature. The spider halted, testing the tension, calculating.

George went back to the chair. He lowered himself into it, into the rigid wood, ignoring the dog whining at his side. Seeing his unwillingness to move, eventually China sank to the floor at his feet, keening and groaning far back in her throat by way of complaint. But George did not hear her.

Under his palms was life solidified, the oak worked by hands over four centuries before, the whole tree naked under him. It was nearly black with age in some places.

Just for a second, George Dale wished violently that he were the insect, the chair. Jointed, lacquered, nailed. As dead as the brittle body hanging in the corner of the window.

Tension flickered at the corner of his mouth, a depressed smile.

The bracelet was worth four hundred pounds.

But that was not the point.

THREE

THE PHONE RANG just as Maggie Spence was getting dressed.

She was struggling into her clothes, into a dress that ought to have fitted. She swore softly to herself, tugging the belt from its loops in exasperation. Around her, the room was in chaos, clothes strewn everywhere, magazines crumpled at the side of the bed.

'Oh damn,' she muttered. The phone shrilled insistently. She grabbed it, and balanced it in the crook of her shoulder.

'Yes—what?'

'That's a nice greeting.'

'Oh . . .' She began to laugh. 'It's you.'

'Expecting someone else?'

Maggie blushed, biting her lip. She stood very still, her gaze fixed on the view beyond the window: the long and deserted promenade, the empty beach. Her flat was four floors up, one of a dozen bedsits crowded into a converted Victorian house.

'No,' she said softly. 'I'm not expecting anyone else.'

'I'm glad I caught you.'

'I slept in—I'm late.' She looked at the clock. Eight forty. She was meant to be at the *Journal* at nine. 'I was late yesterday. *God* . . . I'm only just getting dressed.'

The male voice on the other end of the line made a purring sound. 'What a delicious picture that paints,' he said.

Maggie smiled. She closed her eyes. The only person in the world who was oblivious to her weight was on the other end of the phone.

'Are we still OK for tonight?' he asked.

She held her breath.

'Mags? Still there?'

'Yes, I'm still here.'

'And?'

'I don't know . . .'

'Oh, Maggie.' The disappointment was laboured. 'We're not going back over this again.'

'I'm sorry,' she said.

'You know that I hardly ever see her. What more can I do?'

She looked at the sea, flat and grey, stretching to a dim horizon. 'Get divorced?'

Once said, she immediately regretted the low tone in her voice. She ought never to mention his wife.

He had told her a hundred times that it was over in all but name, and she believed him . . . at least, she believed him when he was with her, his arms around her, his lips on her skin.

The doubt and the coldness crept in later. When she was alone, standing at this same window. Or when she came home at night to an unlit room.

He was such a handsome man. Kind, respected. He was older than her, of course, but he didn't seem to mind that. In fact, he told her that it was one of the things he most loved about her.

Loved about her.

She clenched her fist against her side, willing herself to remember, to have faith in, his promises. To remember his constant, unchanging smile.

'Maggie . . .'

'Yes. I'm here.'

'Meet me tonight. Just for a drink.'

She sat down heavily on the bed. 'All right. Just one drink, then.'

'Wonderful.' He named a bar. She agreed to see him there at nine. 'Kiss me, Mags.'

She glanced at the clock, at the debris of the room, its complete disorganisation. She would have to leave work early, she told herself, and rush back here to tidy up. He hated mess, despite the fact that mess seemed to be her natural state.

Even as she had been speaking, she had been under no illusion. It would not be just *one* drink. It never was with him.

She pressed her lips to the phone.

Down the line, he made that soft, guttural sound in his throat; the very same, secret and needing, as he would make tonight.

'I'll see you later,' she whispered.

'You will,' he told her. 'You will.'

FOUR

$\mathscr{T}$HE OFFICES OF THE *JOURNAL* sat back from the road, looking like a spinster aunt in a crowd of rugby fullbacks.

They occupied the last Georgian house in a street which had long ago fallen to the concentrated assault of the twentieth century. What had once been pretty terraces with a distant view of the sea were now a ribbon of shops, pubs and petrol stations.

The offices of the local newspaper tried hard not to look out of place. A large neon-lit board at the entrance reflected the rest of the street with its garish red, blue and white emblem; and most of the front garden had been turned over to car parking spaces. But the fine lines of the original house still stood out.

Kate's car drew in at nine thirty.

She walked in, and up two flights of echoing concrete stairs; a tall, slim figure dressed in grey. She walked with brisk purpose, her bag held to her chest, her eyes fixed on the ground.

She could hear the noise at the start of the second flight. At the newsroom door it was deafening.

The morning planning meeting was on the point of breaking up. Kate caught the fleeting gesture of one hand brushing away another:

Jack Seward and the editor, Ken Bartlett, were standing toe to toe by the big, rectangular table. It was hard to tell if it had been a deflected blow or not.

Kate glanced at one of the staff, sitting alongside her at a computer screen. She raised her eyebrows, smiling.

The man grinned back. 'PMT,' he muttered.

Kate walked on.

'. . . reliable,' she heard Jack say. He had flushed bright red.

'*I'm* the one who decides what's reliable or not,' Bartlett retaliated. 'What is he? Some stringer, and I've only got your word for it. What if it goes to the fan? I'd have to answer to the authorities. What do you think—'

'It won't,' Jack shouted. He turned, saw Kate. 'I told you, if I'm not there at ten . . .' He picked up papers from the desk, shuffling them into a haphazard pile. He tried a last shot. 'It's just right there, right there. Maybe a week—'

'I won't change my mind,' Bartlett said. 'Wind it up. Drop it.'

Others around the table got up; Bartlett himself went into his office. The meeting, and the argument, were abruptly over, leaving Jack Seward visibly fuming in Bartlett's wake. He turned, saying something under his breath, then moved away.

'Hello, Jack,' Kate said as he passed her. She could feel fury rolling off him. Tangible, touchable.

He walked on. 'I've got to go,' he muttered.

Kate's first reaction on meeting Jack Seward when she had joined the paper five years ago had been to step back, even from his offered handshake. His size and presence engulfed her. He was six foot five; and habitually unshaven, unkempt. He had nicknamed her Snow White, for no better reason than that she had been dressed in a white coat. And then, inexplicably, a month later, he had apologised to her. He called her Miss McCaulay now, too formal to be joking. Too softly to be an insult.

He stopped now at the door, looked back at her, and gave a rueful twist of a smile before he went out. She looked around when the door had slammed behind him. The Features desk was empty.

'Claire in?' she asked.

'No. Must be worn out,' said the girl at the next desk. 'Totally shagged out.' There was a ripple of laughter that found its way along the lines. Kate sat down at Features and began to enter her copy.

'Oh, she will not like that,' the girl said, grinning, a pencil in her teeth. 'Rap your knuckles, Miss McCaulay. Her chair with the Relaxa-flo recline. Ouch ouch.'

McCaulay . . . Kate typed the date.

'I won't be here long,' she said. The keyboard rattled.

Ang/Violin.

Kate had been to Howells yesterday. The workshop was in a village street, a house of picturebook thatch. She wouldn't have known that she had the right place if it hadn't been for the brassplate on the door, *Chords Violins. John Howell.* She had knocked, and the door, unlatched, had edged open.

In the porch was a small child's plastic tricycle and a heap of news-papers.

'Hello?' she had called.

There had been no reply. Kate had stepped inside the house, into a hallway. On the left there was a room with a beamed fireplace, hessian rugs on the floor, a basket of logs, the wicker of the basket fraying. And more abandoned toys. She went down the hall and found herself in the kitchen. Here, on the doorframe, a note was pinned.

Violins? Go straight through.

Someone—a different hand—had scrawled underneath, *Washing up? Stay right here.*

She had smiled.

'Hello?' she called again.

There was a workshop beyond the kitchen, visible through the window. It had a corrugated iron roof whose rust shone bright red in the autumn sun. She went out of the kitchen and straight into a long outhouse.

The first few feet were occupied by lines of dead and empty violins, hanging in rows like meat at an abattoir, suspended from the ceiling on wire rods. She touched the first wooden cadaver; a gutless, string-less instrument.

'Play?' he asked.

She turned. The violin maker stood, smiling, at a curtain that divided the workshop.

'I used to,' she said. 'As a child.'

He walked forward, wiping his hands. 'Forced into it by devoted parents, I suppose.'

'Oh, no. I always wanted to play.'

He was about to say something else. Then, his eyes narrowed. 'Don't I know you?' he asked.

She put out her hand. 'Kate McCaulay, from the *Journal*. I rang you on Saturday to make the appointment.'

'Yes.' He held her hand a fraction too long. 'Do you have your picture in the paper?' he asked.

'Sorry?'

'When the article comes out. Does it have your picture next to it?'

'No.'

She took out her notepad.

'No laptop?'

She smiled. 'No substitute for a pencil and paper.'

'I'm glad to hear it.'

They sat on wooden chairs and he told her how he had started the business; how many customers he had; the pitfalls and successes.

'It's better than working for a living,' he said, when she asked him why he had chosen to give up his previous work—a job in an insurance office. He had laughed loudly at his own joke. 'I'm my own boss and I like to be on my own,' he said. 'I expect you're the same in what you do?'

'Yes . . . perhaps.'

'I've read all your pieces,' he said. He had brought them each a cup of coffee. 'I like them. They're so funny. Very witty.'

'Thank you,' she replied, holding the mug between both hands.

'Going to make me funny?' he asked.

'Not if you object.'

'I don't mind. It'll be interesting.' He paused. 'What do you call them, now?'

'"The Odd Angle."'

'That's it. I like them,' he repeated.

She smiled. She looked around at the violins behind her. 'Would you play something for me?' she asked.

'Yes, all right,' he said.

As luck would have it, he played the one melody she could not bear to hear.

'Bach's Concerto in A minor,' she said.

'Ten out of ten,' he replied.

She closed her eyes. The notes elongated into strands of blue, icy on the higher pitches, glassier, smoother on the low. Even if she opened her eyes she would see them all the time he played, frosty traces superimposed on the workbench, the floor, the cloths. She could feel the notes in her hands, their silky arches, tubes of smooth texture, less concrete than stone, less fluid than fabric.

He stopped and held the violin out to her.

'Now you,' he said.

Abruptly, she stood up. 'I've got to go,' she told him. 'Thank you very much for talking to me.'

'Are you all right?' he asked. 'What did I do? I'm sorry. What is it?'

'I'm fine. Thank you for the interview. It'll probably be two or three weeks.'

He hadn't opened the door for her. 'I've upset you,' he said.

She shrugged; then laughed. It sounded strained, but her expression was bright. 'It's just Bach. It always has that effect on me,' she said. Smiling now, she extended her hand. 'Goodbye, Mr Howell.'

'Goodbye,' he said. He watched her go, the violin still held in one hand.

Kate got back to the street. The car was parked only a few yards away.

But the words of the article, already forming in her mind, battled with the persistent memory.

FIVE

*K*ATE LEFT THE *JOURNAL* AT HALF ELEVEN.

She walked down the long hill towards the town, stopping to buy a sandwich. She ate it on the promenade, sitting in one of the turquoise wooden shelters that faced the sea.

She was almost finished when Maggie Spence came along, swinging her bag exaggeratedly as she walked. She only noticed Kate when she was six feet away.

'Hello,' she said. 'Another expense account lunch, huh?' nodding at the sandwich wrapping.

Kate smiled. 'Been shopping?'

'Just a few bits and pieces.'

As Maggie sat down, Kate nudged the bag open with the tip of her shoe. 'From Mullards? They must have cost a week's wages.' The bags belonged to a pricey delicatessen. Next to them was a jar of crystallised ginger, a loaf of bread, a bottle of red wine.

Maggie stretched her legs, pinioning her hands between her knees. She paused a moment. 'Have you ever been married?'

Kate, used to Maggie's questions that invariably came out of the blue, wrapped the crust of her sandwich in its polythene and put it in the bin. 'He's married?' she asked.

Maggie coloured. She picked up the bag and put it on her knee, and folded her hands over it.

'Do I know him?' Kate persisted.

'No.' The response was very quick.

'Who is he?'

'If you don't know him, what difference does it make?'

Kate stood up. Maggie followed her. They walked in silence beside the beach for another hundred yards. On the sands, a woman was exercising one of the shire horses from the brewery; they stopped to watch it cutting through the sluggish waves.

'What would you do with a million pounds?' Maggie asked.

Kate smiled. 'Give it away.'

'You wouldn't!'

'Well . . . maybe not . . .'

'You wouldn't get a big house? Or go on holiday?'

Kate said nothing for a while; then, turning the tables as usual, she said, 'Tell me what you would do.'

Maggie leaned on the railings. 'I'd buy a tea shop. Like the one at Downborough Lake. You know? With the nice garden, and the plates and teapots on shelves inside, and herbs . . .'

Kate knew the shop at the lake; it only opened in season. It was festooned with bags of lavender and flowery tea towels, and factory-wrapped apple cake. Maggie turned to her. 'Did you see the article about May Porter?'

Kate had. May Porter was an artist, sometime hippy and actress, who owned a hotel further along the coast. Two weeks ago, Claire had featured it. May Porter's autobiography, a hot account of sixties London, stuffed with drug busts and sexual athletics, had financed the hotel; but you would never know it. The May Porter in last week's paper had reinvented herself.

'She runs a restaurant and it's got two crowns,' Maggie was saying. 'She does astrology readings, and makes jam and wine and all that. She sells paintings, and you should see her garden.'

'I know,' Kate murmured. 'Good luck to her.'

Maggie had stopped walking. 'I'd like a place like that,' she said. 'No kids around your feet, and no family, and a little business doing what you liked.'

Kate considered. She could see Maggie at the door of a teashop. She could see her making her own tablemats and curtains. But she could not see her childless.

'You'll get married,' she said.

'No.'

'Why not?'

The breeze blew off the sea, salty and cool. Maggie didn't seem inclined to answer.

'Maggie, May Porter has got four children, all grown up,' Kate said. 'She's had a hundred lovers and two husbands. Family life's not a disease; it won't stop you doing what you want.' She smiled. 'You'll be married and happy. Not to *this* one, though. Married men don't often marry their mistresses. That's not the point of having one.'

Maggie bit her lip. Taking pity, Kate raised a mock fist to the younger woman's chin. 'Lay him out cold, the sod,' she said. 'Just . . . like *that*.'

She began to walk on. Maggie watched her, then hurried to catch up. She saw that Kate's face had that closed expression that Maggie had come to know well: *so far, and no further.* The conversation had finished.

They reached the pedestrian crossing.

'I'd better hurry up,' Maggie said. 'Get back.'

'Yes . . . don't get yourself fired.'

'What are you doing this afternoon?'

'Minding the shop for the headache.'

'George?' Maggie laughed. 'Why, what's he done now?'

Kate smiled. 'Ever since he split up with that Fremley woman, he ogles. Like—' She made a hangdog, bloodhound expression.

Maggie's eyes widened. 'Really? But he's forty years older than you!'

'Thirty.' Kate patted her arm. 'But he'll find another rich old dear in a couple of weeks. It'll pass.'

She slung her handbag across her shoulder, and smiled goodbye.

Maggie watched her walk down the street, face turned towards the shop windows. Kate McCaulay was thin, Maggie thought, without envy. She probably had three or four boyfriends right now. Rich ones, that took her out, that didn't always want to hide her away. She didn't have that option herself; the right to pick and choose. The luxury of being shown off.

She caught sight of herself, a large brown shape in the reflection of a window opposite.

'Lucky,' she whispered. She turned, crossed the road, and started up the hill.

SIX

JACK SEWARD HAD BEGGED THE COPIES from the paper's librarian. Of course, it was strictly against the rules to take back issues from the building. If anyone found out, it was possible that Linda Stark, in the archives, could lose her job. But he had a way of talking women round that occasionally came in useful.

As Jack placed the papers on his kitchen table, he smiled ruefully to himself at that last thought. He hadn't talked his wife round last year, when she had left him. He didn't notice Carol melting under his romantic rhetoric. In fact, he thought, filling his coffee cup, and gazing across at the dismal chaos of the unwashed crockery littering the draining board, if he remembered rightly she had not so much fallen into his arms as smashed him across the face with his own briefcase.

Tough girl, Carol. Would go far.

Had gone far, in fact, he thought, trudging back to the table. As far away as she could get. She was selling training schemes now for computer courses in Bahrain. Having a wonderful time, if the reports that filtered back to him could be believed.

He frowned, sitting down with a grunting sigh in the kitchen chair, and drawing the papers towards him. He opened the first, at the page marked with a paperclip.

Most of these issues were on microfilm now. More recent copies were on CD-Rom. But he preferred to look at the real thing. The heading on the top of the page read *14 March 1985*.

He drew it towards him carefully.

The photograph of the woman was recognisably Kate McCaulay. The surname was different, and her hair in the picture was long. But it was definitely still her. It was a national news item that the local paper had picked up. A news item that had gone on to dominate the scene for a very long time.

The picture had been taken in central London outside the building where Kate McCaulay had worked, on a day when the sun slanted almost diagionally across the crowd of faces caught in late afternoon light.

Jack noted how she held on to the arm of a man older and taller than she. Her husband. His face was set and expressionless, while hers was fractured and distorted by grief. Kate's mouth hung open raggedly, her eyes were almost squeezed shut. It was as if she had given up any semblance of control, unable to hold together even for the fleeting moment in the public gaze.

In the background, other faces milled. Staff from the newspaper where she worked. Someone had their hand on Kate's shoulder—tips of fingers could be seen. Husband and wife, Jack noticed, looked away from each other, despite Kate's grasping of his arm.

All in all, they resembled people who had been cornered, accused of some terrible crime, hounded into a position from which they had no escape. Rather than a couple whose child had been missing for nearly a week.

Jack bent his head, reading the text with rapt concentration.

James Lydiatt, eight weeks . . .

And at the bottom of the page was the most poignant picture of all. A photograph taken of his son by the father, at home.

Their lost child, wrapped tightly in a white blanket, stared unfocused towards the lens.

SEVEN

*T*HE AUCTION ROOM WAS WARM, despite the greyness of the day outside.

Looking up at the enormous circular skylight in the ceiling, George Dale could see the trails of grey cloud, laced with a thunderous yellow. The sale had begun at twelve, and it was now nearly four: four hundred lots were scheduled for that day. The crowds under the washed-out yellow light from above looked sepulchral, the faces waxy. Expressions were strained, and tempers short. The bidders were tired.

He was waiting for the Dutch bureau *à cylindre*. On his chair on the opposite side of the aisle, he could still make out its lovely detail. It was walnut, and the roll-top was set with diamond parquetry; a delicate thing, on narrow feet.

George straightened to allow the nagging pain in his back to ease. His mind wandered up to the skylight where the consciousness of the room seemed to hover: distracted, pervasive.

His need went back a long way.

The first time that he had contracted—and he thought of it like that, like an illness—this quiet avarice had been on a cold day exactly like this.

Tibbs Street had been right at the top of the Midlands town where he had been born. Mr Angel's antiques shop had been very clean. It was white walled, with a Persian rug on the floor. It had a piano and an entire wall of books, and a huge overmantel mirror of bevelled panes, twirly columns and little shelves. There had been a fireplace with a vast herringbone-brick back, large enough to walk into and see up the chimney.

'It's a very old room,' Mr Angel had told him, glancing at him as George hovered near the door of the shop. It was the first time that George had ventured inside, certainly the first time that he had spoken to the owner. And yet it was if Mr Angel were continuing a conversation that they had already begun. 'Did you know it was old?'

'I came to see the books,' George had muttered, embarrassed. There were annuals nearest the door, on a low shelf. Fivepence each. He had glimpsed them from the street. 'You haven't half got a lot of books,' he had said.

'A terrible lot.'

'Have you read them all?'

'The whole.'

George had considered, his eyes fixed on the inch of flesh where his first long trousers did not meet his socks. Then, he had looked further about the room. On the top of the piano was a photograph of a boy in uniform, not much older than himself.

'Who d'you think that is?' asked Mr Angel. 'Guess.'

It didn't look like anyone that George knew.

'That's me,' Mr Angel said. 'In the first lot, back in 1915.'

'You never got shot?' George had asked.

Angel had laughed outright this time. 'Oh yes, got shot. Got a mine. You know what they are?'

George shook his head.

Angel's hands described an arc in the air. 'Whoosh. Send you up in the sky. Some never came down.'

'You whooshed up?' George's twelve-year-old curiosity had got the better of him. He had stepped closer.

'Right up,' Angel confirmed. He had begun polishing a desk, a tin of beeswax in one hand, a faded duster in the other. 'And when I come down, I'd dropped four toes. 'Magine that, now! I looked for them everywhere, but I had to come back without 'em.'

George's mouth had dropped open.

'Want to see?' Angel asked.

He had nodded dumbly.

Still chuckling, Angel had sat down on the nearest chair.

Perhaps it had been a particularly slow afternoon. Perhaps the old man had been bored, even lonely. What had exactly possessed him, though, to sit there and unlace his brogue shoes, and roll off his sock to reveal his foot, there in the High Street daylight, when anyone might have walked in, was still a mystery to George even now.

Angel had held up his right foot. There was a reddened stub of a foot with only the big toe remaining. The end where the toes should have been was beautifully shiny and smooth. 'Me and the poor horses,' Angel had murmured, putting the shoe and sock back on.

George's eyes had flickered to the fireplace, where black wood was burning in a black hearth. Something deliciously fearful rumbled in the pit of his stomach, and rose to lodge under his ribs. The image of the shiny stumps of toes danced before his eyes.

'Like Horlicks?'

He had jolted. 'Yes . . .'

'Want some now?'

'All right.'

And the old man went off. While he was away, George had looked at the books. He took down one of the Arthur Mee *Children's Encyclopaedia*. On a higher shelf had been thicker volumes. *The Illustrated History of the Camellia . . . Showmen and Show-women . . . Lardy's Apocryphal Miscellanea*, a book on freaks of nature, which he had touched but dared not take down.

Angel came back in, carrying the mugs on a tray.

'I get 'em off auctions,' he said. He put the tray down on a table. 'Know what they are—auctions? House sales?'

'No.'

George had never heard of such a thing before. Out of Angel's mouth, the word *auctions* seemed heavy with magic.

Angel had settled himself on one of the elaborate chairs, and motioned George to take his drink.

'Well,' he said. 'You go along to a place, and they sell a whole lot of things. If you want something, you have to shout a price, and if nobody else shouts a higher price, you get it.'

'Like the market,' George said.

'A bit,' Angel had agreed. 'But in these places, they sell everything. *Everything*. Whole houses, whole lives. Probably somebody has died, and they've no one to give their things to. Or the family don't want their things. They want to sell them and get the money instead.'

Angel had shaken his head at this, then carried on. 'So, one day, they sell everything that person's bought during their life. I've even seen dentures.' He began to laugh. 'I have! Dentures in a tinplate box. What d'you think of that?'

'Horrible,' George said.

''Tis,' Angel had agreed. 'Horrible. Horrible.'

'But why?'

'Why what?'

'Why'd you go, if it's horrible?'

Angel leaned back, gazing fixedly for a moment at the overmantel. 'Addicted,' he said, at last.

George closed his eyes momentarily now.

He had gone on to work for Mr Angel on Saturdays for ten long months. Until that terrible winter day when Angel died.

The auctioneer's hammer slammed down.

The lot before the Dutch bureau had been sold. George sat up immediately, realising that he had almost been asleep, and might have missed it.

He saw that the room was not quite so full now. These were the last dozen lots.

'Can we start at one thousand?' the auctioneer asked.

'One thousand,' said a voice at the front.

'Thank you. One thousand five hundred? One thousand three? Three . . . thank you . . . one thousand five . . .'

It leaped up like this for another few bids; then slowed. They began bidding in hundreds at three thousand. A woman to George's right, dressed in a loud pink suit, raised her catalogue.

'Three thousand three hundred . . .'

The dealers around the room glanced at her. A murmur whispered through the crowd, touching George as it rolled on its journey. The woman was a private buyer, and it was no use bidding against private buyers.

George raised his hand slightly. 'Three thousand four,' he said.

The woman didn't look his way. 'Three thousand five,' she countered.

They bid to four thousand, then four thousand one hundred. The room, originally silent, began to stir. Dealers whispered that Dale was bidding high. A short flurry of rival bids fluttered round the room.

'Four thousand two . . .'

Now, at last, the woman in pink looked at him.

George smiled. *My need is more than yours.*

'Four thousand three . . . four thousand four . . .'

Last year, he had owned a cabinet just like this. Rather plainer, perhaps, without the marquetry. Before the bureau, Kate had never commented at all on anything in the Gallery. He had never seen her so much as touch anything until she touched the bureau.

'Nice,' she had said.

'It's 1780,' he told her.

She hadn't replied; just smiled.

He had lifted the top; shown her the drawers inside. 'And there's a secret one . . .' He had revealed it for her. She had rested her arm on the top and ran a finger along the edge.

He had sold the desk at Christmas.

As she came in before the holiday, he had gone forward to meet her. 'I'm afraid I sold the cabinet.'

She took off her coat. 'Sorry?'

'Your bureau that you liked.'

She had given him the most lingering look; not quite sadness. 'Good,' she said. 'That's a lot of money for you, at Christmas too.'

'Four thousand eight hundred,' the woman in pink was calling.

It was way over now. The catalogue had a top estimate of four. The woman in pink looked down at her lap and did not raise her hand.

'Five thousand,' George said.

A dealer that George knew, standing over by the door, grinned at him. He lifted one finger to his neck and drew expressively across it, indicating that George was cutting his own throat.

'There are two kinds of people in the world,' Angel had always told him. 'Those who have a price, and those who are worth something.' The dealer by the door, in his greasy Barbour jacket, knocked values down, tearing furniture to pieces to make fakes. He had a price, but he was worth nothing.

The auctioneer's hammer came down.

Conversation buzzed and flowed over the room. The woman in pink got up, hurt scored on her face. The loss was personal to her; George almost sympathised.

But it didn't matter to him if he had cut his own throat or not. Because he had what he wanted.

He hadn't bought the bureau for business.

But for love.

EIGHT

*K*ATE GOT BACK TO THE GALLERY AT ONE O'CLOCK.

The shop was locked because George was at the sale, but she had the key in her bag, and opened up. As she switched on more lights, and stowed her scarf and gloves in a small cabinet by the front door, she noticed that George had not seen to the morning post.

She picked up the pile of letters and walked to the back of the ground floor.

Her breath showed in the cold shop; shivering, she turned on the heating. As was his habit, George had left her a Thermos of coffee. She poured herself a cup and sat down on a couch, her mind elsewhere— at the paper, on Maggie and her nameless married lover—as she separated out the catalogues and magazines to make an orderly pile.

It was then that Kate noticed the envelope addressed to her.

She frowned as she picked it up. She had her own mailbox at the foot of the steps outside. It was true that, occasionally, letters for the flat arrived at the Gallery—it was easily done. But usually she could recognise the sender.

She turned this letter, now, over in her hands. It was a foolscap white envelope with a typed address. It had been sent yesterday, franked with an evening collection time. She opened the envelope and unfolded the single sheet of paper.

There was no sender's address. No reference, no heading. No signature.

Just one sentence in the centre of the page.

I KNOW WHERE HE IS.

She stared at it, motionless for perhaps a minute. She read it three, four, five times.

Then she put the paper down in her lap. The room jolted, the colours mixing.

She looked down the aisle. The letter fell on to the top of the couch. She snatched it up almost at once, crumpling it to her chest.

Alongside her, in a glass booth, marching lines of minature toys— bright green and red cars, small ceramic houses, flat-faced golliwog metal brooches—rose in an orderly phalanx, seeming to press forward. She stood up and, in doing so, knocked over the cup of coffee. The stain spread quickly on the carpet at her feet.

Turning away, she ran back to the front door, fumbled with the catch, ran out into the yard, and round to the porchway to her own flat.

She had no idea at all of where she was going, or what she was doing. The blood thundered in her head, squeezing tight. The skin of her face was cold. As she stood in the porch, the stairs loomed at her with the old immediacy of the dream; higher, steeper, wider than they should be.

'God,' she whispered.

The letter hurt her hand where she had crumpled its thick, grainy page. But she dared not look at it again.

Up the hundred treads, each one higher than the one before, each depth too huge to be real. Up the never-ending flight. Up the stairs of the house . . . up, up . . . into the dark.

NINE

*I*T WAS DARK WHEN MAGGIE WOKE.

For a moment, the shadows struggled with a dream; then she stretched her hand across the bed.

But he was not there.

She called his name. Lifting herself on to one elbow, she looked at the luminous dial of the clock. It was half-past two in the morning. The narrow bed was still warm where he had been; she could still smell him on the sheets. For a second, her hand hesitated next to the bedside light, then dropped away. She had no desire to see the empty room he had abandoned.

She got up, shivering, pulling on a sweater that was within reach, and went to the window.

Across the promenade, the sea was high on the flat beach. The long stretch of bay, a mile or more of horseshoe-shaped sand, looked eerie in the night, almost as though lit from under the water, a thin depth for hundreds of yards out. In the summer, you could walk into the sea for five minutes and still it would only be waist-high. Now, at night, in the oncoming winter, it looked like a rippled grey sheet.

There was no traffic, no movement at all along the street. A light shone at the end of the stone pier, at the edge of the harbour; the street-lights were yellow circles at intervals along the blue-railed pavement. If she craned her neck, she could see the clock, a Victorian monument trying to be the Albert Memorial. She could see its face now, a floating disc two hundred yards away, above the road.

She turned from the window and stood with her back against the glass. She could make out the lines of the bed vaguely, the back-turned white cover and the pillows; she could see the faint figuring of the rug at the side of the bed, a cotton throw she had bought last week, with geometric squares of white on pink.

By the door there was a chest of drawers that belonged to the land-lord. There were pictures of her family here. She walked through the dark towards them; she reached out and touched the drawer top, and her hand immediately connected with a wallet.

For a moment, she didn't realise what or whose it was. Then, it dawned on her. She fumbled back to the bed, switched on the light, and saw that it was his.

It had a black cover and was about two inches thick, the edges zipped together. She picked it up and weighed it experimentally in her palm. It felt very heavy. The binding was soft leather; there was a clasp at one side that showed it was possible to lock it.

But it was not locked.

She smiled, as though balancing him, holding his weight. He was very protective of all his belongings; he didn't like her to touch his clothes, for instance, even to move them so that she might sit down.

He didn't like her to touch him when he was dressing; she was not allowed to straighten his tie, or even smooth the shoulders of his jacket as he put it on. It was the same undressing, too. There was no intimate discovery; he took off everything he wore while standing apart from her, as if he were preparing for a medical examination.

He was private, she thought. *A private person*. You heard that all the time: it wasn't unusual. Such people existed—even if, in her own crowded childhood, she had never come across it before. Maggie had been brought up in a house where you lived shoulder to shoulder, always jostling for air, always treading on each other's toes. There had been no privacy in her past, and so she could see—she could understand—those people, like him, who didn't especially like to be touched or explored or smothered.

A small thread of disquiet strained as she considered it, nevertheless.

She pressed the clasp and the little book fell open.

She didn't read anything. Or look at anything. She just pressed it momentarily to her face, inhaling him, absorbing his life, his preoccupations, the contour of his day, through the pages. When she lowered it from her face, she saw an inner file of pockets: stamps, business cards, receipts. Slowly, she lifted the cover of the diary compartment.

And the door behind her opened.

'What the hell are you doing?' he said.

She jumped guiltily; he snatched the wallet from her.

'I . . . I thought you'd gone.'

He glanced over it, then snapped it shut, putting it into an inside pocket of his coat. 'I forgot this.'

She smiled, and put her arms round his neck. 'But why were you going at all?' she asked. 'You can stay all night.'

'No,' he said.

'Just once. Please.' She looked up at him. He had made no effort to respond to her gesture. His arms hung at his sides. 'Why not?'

'Not tonight.'

'But you told me she was away!'

'She is.'

Don't push it, she thought. He doesn't like it. Still, the reply was already out of her mouth. 'I don't see why you can't stay. Just for once.'

He took hold of her hands and pulled them down from her neck. 'Don't tell me what I can and can't do,' he said.

She ignored the warning in his voice. She looked in his eyes, trying to read them. 'You don't want to, do you? That's it, isn't it? You don't really want to.' She felt a knot tighten in her throat, a first transmission of tears.

'Maggie, don't start this.'

'But, I—' She stopped. He was holding her wrists in front of them both, his fingers pinching her skin, the flesh whitening.

'You aren't who you should be,' he said.

She glanced at her hands, then back at him. 'What?'

He began to turn her arms inwards, so that her elbows locked. 'Who you should be,' he said.

The pain flashed along her arm and into her shoulder.

'Don't try to tell me what to do,' he said. 'Because you don't understand.'

'Let me go.'

'Don't *try*—'

'I won't! I won't, I won't.' Her tone spiralled down into a plea. The pressure was now intense on the joints in her wrist and elbow; she pitched forward, bending from the waist in an effort to relieve it. 'I promise I won't . . .'

He bent down with her, pressing his face to hers, his lips close to her ear. She was almost on her knees. 'Do you hear what I'm telling you?'

'Yes . . . yes . . . I do. I do hear it. I promise . . .'

He let her go.

She dropped to the floor, gasping, one hand desperately trying to rub the other, her fingers straying up the length of each arm.

She saw him feel once again in the pocket of his coat, as if to reassure himself that the wallet was there. Then, he turned, pulled the door open, and was gone.

She listened to him descending the long stairway. She sat on her heels, breathing heavily, staring at the place on her arm where his fingers had made a mark.

TEN

*T*HE FOLLOWING MORNING, foggier and colder than the previous day, an ancient grey Mercedes drew up outside the Gallery.

George, standing in the window, saw Isabelle Browning get out: in her late seventies, she was dressed in dirty green jeans and a blue sweater. She slammed the door, looked up just once at Kate's window, and came into the shop at a brisk pace.

'Anything?' she asked George, pausing briefly to pat China.

'She hasn't come down.'

'And you knocked on the door?'

George gave an apologetic shrug. 'I don't like to.'

'Oh, *really*.' They had known each other for some years; Isabelle was the stronger character, and the elder.

'What am I supposed to do?' George asked. 'You know how she is.'

Isabelle fixed him with a look. She said nothing else, but went out again, crossing the yard and opening the door to the stairs. Climbing to the top, she saw, to her surprise, that Kate's door was open wide. There was no sound from the room, and no movement.

'Kate?' she called. 'It's Isabelle. Are you there?'

She paused, waiting. Hesitating, because, in truth, she hated to trespass. 'Kate . . .'

'I'm here,' Kate said. 'Come in.'

Isabelle did not quite know what she had expected. But the voice from the room was perfectly calm. She walked forward.

Kate was sitting at the table where she ate her meals. Paper was neatly spaced across the surface. She was writing, or had been. She waited for Isabelle to come in, pen poised midair.

'Well,' Isabelle said drily. 'I see I've made that bloody climb to no purpose at all. George said you were ill.'

'Did he?'

'Why didn't you answer when he called?'

'I didn't hear him call.'

Isabelle snorted softly to show that she didn't believe her. 'Why haven't you gone to work?'

'I'm going out this afternoon.'

'What's the matter with you? You look grey.'

'For God's sake! Don't fuss.'

Isabelle regarded her silently. Kate had never broken her routine in the five years she had known her. She had always left for work at precisely half-past eight in the morning. It was this lapse that had worried George. Worried him enough to disturb Isabelle's breakfast and make her drive eight miles through fog on the top roads. She noted that Kate would not look her in the eye. There was only one chair in the room, and she took it.

'Oh, this *thing*,' she muttered. 'I can't feel my arse in it after two minutes.'

'Would you like some tea?'

'No,' Isabelle said. She looked severely around herself, at the two-bar electric fire that hardly warmed the room; at the thin curtains and beamed ceiling. She sighed in exasperation. 'Why do you condemn yourself to this godforsaken garret?' she said. Then, getting no reply, she added, smiling, 'You should have heard George on the phone. Have you ever heard a sixty-year-old man squeak? He *squeaked*.' She laughed, and at last secured the ghost of a smile from Kate. 'You ought to take pity on him,' Isabelle continued. 'Poor old George. Why didn't you call down that you were OK? The poor old fart was worried. And here I am, half a breakfast . . .'

'I'm sorry,' Kate said.

Isabelle gestured at the papers on the table. 'Well, what are you doing?'

'A few notes for interviews.' The voice was brittle. Kate put one hand, briefly, to her forehead.

'What notes? Why do you need notes?'

Kate put down the pen, slowly, almost disjointedly. She ran her finger along it, rolling the clip on the cap backwards and forwards.

Isabelle stared hard at her, at the crown of her head as the young woman looked down. The centre parting was clean, like a white line drawn in the blonde.

She had first seen that head, that neat white parting, that downcast, careful look, coming through her own back garden on a summer's day.

Isabelle had been weeding the back border, and, though she knew she was due for a visit from some woman from the *Journal*, she was not particularly predisposed to be interviewed. She had been hoping that this female reporter wouldn't cross the threshold, the wooden door from the street that led through an alley. But Kate McCaulay had come: slow, particular, her step measured, as if assessing every stone along the way.

Isabelle's house was four hundred years old. Its timbered front wall bordered a narrow pavement; the top storey overhung the first. It was a picturebook house, and, to Isabelle's mind, photographed by tourists with irritating regularity. It stood close to a medieval stone cross in Lovatt's village centre.

Isabelle had watched the slowly advancing head above the stone wall, between the trees. At the gateway, Kate McCaulay had stopped and looked up. Isabelle had got to her feet grudgingly.

Kate had not extended her hand or introduced herself. Instead she said, 'This is the most beautiful house I have ever seen.'

Of course, in any other person, it might have been designed to curry favour. It was also a reaction that Isabelle had heard a hundred times before, and so, while being complimentary, was also rather boring. Nevertheless, The Linen House *was* a beautiful place, the subject of various magazine articles, the last being only the month before. Which was how the local paper—the *Journal*—had picked up on her. But Kate was different: there was no envy or flattery in her voice.

They had shaken hands. Kate had a file clamped, with the other arm, to her chest; she had looked about her, and finally, across at Lovatt's grey stone church a hundred yards away through the trees.

Seeing that Kate wasn't inclined to say anything more, Isabelle had found herself doing all the talking. They walked through the borders, along the soft and springy grass.

'With the garden walled, I have a lot of climbers,' she had said. 'This is "La Belle Sultane"—you see? The crimson one?—and this is "Duchess of Edinburgh," the clematis . . . and this is "Rosa Mundi," and "Madame Isaac Pereire" . . .'

She had looked behind her. Kate had stopped, her eyes closed.

'Are you all right?'

'The scent,' Kate said.

'Yes . .'

'What a texture.'

Isabelle had smiled. Kate opened her eyes. 'Do you grow anything?' Isabelle asked.

'No, I don't. Not even a window box.' Kate bent to a long-stemmed white flower.

'Astrantia,' Isabelle said.

'You know every name?'

'Of course.'

'And the Latin names—of these?' She was touching a crowd of old-fashioned roses.

'*Rosa gallica officinalis*'

They went, eventually, into the house.

The sun came to the south-facing back all day long; but the front, the room that faced on to the street, was dark. Isabelle had not tried to brighten it; instead, it was richly red, gold, ochre, and velvet brown. The walls were lined with books; the carpet was thick.

Kate sat down, tucking her legs underneath her on the couch.

'Aren't you going to take any photographs?' Isabelle asked.

'The photographer is coming at one.'

'I see.' Isabelle hesitated for a moment, not knowing quite what to say. In other interviews, the questions had come thick and fast. She usually had the sense of her feet being swept from under her. But Kate seemed to be making very little effort even at conversation. Much later, when they knew each other better, Kate had confided that she had felt low that day, disinclined even to ask the most expected questions.

'How do you like my room?'

'Too dark for me.'

It was almost a rebuff. 'Oh? And how should it be improved?'

'It can't.'

'Well. I *am* mortified.'

Kate glanced up—she had been looking at the window. She smiled. 'Do you have any ghosts?'

'Heavens! No.'

'Readers love ghosts.'

'I am sorry to disappoint them.'

'They won't be disappointed. Have you ever opened to the public?'

'Only for the annual weekend. The village raises money for charity, we all open our houses . . .'

'Oh, yes. I've heard of it.' Kate's voice was offhand.

'Ah . . . not appealing, that line of enquiry?'

'Tell me when you first came here,' Kate continued.

'In 1942. To get out of London. This was being sold by the wife of a colonel who had bought it in Libya.'

'Bought the house? In Libya?'

'No.' Isabelle laughed. 'Bought the afterlife. He was *killed* in Libya.'

Kate had smiled acknowledgement. 'And was it like this when you came here?'

'Not at all. It was dreary, a god-awful prim, panelled, deathly place,' Isabelle had replied. 'Very cold. Dreadfully cold. I put in a proper central heating system, you know. A new kitchen. I took out the panelling. Fearful! The conservationists would kill me, probably *should* have killed me.' She had pushed a wing of grey hair back from her eyes. 'But I had lived for the previous two years in a dark wood-lined Victorian house in Kew, with a dark ten-foot yard, five storeys, dark stairs . . .'

She had seen Kate's expression flicker just for a split second. 'Aren't you going to ask why they call it The Linen House?'

'This was a wool town, but here was the only place where linen was sold. So it was an oddity . . . the only linen house,' Kate replied.

Isabelle had crossed her arms. 'I must say, you're very infuriating. I am usually told that is a fascinating snippet of the past.'

'So it is. But they read that four weeks ago.'

'Ah.'

'It must have been very quiet after London,' Kate observed.

'Blessedly so.'

'After the war ended, you weren't tempted to return?'

'No.'

'No husband coming back from the conflict?'

'Yes. No . . .'

'He didn't come back?'

'*He* came back. I didn't.'

'You separated? Why?'

'I wanted to be here.'

'A house kept you from your husband?'

'Not just the house.'

'What then?'

'This area . . .'

'Just the area?' Kate persisted.

'Of course.'

'Just that?'

'Well . . .' Isabelle felt the direction of dialogue, which she was used to controlling, slipping away from her.

'A man?' Kate asked.

'No, indeed.'

There had been a long pause. Kate's whole demeanour had altered. She is just like a cat, Isabelle thought. She owned several herself— beloved houseguests, when they bothered to be—and she knew and understood the quiet languor replaced by instant rapt attention. She saw that Kate's eyes were a remarkable blue, rather pale, very striking.

'Excuse me,' Kate said. Even her voice had dropped and changed. 'But was it a man that made you love this house?'

'Would you like some tea?' Isabelle asked. She went out to the kitchen. Kate followed her.

'Was he local?' she asked.

Isabelle, in the act of filling the kettle, stopped. 'I thought you came to hear about the house, not me,' she replied in a tone that was meant to discourage any further probing.

Kate's eyes held hers. 'I can't write about the house without writing about you,' she said. 'You're one and the same.' She smiled, very gently; then, she looked across at the panel decorating the wall behind Isabelle's shoulder. It was a section of brick which had been smoothed and painted with a square foot of intricate mural. 'Clarice Cliff,' Kate remarked.

'Yes. The "Bizarre" pattern. He painted that.' Damn it! she had thought. It was out, as easily, as unguardedly, as that. Isabelle had taken a breath. 'You see the little Chinese salts on the shelves?' she asked. 'That was his collection. The colours in the sitting room, the books—all his.'

'This was your home?'

'Yes, our home.'

'Did you have children?'

'No.' Isabelle paused. 'No, Michael was married.'

Kate had explored the painted panel with a fingertip. She gave no sign of being surprised or shocked. 'And the garden? Did you plant the garden together?'

'Yes. The vine in the corner, the little orchard.'

'The roses?'

'Descendants of the first. Michael adored roses.'

'And you and he . . .'

'He died of cancer in 1951.'

Kate looked up. Up to that moment, Isabelle had been studying Kate's face, recognising its intelligence, and also its secrecy.

Kate had called the newspaper article 'Descendants of the Rose'.

Once she had got over her initial disconcertedness, Isabelle realised that she did not mind being found out, or, rather, rediscovered, in her affair. The whole village had once known about it, and had been divided, more or less equally, between supporting her and ignoring her.

She had expected the same divisions when the article was published; but, to her surprise, found that most of her contemporaries, seasoned perhaps by age, now gave her conspiratorial smiles, or patted her arm as they passed her in church. Even those who had been implacably opposed all those years ago.

The revelation hurt no one. Michael's wife was long dead, and, like Isabelle, had been childless. Only Isabelle's sister remained stoutly disapproving to the end, until she, too, had died six months ago.

Kate has redrawn me, she thought one day while she gazed at the 'Bizarre'. Michael would have approved of it. He had always said that the world took itself too seriously, and judged others too harshly. She and Kate had met regularly after the article came out. And, with each meeting, she had found that she liked Kate McCaulay more, and their friendship had deepened.

She had even, at last, found out Kate's secrets.

She looked at Kate now, at that downcast face.

'Why don't you tell me what it is?' she said.

Kate shook her head.

'Kate, dear . . .' Isabelle got up.

Kate raised one hand, palm outwards, a signal to stop Isabelle's advance. Isabelle saw that the hand was trembling.

'Tell me,' Isabelle said. 'Please . . .'

Kate's hand fell. It passed to a piece of thick paper that had been lying face down on the table, close to the edge. Kate turned it over and, without looking at it, or even looking up at Isabelle, held it out towards her.

Isabelle took it.

The paper was rather coarse, more like a drawing paper, or a watercolour paper, than typing paper. And yet it had been typed on. One sentence in the dead centre of the sheet.

I KNOW WHERE HE IS.

Isabelle looked up from the letter, straight into Kate's eyes.

'When did it come?' she asked.

'Yesterday.'

'By ordinary post?'

'Yes. It was waiting here when I got back from work at lunchtime.'

'Let me see the envelope.'

Kate gave it to her, saying, 'I've already looked at it a hundred times. You can't read the postmark.'

Isabelle examined it carefully. 'The time is clear enough. Five p.m. It must have been posted fairly locally for it to have got here by first post.'

'Not necessarily.' Kate got up suddenly. Isabelle tried to give the letter back to her, but she refused it, shuddering, her shoulders hunched. She walked to the window, staring at the view of the road between the trees, the roofs of the village, the rolling downland beyond.

'It can't mean what you think it means,' Isabelle said. 'It can't possibly.'

Kate turned back to her. She was trembling visibly; she put her hand briefly to her mouth.

'Can't it?' she asked. 'What else could it possibly mean?'

ELEVEN

*S*HE WAS STANDING WITH RICHARD on the steps of their home.

It was impossible, Kate knew. Even in sleep—now, ten years later, after so many changes—her brain tried to assert reality. Messages blinked across Richard's image, flashes of light weighed with invisible words. *This isn't happening. Not now.*

It made no difference. Suppressed for so long, the picture wanted to be seen again. Ripples on each side of the frame straightened, and the day in the dream became the present, surging out of the past.

In the darkness that night, Kate squirmed while asleep. Her fists were clenched on the outside cover of the bed, her body rigid.

But she could not stop the dream's advance.

'You'll never cope,' Richard had said as he dressed for work. It was barely light, just seven o'clock. Kate had already been up for two hours. The baby was crying in jagged, hitched loops of sound; they could barely hear each other speak.

'I want to see Cathy,' she had replied. She knew how she sounded: aggressive, tearful.

'You just won't cope,' he had repeated. 'Drive—what? It must be eighty miles, right through the city? Find the motorway, find the town? Feed *him*?'

He had glanced down at their son. Sometimes Richard voiced what she herself had felt: the total bewildered exasperation at the tyranny of this interloper.

Jamie, then, had been lying on their bed, his feet drawn up almost to his stomach, his face screwed up into an expression of painful fury. His cry had sliced through her, making the muscles across her stomach contract in a parody of birth. She wanted to pick him up and comfort him. But she had tried that already, walked incessantly to and fro since five a.m. She was tired and hungry herself. And Richard had not even made her a cup of tea, furious with her as if she had purposefully *made* James cry.

Their son had been premature. He had arrived thin and angry and jaundiced, with his two tiny fists clenched. He was not at all the idyllically perfect baby they had imagined. He had slept erratically, waking at half-hour intervals through the night. Nothing placated him. He brought back his feeds. Jamie had even turned his head away from the mobile with its musical lullaby.

And the pretty nursery that they had dedicated to him—spending so much time on rag-rolling the walls, hand-painting the nursery-rhyme mural—was lost along with all the other fantasies. It was now just a disaster area, heaped with bags of Pampers, scrunched tissues, discarded clothes.

'I'll manage,' Kate had retorted. She could not say what was really in her mind. She had to get out of the house. She *had* to. She had to see her friend. She had to talk about something other than babies for a few hours. Cathy used to work at the paper—oh Christ, Kate had thought, closing her eyes momentarily, recalling the frenzy of her job with unadulterated longing. Cathy would willingly talk shop all day. She would also welcome Kate with open arms and a bottle of wine. All the things that Kate needed right now. Right *now*.

Jamie began to scream in earnest, arching his back. Richard had gone downstairs by now. Distractedly, Kate had scooped Jamie from the bed and run downstairs with him in her arms.

Richard was already at the car, the alarm unlocking to its usual high-pitched three notes. The sounds went through Kate like knives. She had glanced down at James's contorted face with something like sympathy.

'So you won't be back tonight?' Richard had said.

'I told you. She invited me overnight.'

Richard had shaken his head in disbelief. 'You're insane,' he told her, door open, and one foot already inside the car. 'You've hardly left the house since you got back from hospital. You've only walked down the road twice in four bloody weeks! And you think you can—'

'I'll be *fine*,' Kate had replied.

He grinned. 'Mad,' he told her, and got into the car.

She had watched him drive away along the crowded suburban street. 'Drive carefully,' she muttered.

She had finally got out of the house three hours later. It did take her more time than she had hoped to get through the London midday traffic and out on to the motorway. And all the way she had cursed the other drivers on the road. She had even almost driven into the back of one car in Earls Court.

She sighed now, squinting at the blue motorway signs looming ahead. Visibility was poor. Other cars began to switch on their head-lights. It was only one o'clock in the afternoon.

She had seen the sign, *Services 2 miles*.

She had glanced back to the baby seat.

Jamie was, unbelievably, blissfully, asleep; lulled at last by the motion of the car. He had yelled non-stop for the first hour, despite having just been fed and changed. She had pulled up at a set of traffic lights in Lewisham, and seen a woman in a car alongside glancing at the back seat, and then again at her. The woman had long dark hair; her gaze was fixed. Probably she can hear him scream, Kate had thought. Probably she thinks I'm an appalling mother. She had gripped the steering wheel, her eyes fixed on the lights, praying for them to change, while Jamie's cries filled the car.

Another five miles on, he had still been wailing. To her horror, glancing back at him momentarily, Kate had realised that he was turning blue in the face. She had screeched the car into a lay-by, jumped out of the car, opened the back door, and pulled him from his seat. As soon as she touched him, he had stopped crying and lay in her arms, his face blotched and swollen, overheated.

Frantic, wordless anxiety coursed through her, all the more piercing because it was so irrational. There was nothing obviously wrong with him: the Health Visitor had told her so only two days before. *He's just a crier*, she had said. So soothing, such a little phrase. It hardly summed up the surging desperation she felt.

She had paced up and down on the windswept tarmac while lorries and buses thundered past, blowing her hair blindingly across her eyes.

'What's the matter with you?' She had said, holding him in front of her, trying to resist the urge to shake him. 'Please, *please*. Tell me what's the matter.'

As she had got to the edge of London and joined the motorway, the noise from the back seat had lessened. She kept turning round, snatching looks at him. Eventually, she turned to see him asleep, looking like an angel, a baby from a TV commercial, a wisp of blond hair stuck to his forehead, escaping from the blue knitted cap. Her throat closed, choked with frustrated love.

Services 1 mile.

She felt her eyelids droop, just for a second. It was risky to pull in, she knew. Dangerous to slow down, to interrupt the rolling drone of the engine. It would undoubtedly wake him up again. And yet it was more dangerous to go on, tired as she was.

She had only grabbed a slice of toast for breakfast, and had missed lunch altogether. More than that—she looked at the looming sliproad for the service area, only a hundred yards away now—she simply had to stop because she needed the loo.

She had signalled left.

Perhaps she could wake him and feed him. Her heart immediately sank at the thought; trying to feed him, in public, while he turned his face away.

'Please,' she had sighed. 'Please don't let him cry.'

She had pulled in close to the entrance, and turned the engine off, holding her breath. She had stayed for a while, looking at the people going in and out. Jamie, miraculously, did not stir. Cramp flashed across her stomach: she really did need the loo at once. Fatigue made the bleak prospect of the service forecourt swim in and out of focus. She had never felt so utterly drained. She glanced up into the driver's mirror, and saw her own face. She looked terrible: tired, white. What little make-up she had put on that morning was now smudged, the mascara describing two panda-like circles under her eyes.

She wet her finger and rubbed determinedly at them. God forbid that she should turn up at Cathy's looking like this, she thought. The last time she had seen her friend, they were at an awards lunch. A thousand years ago, in another lifetime.

She had got out of the car. Like a sleepwalker, she felt numb.

Opening the back door, she leaned down to James. With her face close to his, she could hear that his breathing was deep and regular. She had looked at him closely, knowing at once that she couldn't bear to break this wonderful silence. The poor child was obviously as tired as she was. Her hand had remained on the childlock on the babyseat for a long time. Then, she had straightened up.

She had left the car, and started to run.

She could see the toilets, just inside the door of the building ahead of her. She had run in, grabbing the first empty cubicle. When she came out, she stood for a second to run water over her hands. It had perhaps taken ninety seconds. Ninety seconds; two minutes at most.

And here—and now—the knowledge that she was dreaming reasserted itself. The picture created by the dream began to waver, to shake. Sounds accompanying the image ballooned and dropped alternately. In the dream, in reality, her heartbeat quickened, her body ached and tensed.

The car door, the dream whispered. *Such a hurry, such a hurry . . . dear, dear.* Disapproval in the disembodied voice of the dream, a voice faintly reminiscent of her old headmistress's critical tone. *The car door, Kate . . . did you lock the car door?*

She came out of the building. She could see the car clearly. She could see the edge of James's seat, a curve peeping behind the driver's headrest.

She had taken the ignition from her pocket, glancing at her watch. Another forty-some miles to go. She looked up at the darkening sky, and realised that a few dry, light flakes were falling.

'Snow,' she had murmured. 'Oh, great.' She didn't register then, even with the key in the lock, that the door was actually still open. No lock. No resistance to the key. She had run across the forecourt in that dazed, exhausted, racing panic, taking the key . . . but not locking the door.

I was only a few seconds, she thought.

Only a few short, short seconds . . .

Snow . . . snow . . . snow.

Thick flakes drowning her. Thick solid drifts through which she tried to find her way now, the dream flakes fictionally huge, threatening to engulf her. Snow drowning her, entombing her.

She had got in the car.

Turned round, smiling, in her seat to check on him.

But the seat had been empty.

Her son was gone.

TWELVE

*I*T WAS VERY LATE, but he could not sleep that night.

At last, he got up, pulling on the clothes that he had taken off only an hour ago. He went up the steps, and opened the door to the roof space. He didn't put on the light tonight: the house was full of women, and he wanted to feel them round him. He went to the sloping window and opened it, breathing in the cold night.

There were no other lights anywhere. He might have been alone, the only person alive on earth. He left the window open, savouring the cold, as he walked to the first of the cabinets under the typewriter shelves. In the drawers, he kept their files: more than a hundred now, all in their neat blue folders.

He put his hand randomly into the drawer. When he opened the first file, newsprint stared back at him. He stood with her in his hands, a woman of forty who had been so confused and afraid. When the article in the newspaper came out, she had already been missing for a day, and it was a week later that her body had been found, washed up on the shore near Kingsley.

Appropriate. She had been a kind of flotsam, washed up by life on a variety of foreign shores. A drinker, an addict, she was not really wanted anywhere. She had even shunned the short consolation that he had given her.

He put the folder down, and tried another.

This one was far more interesting. This woman had been seen walking down a busy December street two years ago. A well-dressed, cultured person, who bore inside her a seed that only he and she knew existed. He had found that out as she talked to him. She had been the daughter of a distant, uncaring father. Such women invariably tried too hard. Dressed too well, worked too frantically, raised too-perfect children.

She had vanished the same afternoon, and never been found. Mourned by her family. Hunted by them and the police to absolutely no avail. To all intents and purposes, she had simply evaporated from existence that December day, leaving no trace at all, except the empty car in a deserted car park. He smiled briefly. She had excelled herself.

The best games were silent. Conceived in silence, exacted by inches, by degrees. Little pressures, little stresses. Touch this string and watch her dance. Touch another and watch her drown. Pull a little this way and watch her climb. Pull a little the other and watch her fall.

Even if she ignored him now, one day Kate McCaulay would know him. One day, when it was too late, she would recognise him, and understand the damage he had inflicted on her.

And the reason why.

He looked down at his desk, sheltered by its partition. At the typewriter covered by its black lid.

There on the desk top, the second letter was waiting.

THIRTEEN

*J*ACK SEWARD PAUSED AT THE CORNER of the London street, and, taking a piece of paper from his pocket, he checked the address.

The road looked as affluent as he had expected; after all, when he visited the estate agents an hour ago, and saw the brochure for the house, he had given a low whistle at the price.

'It's an extraordinary property,' the salesman had assured him.

'I'm sure it is,' Jack had replied. 'It would have to be.'

They didn't question his interest in the place. It seemed that, looking as he did, with a day's growth of beard, almost bare-kneed cords, and a worn leather jacket, was entirely the kind of look deemed appropriate for South Kensington.

'Would you like to view?' the man asked him as he sat sorting through leaflets.

He held up the brochure. 'Has this place always been this pricey?'

'This particular house . . . ?'

'No. The street. The area.'

The salesman shrugged. 'Perhaps not so exclusive a while ago. Certain areas come up, others go down, of course.'

'But it would have been, say ten years ago . . .'

'Attractive.'

'Many people moving in and out?'

'Oh, yes. The Baron's Reach development began around that time. The whole area changed.'

'I see.' Jack had stood up, stowing several brochures, rolled, into his jacket pocket.

'Would you care to view anything?'

'I'll think about it,' he said.

He was as good as his word. He thought about it through lunch, a sandwich that he ate sitting on a park bench, watching pigeons picking desultorily at the grey grass. He thought about Kate McCaulay, and the file of photographs he had at home, carefully kept apart from his work.

When he left the park, he made for the street. It was a line of Georgian houses, narrow-fronted, each with an iron railing and a basement floor. In occasional windows, he could glimpse well-furnished rooms; in one, as a woman came out as he passed, he saw a white hall of such grandeur that he stopped momentarily, surprised at the polished stone flooring, the airy staircase behind her. She gave him a suspicious look.

'Could you help me?' he said.

She paused, key in hand, a briefcase in the other. Then she took a small step backwards.

He showed her the press card, holding it out to her so that she could bend down to see it and still keep him at the safe distance at the bottom of her steps.

'Chasing a story?' she asked. The tone was sarcastic.

'An old one,' he said. 'Have you lived here long?'

She was still assessing him. 'Three years.'

'I see. Would you know of anyone who has lived here longer?'

'Why?'

'I'm looking into something that happened ten years ago. An abduction.'

She raised her eyebrows, interested at last. 'In this street?'

'A child.'

'Really?' She looked him up and down. 'What are you, a private investigator?'

'No.' He waved the card.

She smiled. 'Listen, I know a lot of people on the nationals,' she said. 'And you don't look like them.'

'Good,' he said.

She laughed, finally locking her door. She came down the steps with a supercilious smile on her face. 'If you're that keen on a dead story, ask at number 30,' she said as she passed him. 'There's some old dear there who wouldn't shift for the developer. The green place—green paint, green door. Hideous.'

'Thanks,' he said.

He watched her go, waiting for at least a minute to see if she looked back. Rather to his relief, she did not.

FOURTEEN

$\mathcal{G}$EORGE WAS SITTING IN THE BACK OF THE GALLERY reading the morning paper when he heard Kate descending the stairs from the flat.

He glanced at his watch; it was eight o'clock. He got up immediately, and walked to the front door. He paused for a second, weighing up what he should do. Then he saw her start to cross the yard, dressed in jogging sweatshirt and pants. She looked as if she had several layers on, he noticed; her figure was obscured by squarish, padded shoulders and hips.

He opened the outside door. 'Kate!' he called.

She turned to look.

She seemed actually to be frightened for a second. Then, her expression relaxed.

'I'm sorry,' he said at once. 'I wanted to catch you before the shop opened. I've got Henry Phelps coming in first thing. You know how he goes on.'

She stopped, looked at her feet, then walked across. 'What is it?' she asked.

'Come inside a moment,' he said. He let her go through the ground floor ahead of him.

Reaching the back, he motioned her towards a table that he had already set with a coffee service. She questioned him with a raised eyebrow. 'What's the occasion?'

'No occasion.'

'This is your best set.'

'Well . . . just a whim. Do you want a cup?'

'George, I'm just about to go running.'

'What are you doing today?' he asked. 'Anything interesting?'

She frowned.

'Are you cold?' he asked.

'No, no.'

'I'll put the Calor Gas on.'

'No. Don't bother.'

'It's no bother.' He lit the stove and pulled it closer to them.

He poured his own coffee, trying desperately to think of a neutral topic of conversation. At last he nodded in the direction of the newspaper. 'Another cock-up with the Government,' he said.

'Is there?'

'Some witless MP with his secretary.'

She smiled briefly.

'You never read the papers, do you?'

'No.'

'Why is that?'

She shrugged.

'I thought journalists read all the opposition,' he said.

'I'm not a journalist, George. I just write the odd piece. Look, I have to go—'

He gazed at her, seeing her mouth become a thin, obstructive line. For five years she had lived here, he thought. Five years of being under his own roof. That was longer than a lot of marriages. And yet she never let him get close to her.

Last year, after letting in a workman to do a routine repair—the shower, Kate had told him, wouldn't keep a constant temperature— he had stood on the threshold of her flat, knowing how much she valued her privacy, and yet unable to resist looking at the way she had left the room. He couldn't get over the coldness, the stark emptiness. It had struck him as dreadfully sad. The image had stayed in his mind.

The clatter of the post on the mat interrupted his train of thought. He saw Kate jump; she glanced back at the door. He put out his hand; she immediately withdrew, stepping backwards.

'I've got a surprise for you,' he said.

'Sorry?'

'Surprise. In the house.' He indicated the connecting door. She looked from it to him. 'It won't take a minute,' he said.

She opened her mouth as if to say something, but did not. She gave a short sigh of resignation.

He tried talking over his shoulder as they walked through to his cottage, keeping up a stream of noise to hide his nervousness. 'I'm going to redecorate this hall. What do you think? I had an idea, maybe the walls striped, very pale, not Regency . . .'

She didn't reply. They emerged into his sitting room.

The desk was standing in the centre. He had spent the previous evening polishing it, cleaning the locks, the metal keyholes in the drawers.

'What do you think?' he asked.

She stood for a second; then walked around it. 'It's lovely.'

'You really think so?'

'Yes, I do.'

'I bought it two days ago.'

'It's very nice.'

'Is it the same?'

She looked up. 'Pardon?'

'Is it the same as yours?'

A trespass. His heart banged hard in his chest. When she had first come here, when he had first shown her around the shop and asked if she might help occasionally, and whether she knew anything about antiques, she had told him that she once used to go to auctions herself. 'As you do, when you're setting up home,' she had said. It had been a very quiet, thrownaway aside. And she had added, as quietly, 'I once bought a Dutch bureau. That was my star purchase.'

She had described it exactly as this one.

'Mine?' she asked.

'The one you used to have.'

Her gaze fixed on him. Don't be angry, he thought.

'I never had anything like this,' she said.

'A Dutch bureau.'

'Oh . . . a . . .' She seemed to make an enormous effort to remember. 'A small one, much smaller.' She looked away. 'George, I must go.'

'But this—'

'It's lovely. I'm sure it'll sell.'

'But it's not for the shop,' he said. 'It's for you.'

She stopped dead, in the doorway of the room.

The words poured out of his mouth, stumbling over each other in his haste. 'I want you to have it,' he told her. 'As a gift. I know you haven't got too many things . . .' Damn. That wasn't right. He didn't want her to think that this was a charitable gesture. 'I mean, I saw it, and I thought it was you exactly, just what you might like, and it would be useful, for your papers, to put your files and your papers in, things like that—'

'George,' she said, cutting through him, 'I can't take this. First the bracelet and now this.' She eyed him thoughtfully. 'Why are you doing this? I don't understand.'

Embarrassed, he began to laugh. He thought at once that his voice made a booming, unnatural sound in the low-beamed room. 'But I *want* you to have it,' he said.

'George—'

'Look, dear,' he said. 'I don't want to make a big deal over this. You do a lot of work for me, you stand in for me at short notice, and you never let me pay you—'

'I don't want paying. That's what the low rent was about, wasn't it? A low rent on the understanding that I worked in the shop when you needed me. That was the arrangement.'

'Yes, yes. But you really do a tremendous amount.' He tried to lighten his voice. 'I use you disgracefully, you know—'

'George, this is stupid.'

'No. It's not,' he protested. 'It's a nice little bureau and I would like you to have it. A token of my thanks, and my . . . respect . . .' The flush came back to his face with renewed ferocity. Young people didn't say that, did they? A *token of my respect.*

She stood looking at him for what seemed like an eternity.

'I'm sorry, George,' she said, finally. 'You're very kind, but it's far too much. Far too much. I'm sorry.' She began to walk, then hesitated and turned back to him.

'And I can't keep the bracelet, George, for the same reason.'

She left the room, closing the door behind her, moving into the shop. He heard her footsteps along the ground floor.

He closed his eyes, thumping a closed fist against his leg.

FIFTEEN

$\mathcal{L}$ATER THAT MORNING, it began to rain. Kate, too early for her appointment, sat in the lane a half-mile from the farm she was due to visit. While she waited, the drizzle matured into a downpour, splashing the windscreen. She had a feeling of detachment, of unfixed buoyancy, as though adrift in an invisible current.

In the hedge alongside her, the last leaves clung to branches shiny with moisture. They looked surreal: veins of orange against brown flesh.

Through the window, Cinder Break filled the view, a deeply indented valley between two smooth, sweeping hills. The Break itself topped the landscape, a darker green spine of trees. Kate had originally come to this part of the country for the comfort of these places: their emptiness, their breadth. Their isolation had matched hers.

I know where he is . . .

She willed the empty feeling back. She had made the silence in her head, instructed it, enforced it. It was her defence. But, since the letter, it was unaccountably slithering from her.

She wiped a clear space in the growing condensation on the windscreen. The farm ahead was marked with a stream of pale smoke, almost vertical.

'Come on,' she whispered to herself.

Over the phone, the woman she was going to see this morning had sounded robust: shouting so loudly, in fact, that it had been necessary for Kate to hold the phone away from her ear as Mrs Dearsley had given directions.

Kate had almost had an accident in the car as she had left the lane to the Gallery. When she pulled out into the road, another vehicle had swerved to miss her, and had mounted the pavement on the other side of the village street. The driver had stopped; she had stopped. Other traffic had pulled up on either side.

After a few terrible seconds, Kate had managed to raise a hand, acknowledge her mistake. She genuinely had not seen him although she had looked. She did not know how she could have looked along the road and registered nothing—no oncoming traffic—at all.

The sound of the rain increased. In her head, it was thin pricks of grey; she felt them falling through her head and into her mouth like needles. Unable to bear the sensation, she watched her fingers uncurl, saw her hand descend to the ignition. She turned on the engine, and put the car into gear.

Mrs Dearsley was waiting for her in the broad, dirty farmyard, on the steps of the outhouse. Kate got out of the car, and ran across through the rain, holding a sheaf of papers over her head.

'Come in, come in,' the woman said. 'If that en't half changed, though? Bloody weather.'

'Yes . . .' Kate shook the rain from her coat.

'Sit yourself down. I've got the kettle on.'

Kate looked around her. 'So this is your workshop?'

'This is it.'

There was a stone sink in one corner, a small electric stove, and a dozen battered containers spread about on the drainer and the floor. Mrs Dearsley made a living spinning yarns, dyeing them. She was perfect for 'The Odd Angle'.

'I'm doing indigo today,' she was saying, all enthusiasm. 'You see? It'll come out like this.'

She pointed to the wall, where hanks of yarn were pinned to a noticeboard. The colouring was precise, each with a little white tab label—'Number 7, onion red, 1 gramme tartar . . . Number 22, 80 gramme cutch, iron mordant . . .'

The room in Kate's vision rotated a little, lurching and falling gently. The breath sounded loud in her throat. Sitting on the edge of the wooden chair, Kate sensed panic sweeping towards her, telegraphing a message of disaster through the rolling room. *What was the message?* She closed her eyes, waiting for the pitching to stop.

I know where he is.

This is no good, she thought. No bloody good at all.

She opened her eyes. She looked fixedly at the shades of blue on the wall. 'They are lovely,' she said.

Mrs Dearsley smiled broadly. 'You can't get colours like that with chemicals.'

She wasn't at all like her voice. It had betrayed her. She was a slim, friendly-looking person of about forty, with a ring of broken-veined red on each cheek that made her look like a painted doll. She was taking down a canister of tea, spooning the leaves into a pot.

'Does it . . .' Kate's mind suddenly went blank. She had known what the question was—something to do with the time of dyeing— but it had vanished completely from her head. The colour directly in front of her vibrated with a hue that was deeper than blue, brighter than green.

Mrs Dearsley handed her the tea in a large mug with red cockerels dancing around the rim. Kate looked down at herself, absorbing the blankness of the black in her clothes.

It was the colours, the screaming, intense colours, that were the problem, she thought distractedly.

Get a hold of yourself.

Get a hold.

'Fifty years is the most for chemical dyes,' Mrs Dearsley was saying. 'These, though, they'll last hundreds of years. And the dyes are cool. You can put your hand in the water.'

Kate made an intense effort. 'And you . . . you use just goat hair?'

'Oh, no. We've got mohair rabbits, and sheep. Jacob Cross and Shetland. You can see them if you want. D'you want?'

'Yes,' Kate said. 'Yes, fine.'

The woman put on a waxed jacket, taking it down from a peg behind the door. 'Did you find us all right?'

'Yes.'

'I thought I saw you parked.'

'Oh . . . I was early.'

'I saw you coming and then stop. I thought, she's not sure if it's us.'

'I was just a bit early.'

The woman looked at her acutely, then passed out into the yard, into the still-slanting rain.

'You've got good shoes on?' she asked over her shoulder. 'It's muddy.'

They went to the field gate. The rain hammered on them. There were probably twenty goats in the small paddock.

'We clip them twice a year. The rabbits we clip ten times . . .'

Kate looked down at the nearest animal. It raised its head and stared back with slanting, yellow eyes. She held out her hand.

I know where he is.

Abruptly, suddenly, with frightening ferocity, the field telescoped downwards, drawn to a point, a circle of vivid light. Her heart congested, pumping what felt like clay in place of blood. Her palms slithered on the gate.

Someone in the farmhouse opened a window and called: another woman. Behind her in the kitchen, a radio was playing. The noises jumbled, flapping against the side of Kate's skull, a pack of playing cards, fluttering, cracking.

Kate turned away from the gate. The car was fifty yards away, parked at the side of the yard.

'I have to go,' she said.

Mrs Dearsley turned, ducking her head against the rain to look into Kate's face. 'Whatever's the matter?' she asked. 'He didn't bite you, did he? They do, sometimes. Is it bad? Let me see.' And she made a grasp for Kate's hand, the one she had extended over the top of the gate.

'No.' Kate snatched her fingers away. 'No, it's all right.'

She began to walk, her legs numb under her. She had a sudden conviction that she was going to be sick.

'What's the matter?' Mrs Dearsley's voice, raised in high-pitched concern, followed her.

By the time she got to the car, Kate was gasping for breath. Clouds pressed in at each side of her vision, squeezing the picture of her hands, fumbling with the keys, to a thin distortion an inch wide.

She got the door open, and fell in, turning the key, hearing the welcoming roar of the engine. The other woman was at the driver's window, tapping to get her attention.

'What is it?' she was saying. 'Do you want to come into the house?'

Kate shoved the car into reverse. 'I'm sorry,' she muttered, hauling on the wheel. She managed to turn it around, her foot slipping twice from the pedals, while the car bucked and stuttered. She saw that Mrs Dearsley had stopped in the centre of the yard, her hands clasped. She looked desperately upset.

'I'm sorry,' Kate repeated.

She leaned on the accelerator. The car shot up the incline, occasionally clipping the raised verge and the branches of the hedge.

At the junction with the larger road, Kate turned left. The view through the windscreen raced at her, swimming in and out of focus. She felt something on her hands, and looked down to see, in horror and astonishment, that she was crying and the sensation was the tears dropping on her.

I know where he is.

In five minutes, she had reached Easting, a group of houses on a crossroads. She stared at the signpost.

After a minute or so, another car drew up behind her. The driver waited, then blew on his horn. She could not move.

The world had halted, all its significance crammed into the indecipherable words on the black-and-white road sign. Eventually, the other driver reversed, and swung his car around her. She sensed him looking at her, but she could not turn her head.

Finally, she signalled right and moved forward. For all she knew, there was a stream of traffic coming along the main road. It was a high, straight section of Roman road that ran parallel to the coast; cars hurtled through here at eighty. Yet she drove out. She felt detached from her body, rising high over the car.

She looked down at herself, a dark shape in a white box beneath her. The car stood out in the curtain of closing rain, a toy moving along the thread of carriageway.

She was high up now, a hundred feet high, the land smoothing to a sheet of green cartidge paper, the road merely a line, and the air rushing around her.

There was an oak door.

A sign at the side of it, handwritten in an italic script enclosed under a strip of plastic, said, *Patients. Please enter and wait in the hall.*

Enter.

Kate tried to fix on what the words meant. She looked at her watch. It was twenty past one. It was two hours since she had been at the Dearsley farm.

Enter and wait.

Two hours . . .

Enter and wait.

The light in the hall was very subdued. There was a yellow upholstered chair, a table with a few magazines. A mirror behind the chair, and a yellow rug on the polished floor.

'Hello,' said a man's voice.

She glanced up. 'Hello. Is it . . . it's Dr Reeve?' She really meant the question. She had been convinced, a few moments ago, that she had the right place, but now was not so sure. She couldn't recognise him.

Twenty past one. Two hours . . .

'Not Doctor. Just Mister.' He held out his hand, smiling warmly. He looked vastly pleased to see her. 'Jonathan.'

She didn't take it. She felt that she couldn't. Couldn't touch anyone.

'It's Miss McCaulay, isn't it?' he asked.

She continued to stare, locked in place, rigid.

Two hours . . . Where have I been for two hours?

'We met a little while ago,' he said. 'Last Christmas?'

'Yes,' she said.

'How are you?' he asked. His voice was very smooth, flowing. He had moved a little closer.

She saw, as if for the first time, that Jonathan Reeve was a handsome man, perhaps a little younger than her. He had thick, light brown hair, grey eyes. He was her own height. His expression was kindly and concerned.

'I'm sorry to come here,' she said.

'Not at all. You've been before, to interview me. After Christmas ...' His tone was gently cajoling. 'You wrote a very good piece about me for your newspaper column. We talked on the phone.'

'Yes.' She didn't remember. He sounded as if he wanted her to remember. She tried, and recalled only the house, down a lane just a mile from the crossroads where the other car had moved around her. She remembered the name of it—Kilcot Down House—written on a white stone at the edge of the road, and the trees lacing overhead. 'I shouldn't just come here,' she murmured, 'without arranging ...'

What? Without arranging what?

Two entire hours.

Jonathan Reeve put his hand on her arm. 'That's all right,' he said. 'It's lunchtime. You don't need an appointment. I don't have any patients until three today.'

She heard her own voice tremble. 'Mr Reeve,' she said, slowly, 'could you please help me?'

SIXTEEN

*T*HE POLICE HAD HEARD FROM THE OLD WOMAN BEFORE.

It was not that she was deliberately time-wasting; she was just lonely. She had lived in the same seafront block of flats for twenty years, alone; and sometimes the nights were fractured by noises, and sometimes the days were too long, and sometimes she simply felt bad. Whatever it was, the Sergeant would patiently come, because he knew her, and because his own mother lived alone too.

Mrs Westham was on the step, waiting for him.

'Upstairs,' she said, before he had even reached the door where she stood. She waved her arm behind her. 'The flat upstairs from me.'

He took off his hat as he came inside, shutting the street door against the cold wind blowing across the bay.

'Do you know who lives there?'

'A girl.'

'Do you know her name?'

'No. Passed her on the stairs once or twice. Come and see . . . you come and see . . .'

She ascended slowly, complaining about her arthritis. 'I always

70

know when he comes,' she was saying. 'It's always in the evening. I hear voices in the evenings. Not at weekends. Not in the day . . .'

The Sergeant tried not to look at the stocking tops, hitched just above the knee, that flashed above him with every tread of the stairs.

'He come last night,' she was saying. 'It would be about ten. I heard him knocking on the door. She must have already gone to bed because he knocked a long time before she let him in. I heard them talking, then nothing. Then, about one o'clock, they woke me up . . .'

She had reached the last flat in the block, the little square landing outside Maggie Spence's room.

Mrs Westham made no attempt to go any further forward. She turned to look at the policeman's face.

'I don't like to go in,' she said. 'The door's open, and you can . . .' she leaned forward slightly, 'see something, just on the floor there . . .'

The Sergeant gently edged past her. 'You heard the girl arguing with a man?'

'Oh, yes. Woke me up, lasted . . . maybe three or four minutes—'

'At one o'clock this morning?'

'Yes. Then I heard him going down the stairs. Very quick. I heard the outside door close. I tried to get across the room to see him in the street, but I can't move quick enough.'

'So you didn't see him?'

'No.'

'Have you ever seen the man who came here?'

'No.' The old lady shook her head emphatically. 'Never seen him. Just heard him.'

She grasped his sleeve between bony thumb and forefinger. 'Just inside the door? Am I right? Is it her?'

He stepped forward.

Maggie Spence lay on the threadbare red carpet just inside the door. She was on her side, her head tilted upwards to face the ceiling, her legs curled beneath her. One arm was bent to rest in front of her, the other was extended straight out under her head. It was the tips of her fingers that Mrs Westham had been able to see.

The Sergeant bent down and tentatively touched the side of her neck, feeling for a pulse.

She was cold.

He looked at Maggie's open eyes, the tip of the tongue resting on her lips, the bluish tinge to the tongue and mouth, the red specks on the skin. On the throat, just under the line of the jaw, were a series of bruises.

Sighing, he stood up, and glanced back at the room.

The bed had been slept in. Clothes were scattered about. A book was open and turned face down on the chair beside the bed. It was a paperback romance.

'What's happened?' Mrs Westham asked. He heard her shuffling forward.

'Keep back a minute, love,' he said, depressing the switch on his radio.

'Is it her? What's happened to her?'

'Keep back, sweetheart. You and me'll have a chat in a second.'

He looked down at Maggie's face. Pity, he thought. She was such a pretty girl too.

SEVENTEEN

'KATE, WHAT CAN YOU SEE?'

She is standing in darkness. The shapes overhead might be clouds, ink over ink, black over black. Or trees, or hands. Or high ceilings. Or she is looking down, into a fathomless pit.

'Kate, what can you see?' he repeated.

'Nothing.'

'Nothing at all? There *is* something.'

'Just black.'

'Walk forward. Far forward, into where it's lighter.'

She rolls her head, resisting.

'Kate, take me to see Jamie.'

'No . . .' It is a breathed sigh, almost childish.

'This is his room,' Jonathan Reeve prompts.

She says nothing this time.

'Kate, can you see Jamie?'

She doesn't see him, or hear him. But she *feels* him, the centre of his hand, the palm already lined, the fingers curled round the inch of soft skin. His small hand is pressed to her face, investigating the texture.

'Kate, can you hear me?'

'Yes.'

'What is happening? Tell me.'

Jamie was born four weeks early, barely five pounds in weight.

Kate had woken after being taken back to the ward; it had been an eight-hour labour and she was exhausted. She had really slept. Then, when it was still barely dawn, she had woken, and looked to the empty cot beside the bed. He had gone; they had wheeled him to the nursery.

She had gone down the corridor, frantically tying her dressing gown around her, her feet cold on the polished floor, looking for him. Five forty in the morning. She got to the door of the nursery out of breath, and saw the night staff sleepily talking, two cups of tea at their side on the table.

'Where is he?' she had demanded. 'Can I see him?'

Two other babies had been born in the night. They were full term, and huge; next to them Jamie, in an incubator, was tiny, doll-like, naked, on his stomach, the legs drawn up. This first sight of him had appalled her with its utter defencelessness.

'Get him out of there,' she had said. 'Get him out, get him out.'

They had put him in her arms, soothing her, explaining. She didn't hear a word. She had looked at him in amazement. He had come out of her. Been like this, perfect, inside, while she rushed about working, made love to Richard, cooked meals, slept. Perfect, perfect.

It was still dark. January. She walked to the window with him in her arms and showed him the snow, coming down in lazy, loose flakes, filling the window sill, icing the roof opposite. There was a pinch of light in the early morning sky, a reflection from the city.

'Look, Jamie. Snow . . .'

'Kate. What is happening?'

Here comes home.

Richard on the step, laughing, trying to get the Moses basket in through the hallway. Their next-door neighbour is in the house. She has made them coffee. There is a crowd; Richard's boss and his wife, the neighbour, someone else, a milling sea of faces. Richard gives her a glass of champagne.

The neighbour comes forward, smiling broadly, holding out her hands. 'May I hold him?'

Whether or not it's the champagne, she doesn't know. But she refuses. And laughs. 'I'm never letting him go,' she says.

'You used to say that about me,' Richard calls, across the kitchen.

'I'm never letting *either* of you go!'

No. She can't have that in her mind. She can't carry it. Jamie's hand evaporates. It is dust, or air, or water, taken back wherever he came from.

Out of nothing into nothing.

His hand, Richard's voice, the house, the noise. They all shrink and stop, every face, every word, every sound. A film on pause.

Erase, erase.

'What can you see?'

She plunges away from the agonising scene. At last, coming up from below, a wall without a top, without an end on either side, left or right.

Jonathan Reeve's voice is melodic and low. 'What is the wall made of?'

She laughs, her eyes firmly closed. He suddenly strikes her as funny, transporting her about like this, like Merlin. 'Stones. Big stones.'

'Just stones?'

'What else?'

'You tell me. What kind of stones?'

'Big, greenish ones. Grown over. Lichen.'

'What are you going to do? Are you going to climb it?'

She begins laughing out loud. Ridiculous man. No one could climb something that size.

'Is there any gap in the wall?'

'No.'

'Look harder. There's a gap.'

'*Nothing.*'

'There's a gap. Just a small one.'

She moves her head from side to side, the smile disappearing from her face. Her eyes are tightly shut.

'Lift your hand to the wall and feel the space between the stones.'

She crosses her arms.

'Kate, don't you want to see the gap?'

She doesn't want to see the wall. She turns round, ready to plunge back into the pit yawning behind her. Invisible, invisible.

'Kate, I am with you all the time. You can come to no harm. Look at the wall. Where is it?'

She relents. 'Just ahead.'

'Why? Where are you standing?'

'In trees. In the dark somewhere.'

'Why is there a wall where there are trees?'

'*I* don't know.' Petulant.

'You do. Who built it?'

'I don't know.'

'You do. Who built the wall?'

She sees Reeve. Coming down the line of the wall, on her side, through the overhanging leaves. She stiffens, seeing his feet moving towards her, breaking the branches underfoot, his face sliced by intermittent light.

'Kate, come back to the wall.'

She begins breathing heavily. Her hands move on the arms of the chair.

'All right, Kate. All right.'

Reeve's image flattens and fades. His threat recedes. The wall fades too, losing its detail, growing taller, curving over, until the ground underneath her and the air around her are all the same fabric. Not stone, not solid. A flexible, moving mask. A covering.

'Kate, come forward. There's nothing to be afraid of. Nothing can happen, nothing any worse than has already happened. You can take away the fear if you turn and confront it. Do you understand?'

She has relaxed, but only marginally. He notices what he saw the first time she came into his house, that curious flatness in her expression.

'Kate, you have to reply.'

'Yes . . . all right.' Angry with him.

'Do you understand about facing the things that worry you?'

A long pause. 'Yes.'

'All right, Kate. Come back now. See the road. A flat road. Walk back with me . . .'

* * *

By now, it was five thirty.

Jonathan Reeve had cancelled the two other appointments that afternoon.

He came back into the consulting room, carrying a tray of tea.

She had slept for a while after the sedation and the subsequent visualisation. As he walked into the room, she sat up gradually, rubbing her hands over her face.

'How are you feeling?' he asked.

She shook her head. He took her pulse, and she submitted to him hangdoggedly, as if she ought but did not want to.

'Are you tired?'

'Yes.'

He gave her the tea.

'What is it?' she asked.

'Just herbal. Camomile. Try it.'

She did, but with obvious mistrust. Eventually, she sat back and looked at him. 'I don't know what happened today,' she said.

He paused to think of a way of phrasing it. 'Think of it like a system breakdown on a computer,' he said finally. 'The files were too full, the capacity too small. It is a cardinal fact that you can't store away disturbances and expect them to disappear. They will re-emerge. It might be years later, but emerge they will, sometimes in the oddest ways.' He leaned forward. 'Would you show me the letter?'

She had given a garbled version of the last few days when she had first arrived. Now, she gave him a stricken look.

'It's all right to let other people share your problems,' he said.

She shuddered, almost from revulsion.

'You don't want me to know?' he asked.

'I can't . . .' She tried to find the words. 'I just can't bear anyone knowing,' she said.

'Why do you think that is?'

'I . . .' She really did not want to have this conversation. She wanted to go back to her flat and shut the door. Not come out again for a long time. Until the days were smooth and uneventful again. 'It was everyone's property when it happened,' she said. 'Now it's mine. I don't want to belong to anyone. I can't stand it.'

'You mean you don't want Jamie's disappearance to belong to anyone, to be studied by them?'

'Yes.'

'That's not what you said.'

'Pardon?'

'Never mind. Pass on that now.' He smiled, drank a little tea, and sat back, crossing his legs. 'Tell me why everyone knowing was so hurtful. Surely people were supportive, comforting?'

'No.'

'But they helped you? The police, the counsellors?'

'No.' She pressed her hands to either side of her head, her elbows on her knees. 'Yes, yes, they did everything. They were forever in the house, they rang up all the time, they sent social workers, we saw two women who did some sort of stress counselling . . . it was no good. You can't . . . touch the pain. And the newspapers, Christ . . .'

'You worked on a newspaper yourself, then.'

'Yes.'

'What did they do?'

'Don't you remember?'

'Tell me.'

She sighed. The force of it shook her body. She collapsed backwards in the seat, her eyes fixed somewhere beyond the room. 'They ran a campaign. *Have You Seen Jamie Lydiatt?* It went on for a week. Then again after another week. *Where is Jamie Lydiatt?* Then again after a month. *Have You Seen This Child?* They printed his photograph, and the headline: *Don't Forget Jamie Lydiatt.*'

'Surely that was a very good thing?'

'Was it? He didn't come back. No one ever found him.'

'But they tried for you.'

'Yes,' she admitted.

It had driven a stake through her soul every time she saw the newspaper and his picture. The very fact that they carried it much longer than was normal was something she knew she had to be deeply grateful for. But she could not be grateful. The sight of him, on the front page, exposed to the world and belonging to them now as well as her, had broken something in her.

'Would you show me the letter?'

She came back to the warm, quiet room. She had been remembering standing on the pavement at Holborn, arguing with her editor. She had slapped his face. Actually slapped his face after all he had done. She had been drunk. God forgive me, she thought. Her child missing a fortnight. Drunk. Out of control. Richard couldn't speak to her any more. She wouldn't let him. She didn't want Richard. Only Jamie. Only Jamie. Only . . .

She looked at Jonathan Reeve.

'This is something you can't explain if you haven't experienced it,' she told him, her voice low and even. 'It just doesn't have a name. There isn't a convenient box you can label for me. I'm sorry if that sounds arrogant. It just happens to be true. There are relatively few people whose babies are stolen, and none of us could possibly tell anyone else what it feels like. And I don't even want to *begin* to try. You understand? I don't want to begin. I won't begin. I *can't*. It's mine, just mine, that's all there is to it. I shouldn't be made to.'

'I'm not trying to label you,' he said. 'Could I see the letter?'

She reached down and picked up her handbag. The letter was in the inner pocket, folded into a tight, two-inch square. She handed it over.

He unfolded it and looked at it for a long time without comment. Then he gave it back to her.

'What did you do when you got it?'

'Went upstairs. Hid it.'

'Do you think anyone knows where Jamie is?'

She frowned, the letter in her hand.

'Kate?'

'No,' she said. 'Jamie is dead.'

There was a protracted silence. Outside in Reeve's hallway, a clock chimed delicately. Six o'clock.

'I must go,' she said.

'No,' he replied, holding up his hand. 'Wait a moment. How do you know that Jamie is not alive? Tell me.'

'The police told me.'

'What, exactly?'

She shifted in her seat. 'They told me after Jamie was taken that there are two kinds of people who steal children. Babies.' She spoke without tone or inflection, as if by rote, as if she had learned every word and committed it to memory. He leaned forward, intent. 'There are the kind who have lost a child themselves, or can't have children,' she went on. 'They take a baby to replace what they can't have, and they are kind to it, and look after it. Usually they're caught within a week, because friends or family or neighbours tell the police.' She put the letter back into the handbag, slowly. 'Then there are the other kind,' she said. 'They take children for some perverted purpose. For a sexual reason, or for revenge, or . . . a dozen other unspeakable permutations.' At last she looked up at him. 'They usually kill the child.'

'I see,' he said.

'There's a general rule that if a child hasn't been recovered within a week, it probably won't *ever* be recovered,' she continued. 'Because I worked on the paper, I got a lot of extra publicity, so it stretched the exposure for longer than was normal. But it still didn't work. It ought to have brought Jamie back, even if he was with that one per cent of kindly abductors who aren't caught after seven days. But it didn't. The police didn't tell me in so many words that Jamie was dead. But they did tell me those facts.'

'And you drew your own conclusion.'

'Yes.'

'And this is something you believe in your heart? With a mother's instinct, shall we say? That Jamie is dead?'

'Yes,' she said. 'Yes . . .'

Her gaze trailed away. In that second, Jonathan Reeve knew that Kate harboured a hope. It might only be a fraction of hope. And it might be suppressed by her rigid reasoning, her ability to compress her instincts until her world turned grey. But it was still there.

She still hoped.

'So . . . what do you think the writer of this letter means?'

'I don't know.'

'You think perhaps that it's a lie?'

'Oh yes.'

'Why would anyone want to say such a thing—the worst thing in the world—to you?'

'I don't know.'

'Is there anyone that you know who would want to hurt you in such a way?'

'No.'

'What about your husband?'

She bit her lip. 'We separated six months after Jamie disappeared.'

'Where is Richard now?'

'He lives in Cumbria. We both left London.'

'Would he wish to hurt you with a letter like this?'

'No.' She glanced up at him for a moment. She wondered how he had known Richard's name. Then, she realised that she must have told him, perhaps in that first babble when she arrived—she had talked complete nonsense, she was sure, for some minutes. It was amazing that he had the patience to listen to any of it.

'How can you be sure?' Reeve persisted.

'I *am* sure. I *know* Richard.'

'Even after all this time?'

'Yes.'

'There might not be a chance that Richard too has suffered, and is breaking out of that suffering, making some sort of contact?'

'Like this! God . . . !'

'Suffering is damaging.'

'Richard isn't *like* that.'

'How long is it since you've seen him?'

'Nine years.'

'And you can still say that you know what he's like, even now? With absolute conviction?'

'Yes . . . Look, what the hell are you saying?' She was sitting upright now, staring at him.

'Nothing at all,' Reeve replied evenly. 'I just want to show you avenues. You are the one to speak about them.' He dropped his voice to a softer level. 'What happened after the separation? Did you come straight here?'

'No. I travelled. Took various jobs. Stayed with people, I don't know . . .'

'It's a blur?'

'Yes. Some of it.'

'How long a blur?'

'Three years. I worked abroad for a while. Changed about quite a bit.' Kate bit the corner of her thumbnail. He had penetrated her composure: she looked rattled, confused.

'So that no one got to know you? Got close to you, perhaps?'

'Maybe.'

'You cut yourself off from your friends?'

'No. Maybe.' She took a strand of hair, began twisting it in her fingers.

'Did you work as a journalist?'

'No.' Emphatically.

'That experience was all tied in with Jamie?'

'I . . .' She frowned. 'I can't tell. I don't know.'

'But you came back to journalism here,' he observed. 'Yet, in these intervening years, the lost years, you took any work that you could find?'

'I was a courier for a travel company for a while. Then I cooked for someone for a couple of months, in Italy, in a villa . . . I can't think, I can't remember . . . I was a cleaner once . . .'

'And when did you come back to England?'

'Five years ago.'

'Why did you change your name?'

'Richard had divorced me.'

'How did you feel about that?'

She laughed humourlessly, shot him a look, and immediately got to her feet. She took a deep breath. Then another. 'Look,' she said, 'you've been very kind, really very kind, but I just can't do this. I just don't want to do this. I know you think I should, but I'm afraid it's not on.'

She leaned down, picked up her bag, and was trying to get into her coat, juggling it in her hands, trying to find the first sleeve.

'All right,' he said.

She looked at him. 'It won't work,' she said.

'OK. That's fine.'

'I'm supposed to come round if you back off? Ring you up?' She smiled. 'I won't. Sorry.'

She walked to the door.

'Don't forget where I am,' he said.

She smiled grimly. 'You see? But you're wrong. I've coped with this for a long time. I know how to handle it. I really don't need a psycho-analyst.'

'Fine. But I'm a psychotherapist.'

She held out her hand and shook his firmly.

'You shouldn't really drive,' he told her.

'I must,' she replied. They went out into the hall.

On the doorstep, she turned to him briefly again. 'Please don't forget to send me your bill,' she said.

It was his turn to smile.

'There'll be no charge, Kate,' he said.

EIGHTEEN

*T*HE NEXT MORNING, Kate went into the *Journal*. She climbed to the second floor, and walked straight through the main office to the editor, Ken Bartlett.

Bartlett was sitting in his office. He looked as usual—almost funereal in his dark suit, white shirt, and grey patterned tie, his hair combed into a neat style, and his skin the yellowish shade of the confirmed smoker.

She knocked on the door. 'Could I see you a minute?'

'Come in,' he told her. She noticed the emptiness of his desk. 'Sit down, Kate. How are you?'

'Fine,' she said. She glanced at him, wary because his temper was well known. 'I have some news you won't like,' she went on. 'I can't do any more articles.'

His face bore no expression. 'Is this to do with Maggie?'

She was surprised. 'Maggie? No.'

'What, then?'

'I've no interest in them. I'm sorry.'

He smiled coldly. 'Never mind the interest,' he said. 'You have a contract.'

'I know. But you wouldn't hold me to it, surely?'

'Why not?'

'OK. Tell me what the penalty is. I'll pay it.'

Bartlett seemed to relent, to unwind. He leaned forward, his arms on the desk between them. 'It's that urgent?' he asked. 'Where are you going?'

'Nowhere.'

'What's the other job?'

'No other job.'

He frowned. 'The reason, then?' She looked away from him. 'Have the police seen you?' he asked.

'Police?'

'Didn't they call round?'

'About what?' she asked.

He opened his mouth to tell her, looking intently into her eyes. Then he got up. 'Come here,' he said. They went out into the main office. 'Where is Jack?' he called.

'Just gone out.'

'Go and get him.'

Bartlett had taken hold of Kate's wrist. Not her hand, but the narrow band of bone, as if she would try to escape from him. She shook his hold. 'Ken, please don't do that.'

'Nobody rang you, or came to see you?' he asked.

'I haven't been at home.'

She had stayed last night with Isabelle, but could not see how that was any of his business.

'Don't you watch morning television? Listen to the radio?'

'No. Not today.'

He hissed, almost laughing. 'And you call yourself a journalist.'

Jack Seward came in at the far doors. He took two paces forward, saw Kate and Bartlett, and stopped. 'What d'you want?' he called across the long office.

'Come here, Jack.'

'I was halfway down the road.'

'Come *here*, Jack.' Seward came forward grudgingly. 'Tell Kate about Maggie.'

Bartlett dropped her hand, and walked back into his own room, leaving them stranded, two exhibits with the eyes of the newsroom staff on them. Jack looked witheringly at Bartlett's turned back.

'Bastard,' he muttered.

'What is it?' Kate said.

Jack looked at her. He was more ruffled than usual this morning, coarse dark hair falling over his eyes. He hadn't shaved. He nodded towards the editor. 'Do you ever see him doing anything?' he said. 'It must be osmosis. Do you ever even see him do the "Comment"?'

'Jack,' Kate repeated, 'what is it?'

'Have you had any breakfast?'

'Jack, please.'

'Just come out of here. Let's get something to drink, find a corner ...' He stopped, hearing how angry she was. He sighed. 'The police were called to Maggie's flat yesterday afternoon,' he told her quietly. 'She'd been killed in the early hours of yesterday morning. Strangled.'

She looked at him for a second, then turned back to look at Bartlett's office. 'Why couldn't *he* tell me that!'

'He assigned me yesterday; maybe he thinks I know all the answers.'

'And do you?'

'No. A man used to visit her; that's all there is. Nobody ever knew who he was.'

Kate walked on; he followed. At the door, she asked, 'Why would the police want to see me?'

'They want to see all of us.'

'They've been here?'

'Been here and coming back.'

'Christ,' she said. She shoved open the doors, made for the stairs.

'Kate!'

'What?'

'Did you know who he was? Maggie's lover?'

'No.'

'Hadn't you better stay and wait for them?'

She hesitated. 'I don't know anything.' She put her hand to her forehead. 'Oh God, poor Maggie.'

She swayed where she stood, at the top of the stairs. Jack was suddenly sure that she was going to fall headlong down the flight, and rushed forward, slipping in front of her so that he stood on the first step down and was level with her in height. 'Are you all right?'

'Yes,' she said, looking nothing less than terrible.

'Hold on to my arm.'

'I don't need your arm, Jack.' She closed her eyes.

'Look, just—'

They were interrupted by the girl from reception coming up the stairs. She held a pile of post in her arms and ascended slowly, dreamily. She didn't seem to see them until she was almost upon them. 'Oh—sorry!'

'That's OK,' Jack said.

She passed, smirking at their closeness. Kate began to step down; Jack stood out of her way.

'Oh—Miss McCaulay?' The girl had come back.

'Yes?'

'Letter for you.' She held out the foolscap white envelope. Kate took it and looked at it, at the typeface, at the postmark. The girl walked on, into the newsroom.

'What's the matter?' Jack asked.

Kate tried to put the letter away. Missing her bag, the envelope fluttered down the steps. Jack started down after it. He picked it up, querying her obvious distress with a puzzled expression. 'I feel that way about *my* bills,' he said.

She snatched it from him, but he held the other side. The paper began to tear.

'What's in it?' Jack asked, almost conversationally.

'Give it to me, Jack.'

'You really want it?'

She looked hard at him, frozen. Outside, the traffic of the main street droned, stuck in the road alongside the offices. A motorbike engine revved unmercifully.

She began to shake. Helplessness chased across her face. She glanced at the scene beyond the glass on the stair landing, as if expecting whatever invisible object that appalled her to come hurtling out of the crush of cars and pedestrians.

'Here,' Jack said. 'Here, let me help—'

'I don't need any help,' she said. She pushed past him, turned for the last section of the stairs and immediately lost her footing. He saw her tip forward, her hands brush the rail.

She landed on her side halfway down, fingernails scratching the wall, her legs bunched under her, then tumbled to the bottom, another five steps, finishing up on the harsh needlecord of the empty foyer.

He rushed after her.

'Don't touch me,' she warned.

'For fuck's sake, shut up,' he told her. 'Show me your hands. Can you flex them?'

She did so, mute.

'Can you stand? Feel your feet?'

'Yes,' she muttered.

'Show me.'

She got up, grimacing.

'Did you knock your head?'

'No. Stop it,' she told him. He was testing the hand that had knocked the wall, looking closely at her.

He started to laugh. 'You really can't stand anyone near you, can you?' he said.

'Let's not start,' she responded. She was looking around for her bag. Its contents were littered over the treads. He grabbed what he could, returning things to her. Even the letter. As he handed it over, he held on to it a fraction too long, looking into her eyes.

'Start what?' he said. 'Come for a drink.'

'At ten o'clock? No thanks.'

'I didn't say alcohol,' he told her. 'Come with me.' He walked ahead, held open the outer doors. She stood glaring at him, rubbing her hip.

'Come on,' he said. 'Just for a while. I won't bloody kill you.'

He took her to a café on the main street, on the hill that looked across the edge of the bay. The place was the original greasy spoon, with oil-cloth tacked to the tables, and a list of prices—black inch-high letters on an orange paint background—taped to the wall.

Kate stood near the window, arms crossed. Jack bought two teas and two doughnuts.

'Sit down,' he instructed.

She squeezed gingerly on to a stool, watching while he stirred sugar into his mug. He seemed deep in thought for a while; then looked up at her.

'Kate, how long have we known each other?'

'*Do* we know each other?'

He ran his hand through his hair. 'God, you're the most prickly individual,' he said. 'Just let up a bit, will you?'

'Five years,' she said.

He smiled. 'Five years of standing at the other end of the bar from me at office parties. *If* you ever come to them, which, let's face it, is rare.'

She offered no comment. She had left the drink untouched, and sat with her handbag clasped tightly in her lap, trying not to touch the cracked plastic of the table top. She looked everywhere: at the serving counter, at the street, at the other customers. But only rarely at him.

'Do you know what you remind me of?' he asked.

She shrugged.

'You look like Nancy in *Oliver Twist*. Keeping one eye on the door in case Bill Sikes comes in.'

She still said nothing.

'All right. Not a very good joke,' he said. 'You're not going to help me out at all, are you?'

She eyed him. 'What do you need help with?'

'I want to tell you something,' he said. He paused, wondering what her reaction would be. 'Didn't your name used to be Lydiatt?'

She simply stared at him.

'Didn't you used to live in London, in South Kensington, in a street called—'

'How do you know?' she said.

'I've known for some time. Since you first came here.'

'Since . . .'

'Well, perhaps not straight away. The first time you walked into the office, I thought that I recognised you.' She looked more than shocked;

assaulted would have been a better description. 'Of course, your name was different, your hair . . . In the photographs, your hair was long. Since you came here, it's been short . . .' His glance descended to the handbag still held tightly in her hand. 'I looked you up in the archives, Kate. I knew it was you.'

'And you told them all here, I suppose,' she murmured. 'Is that it? Is that right?'

'No. I told no one.'

'Why?'

'Whose business is it?'

'It's not your business either,' she said.

He rested his head on one hand, looking intently at her. 'No, that's right,' he agreed. 'It's not my business. And you've never given me any reason to think you would welcome my interest. Or help.'

'I don't need help.'

He gave a gusty, short laugh. 'Oh, that's right,' he said. 'I know that. Kate McCaulay works on her own and lives on her own and doesn't need friends.'

She bit her lip.

He traced a circle in the stained surface of the table. 'What's in the letter, Kate?'

She leaned forward. 'Who did you tell about me?'

'No one. I've already said—'

'You must have told someone.'

'Why?'

'Because—' She lifted the letter slowly out of the bag. 'It's got a local postmark.'

'What's it about?'

She had been going to open it, but stopped and looked up. 'If you know who I am, then that means there are two people—only two people—here who know. And the other person would never send a letter like this.'

'Who's the other person?'

'Isabelle Browning.'

'Who?'

Kate waved her hand. 'She'd *never* send a letter like this.'

'You mean to say . . . you think that I *would*?'

She stared at him.

'Give it to me,' he said.

She didn't move.

'For God's *sake*—' He snatched the letter out of her hand, ripped it open, and sat immobile for more than a minute, looking at the single sentence in the centre of the white sheet of paper, and the photograph beneath it.

Kate leaned forward, saw the photocopied picture of Jamie—one of those reprinted in the newspapers when Jamie was first taken, the shot of him when he was just a week old, in Richard's arms—and she let out a small, muffled cry, her hand flying to her mouth.

Jack glanced up at her, looked closely at both the sentence—

I KNOW WHERE HE IS.

—and the picture, and then slid it across the table to her. He saw tears in her eyes.

'How many does this make?' he asked.

'Two. The last one—' She paused, caught her breath. 'The last one didn't have a photograph.'

'And you think I could—I could send you something like this?'

She looked away from him. 'I don't know,' she said softly.

He slammed the piece of paper on to the table top. A man across the aisle turned round to look at them both.

'You know I couldn't do a thing like this,' he said.

'Do I?'

'You *do*. You *do* know.'

'I don't know you.'

He lowered his voice. 'Yes, you do know,' he said. He smiled slowly. 'Look, I'm the guy who stands his round. I'm the one Bartlett loathes. He'd give his right arm to get me off the *Journal*. Remember? Doesn't that count for something?' He waited for a reaction, but got none. 'What do you want to know about me?' he asked. 'I'll tell you anything. Ask me a question. What do I do in my spare time? I'll tell you. I ran that half-marathon for the kids' Christmas appeal, and nearly killed myself in the process. I'm a bloody nice bloke. What's my family like? I'll tell you. My mum lives in Bridport. I do her shopping for her. She's got a dog called Pomfret. I got my shoulder dislocated setting up that second-hand car salesman last year, when his sons caught me in the garage recording him. What do you want to know about me? *I'll tell you*. Kate . . . ask me something.'

She had put her hands to her face. 'I don't want to know anything.'

He stared at the obstruction of her fingers. 'But you want to get back there.'

He saw her wipe her eyes, secretly, behind her hands. As if crying were a crime. 'Back where?' she said.

He waved his hand. 'That place we all want to be. The house, and the family—'

She pushed back her stool, picked the letter from the table. She folded the letter. Her hand hovered, trembled, as she tried to put it back into the envelope.

'Could it be true?' Jack asked.

'What?'

'The letter?'

'No.'

'There couldn't be anyone—someone—who might know where he is?'

'No, no . . .' She was crying openly now. The man in the aisle seat was ramrod straight, obviously trying to decide if he should intervene.

Jack, taking pity on her, tried to put his arms around her. 'Don't cry,' he said. 'I'll find him. Whoever's writing the letters. I'll find him. And Jamie too.'

She was rigid in his embrace; he had to let his arms fall. He found a handkerchief in his pocket, and tried to give it to her as she turned for the door.

'Don't cry,' he repeated. 'Look . . . when I was in London, I saw a woman who used to live there when were there.' She hadn't taken the handkerchief. She stared at him. 'Oh, she wasn't much help,' he added quickly. 'But what I mean is, I can find all those people who lived there, I can go back over it.'

'Why?'

By now, they were standing in the doorway.

'What do you mean, why? It's what I can do,' he said. 'Investigative reporter. Remember?'

'But why do that for me?'

'For Jamie. Why else?'

Kate narrowed her eyes. 'You must be crazy. Or sick,' she said.

He took a step back, stunned. She might as well have punched him in the face.

'Jamie is dead,' she told him. 'You—him—whoever wrote this letter—you're sick if you think my son is alive.'

He took hold of her arm. 'You only say that to protect yourself,' he said. 'Because you'd go crazy if you thought he was living.'

She tore herself away from his grasp. 'Don't tell me what I think,' she said. 'And don't—*don't*—come near me. I don't want your help. Do you understand? I don't need your help. I just want to be left alone.'

She began to walk.

He watched her go down the street.

Two men who had been trying to get into the café finally pushed him aside, but Jack hardly registered the touch.

He followed Kate's progress until she turned in at the *Journal* car park. He waited until her car emerged from the same spot. He followed it with his eyes until it became a speck down the long street, swallowed in the stream of traffic.

'He's alive,' Jack murmured. 'I know that he's alive.'

At the same time, in Lovatt, Isabelle Browning was just leaving the village shop.

She paused on the pavement, putting on her gloves, and acknowledging the wave of an acquaintance across the street. She decided, before going back to the house, to walk around by the stream, skirting the fields, to get some fresh air.

With her usual brisk step, she set off down the slight slope of the main road, pausing a moment at the bridge.

The river was wide and full, threatening to overflow into the water meadows. The landscape was pleated browns and greys, the fields thin with winter crops, the grass faded, the road muddied. She watched the water with her straw bag balanced on the parapet of the bridge. She was thinking about Kate.

As she turned away to begin walking again, she noticed a car on the other side of the road. It had slowed for the narrower width of the bridge. She glanced at the driver.

He must have passed at about twenty miles an hour, then rapidly accelerated. As they were level with each other, she saw his profile clearly, although he did not glance at her.

For a second, her heart stopped.

She stared after the car, at the shape of the driver's body, silhouetted now.

She hadn't even caught the colour of his hair. She hadn't seen his eyes. She hadn't caught a glimpse of his clothes; even his hands on the steering wheel.

She had told him never to come back.

But . . . She closed her eyes. She was sure . . . yes, she was sure it was him.

NINETEEN

$\mathcal{O}$LD GHOSTS WERE BOTHERING GEORGE long before the police turned up that morning.

He knew that Kate had not come home; guessed that she was with Isabelle. He had stood at the front door of the cottage last night, looking up at the empty, unlit window of the flat, waiting for her, waiting for the light to be switched on.

It hurt him disproportionately when she stayed away. It wasn't often, thankfully: perhaps one night a month she would go to Isabelle's. He kept a record of the absences marked on his diary calendar. A little red cross meant that she had gone. He kept the calendar in the cottage. Never in the Gallery.

He had seen the television news last night. They had showed a picture of Maggie Spence. There had been some footage of the *Journal*, and the editor standing outside, mouthing the usual regrets. No one knew very much about the girl; no one knew who the mystery man had been.

George had watched it standing up in his kitchen, arms crossed, a strained expression on his face.

They showed an outside shot of Maggie's flat, from the rear. The fire escape winding up the back wall like a disintegrating web; the narrow door that led into her room. The roof slanting, the large Victorian chimney, with its eighteen stacks, towering over it, looking ready to fall.

Every room had had a fireplace once, he had thought, biting on the nail of his smallest finger, until he had reduced it, unthinkingly, to the quick.

The fire in Angel's old shop had burned incessantly; it had been one of George's jobs to fetch the wood. He had been only twelve years old, and fetching wood and coal from Firbanks' before school, carrying them up the High Street, into Angel's yard. He used to carry the shop keys on a piece of cord and fish them from his pocket.

The first job of the day was the fire. On his knees in the shop, cleaning out the ashes, piling them on newspaper, he would hear Angel moving about in the bedroom above. He would call down the stairs. 'That you, George?'

'It's all right. It's me,' he would reply.

It had been an icy morning in January. Only a fortnight before, he had celebrated Christmas with the old man. Angel knew how to celebrate such things. There was none of the dreariness, the cold front parlour, the sparsely decorated miniature tree, of his own home. Angel had brought a real tree in, and the shop had glowed.

They hung fortunes from the branches: Johillco bandsmen figures, lead alloy, with paper labels stuck to their bases, between the lights, blowing their bugles, frozen in battle, flying their metal standards. Angel put dolls there too, and tinplate limousines—You will have one of those one day, George, you will have a real one, when you have made your millions—and brisé ivory fans, and cigarette cards, and Schuco animals, and pipes, and scent bottles, and netsuke . . . it had been fairyland.

On Christmas Eve, Angel had given him one of the presents from the branches. It had been one of the cigarette cards, and George had felt pained—embarrassed and pained—to have expected more.

Seeing his face, Angel had asked, 'What's the matter, George?'

'Nothing,' he had replied, stowing the card in his pocket.

The key wouldn't go in the lock that January morning. George had squeezed his hand through the letter box, and opened the door by turning the key in its lock on the other side.

Angel had been lying, still, on the shop floor.

Blood lay around him in a drifted brown pool. He was in his night-clothes, and his feet were bare, the slippers lying by the kitchen in the hallway. George had not been able to take his eyes off the old man's feet, white, even the smooth toe stubs white, the skin on the instep wrinkled like corrugated board.

George had sat down on a chair next to him, saw that Angel lay in the unswept needles of the still-decorated tree. For many minutes, the pattern of Angel's drying blood had fascinated him. Then, he had got up, stepped over the body, and taken what he wanted from the tree.

He took a whole set of the Johillco bandsmen, and the rest of the cards. Then he sat down again, and waited.

A woman came into the shop at half-past nine and found them both. Her screaming had pierced the silence, at last distracting George from Angel's last gory flourish on the floor.

The police had questioned George for three days. They never quite believed he had not murdered the old man; but they never could quite prove it either.

Angel had been about him today, wandering through the cottage, hanging motionless in the aisles of the Gallery. He sat on George's shoulder like the demon he had never been in life, whispering in his ear.

It was a quarter past nine.

George saw movement on the drive, and shot from his chair, where he had been holding—but not reading—the newspaper. He thought that it was Kate coming back.

But it was not Kate. It was a police car, toiling slowly along the gravelled lane. It drew up outside and two men got out. China began to bark, and he shut her into the kitchen.

George welcomed the police into the house. They were in plain clothes; one stood all the time, glancing about himself, saying very little. The other was more talkative, smiling, accepting the coffee that George made.

'You have a beautiful home,' he said.

'Thank you,' George replied. 'I like nice things.' He glanced up at the silent partner, disturbed by him. The man had a sallow face, pale eyes that unnerved him. As the older man leaned back on the couch, appearing perfectly at ease, the younger turned his back, and began reading the titles of books in the shelves, taking one down occasionally.

'Sit down and read one,' George said.

His expansiveness, his enforced jolly manner, made no impression. There was no reply.

He turned to the other man, who was lazily stirring his coffee.

'She's still not here,' he said. 'Did you ring Mrs Browning?'

'Yes. We just missed her.' The man smiled. 'But we shall find her, never fear.'

'She's usually back by now,' George said. 'She comes back early, then goes off again to work.'

The coffee cup went down on the table. 'You keep track, do you?'

'Keep track? No. But when she lives so close it's hard not to notice.'

George had gestured through the window to the old stable block, the edge of the Gallery. The man followed his glance. 'You can keep a good eye on her from here,' he said. The tone was conversational, man-to-man.

'I don't keep watch,' George countered.

'No, no. But you know her friends.'

'Her . . .'

'You would know Maggie Spence, for instance.'

'No.'

'She didn't come here?'

He hesitated a moment. 'She came once. It was some time ago, in the summer. Early summer,' he said. 'She was in Kate's car. I remember Kate said it was Maggie, from the paper. I suppose it must have been the same Maggie? They were going somewhere, for an article.'

'She didn't get out of the car?'

'No.'

'But you're sure it was Miss Spence. Miss Spence came here?'

The younger man turned to look at him.

George ventured a smile. 'Pretty girl like that, one doesn't forget. Large, you know. But pretty.'

George made a pinching movement at the side of his face. It was a habit of his, catching at the skin that had been shaved. He willed himself to stop.

There was a long pause. The older man looked him over speculatively, taking in George's expensive suit, the waistcoat, the regimental tie. Then, he looked down at his own legs, crossed at the knee. He followed the crease in his trousers with the edge of his thumb. He did not look up.

'Does Miss McCaulay have many friends?'

'No, not many.'

'She lives alone?'

'Yes.'

'And works at the *Journal*.'

'Yes, and for me.'

'For you?'

'Minding the shop.'

'But surely she made friends of the customers. You have dealers visiting, colleagues?'

'Yes, perhaps . . .'

'And she might have introduced Maggie to someone here?'

'Oh, no.'

'No? You're sure?'

George felt the conversation drifting out of his control. 'Well, I don't know, of course. Kate might have had Miss Spence in the shop at some time, might have talked to someone with her, I don't know . . .'

'You seem to think it unlikely.'

'It is unlikely, yes,' George agreed rapidly. 'Kate is a private person, very private. She will talk, you see. Talk and be very pleasant. Very pleasant. But she . . . isn't gregarious . . .'

'Not sociable?'

'Not quite that . . .'

'But she would have male friends, a boyfriend?'

'No.'

'Someone she would introduce to Maggie?'

'No. Oh, no.'

It emerged as more of a refusal, an emotional rebuff, than he had meant. The younger man closed the book he had been reading, put it back on the shelf, and came to sit next to his colleague on the couch.

Quite suddenly, it occurred to George that they had not come back to find Kate at all, but specifically to speak to him. They had been yesterday, and he had confirmed that Kate did live there, and it had all seemed very relaxed, very polite. They had barely stayed five minutes. And yet, now they were back. They must have discussed him, found something in his manner, perhaps, that intrigued them. He tried desperately to cast his mind back over the previous afternoon.

'Are you married, Mr Dale?'

'Married? No.'

'Ever been married?'

George blushed. 'Is this relevant to Maggie Spence?' he asked.

Both men looked at him intently, their eyes ranging over his face. He had snapped that reply. He could feel its effect freezing the air between them, almost visible.

'Probably not,' the older man said. His tone was calm.

George stood up. 'I have to open the shop.' He glanced very quickly at the clock. It was barely half past nine. The sign on the door quite plainly said ten. If they looked.

The two men got up. The first man shook George's hand.

'I'll show you out,' George said.

They went to the door, both the police ducking their heads slightly in the hallway. They were taller than he. The young man spoke for the first time. 'Thank you,' he said as he passed George on the step.

It took George by surprise. He smiled. 'That's all right. My pleasure. My pleasure.'

Both men were over the doorstep, turned towards their car, when the younger one looked back over his shoulder.

'How did you know that Maggie Spence was overweight?'

George had his hand on the door, to shut it. 'Pardon?'

'How did you know she was . . .' He seemed to be trying to recall George's word. 'Large?'

'I don't . . .'

'You said that she never got out of the car, and then said she was large. How could you tell, if she never got out, and you only saw her once?'

George frowned.

Angel came back abruptly into his mind, sprawled on the shop floor, with his terrible dark halo of blood.

'It was on the news,' he replied at last. 'A picture of her, last night.'

The younger man considered.

'Thank you for your time, Mr Dale,' he said.

TWENTY

$\mathcal{K}$ATE HAD INTENDED TO DRIVE HOME, back to the Gallery. But approaching the junction where it was necessary to turn for the villages higher up the valley, she suddenly realised that she could not face the sight of her room.

She turned back, taking the loop road across the Downsway. After a couple of miles, she turned left for Bloor Mullen.

It was a large town, relentlessly pedestrianised. She parked the car in a multistorey and walked down through side streets to the shopping centre.

In the first street she came to, she saw that there were two vans parked at the edge of the pavement. Using extending ladders, some workmen were putting up lights for Christmas, stringing them from one building to another over the heads of the crowd below.

She paused, thinking how ridiculously early Christmas came. If she had her way, she would ban every mention of it until a week before 25 December. What a misery I am, she thought wryly.

She looked about her, vaguely aware that she was thirsty, and yet not wanting to sit down anywhere. She didn't want anyone to look her in the face. She didn't want to take a plate, a cup and saucer, or hand money to anyone. It was the thought of someone else's skin brushing against hers.

She walked to her left, evading the ladders, thinking of Maggie.

She looked in the lit windows, seeing clothes and books and colours, and yet barely registering them. All the time the sheet of paper burned in her pocket. She had read the letter again just before she got out of the car, staring uncomprehendingly at the words. Jamie's image became merely a series of lines, an arrangement of subtle, pin-prick dots, grey on white.

She stood now at a pedestrian crossing, waiting for the lights to change. Overhead, she heard the sound of something knocking—empty frame against empty frame—looked up and saw it was a huge, as yet dark, plastic casing of Santa Claus and reindeer, swinging in the wind, red bows attached to the sleigh, the parcels, the cuffs of the red costume.

She had never known a Christmas with Jamie.

When the lights changed, she walked.

On the opposite pavement, a series of cards in a window stopped her. There was also a poster photograph showing a mountain running down to a beach, very lush and green. Green contrasting with the bright blue of the water, and the rim of white sand.

Without thinking or rationalising, she pushed open the door, and went in.

A girl was sitting alone, a catalogue on her knee, staring into space. The shop was empty. She was sitting behind a computer, ranged along-side a half-dozen others.

'Are you open?' Kate asked.

'Yes—' The girl jolted. 'Oh, yes.' The corporation smile was switched on. 'How can I help?'

Kate sat down. 'I'd like a holiday. A break.'

'Right . . .'

'Straight away.'

The girl glanced at her. The thought *October* was plainly etched in her expression; then the smile returned. 'Ah—the Caribbean? Goa? Somewhere like that? Somewhere hot?'

'It doesn't matter.'

'Right. Lovely. Let's see . . .'

'I don't want to be flying for a long time.'

There was a pause. 'No? Ah. Well, of course, anywhere hot would mean maybe eight hours . . .'

'No, not that far.'

'Tenerife?'

'How long is that?'

'Well, four—'

'No. Somewhere else. Europe.'

'But it wouldn't be hot, you see . . .'

Kate looked all around her. On the shelves, the first brochure she saw was for the Mediterranean. 'How about there?'

'Spain? Greece?'

'Yes.'

Kate was distantly aware that she was being ridiculous.

'There's Cyprus, of course, though at half term we're quite well booked for Cyprus.'

'Where *isn't* booked?'

The girl cocked her head, her fingers stilled on the computer keyboard. 'We have villa locations in somewhere like the Spanish islands, a few apartments, or there's always space in the more expensive hotels.'

'OK. A villa. Apartment.'

'Spain?'

'Yes.'

'Nerja is very nice.'

'I don't care. Just tell me where it is and how much it is and when I can go.'

The girl looked affronted. She clamped her mouth shut, furiously typing. Finally, she turned the computer screen to show Kate the location.

'This is a small villa near a beach. Not many amenities, I'm afraid, no bars really . . .'

Kate stared at the green letters; at the orange cursor winking at the top of the page.

Go on? asked the box menu at the bottom of the screen.

She didn't want to see George. She didn't want to see Jack Seward. Or the *Journal*. Or the police.

Most of all, she didn't want to see her stairs, the long, high stairs to the empty flat . . .

'What do you think?' the girl asked brightly.

The villa was vacant the following day.

The flight was at eight in the morning.

TWENTY-ONE

*T*HE PLANE ARRIVED AT TEN IN THE MORNING, to an overcast landscape still recovering from the burning summer.

Everywhere that Kate looked out of the window of the airport bus as it jolted along, the ground was scorched and brown, the towns dusty and tired. Only when they began to travel along the coast did the sea offer the first colour. Kate leaned on the glass, trying to turn off the conversation of the families around her.

She was the only one to get off the coach in Santo Assevio. She listened, smiling, while the courier told her which key was which, and gave her a card with her telephone number. Kate watched the bus go, trundling along the thinly surfaced road and up the hill of the headland.

The house was tiny, set in an equally tiny garden. She opened the door straight on to a very white room with two couches, an open fireplace, and a table and two chairs. The villa smelled musty, of disuse rather than actual neglect. It was tidy enough, with plain dark furniture. The cotton curtains were drawn.

She dropped her case by the door, and walked through, inspecting the place. There was a living room and kitchen downstairs;

upstairs, a double bedroom and a bathroom. More white, more wood. Red striped spread, with a pack of linen on the top. Mercifully clean crisp sheets, but a towel that had seen immeasurably better days.

Looking in the bathroom mirror, she saw herself framed against the blue tile wall behind her: a pale face, drawn skin with a fretwork of fine lines at the edge of her eyes, two deep furrows of anxious concentration in her forehead.

'What do you look like?' she murmured.

She went back down to the kitchen and opened the fridge. The welcome pack was minimal: bread, milk, eggs, cereal. On the ledge near the sink, a pack of tea and two sachets of coffee. She smiled ironically; put the kettle on to boil, opened one of the sachets, and emptied it into a mug.

Now that she was actually here, she felt a little better than she had done on the plane. Getting on it, finding her seat, she had thought that the roof had seemed lower, the aisle narrower than usual. She had fumbled for a while with the seat belt, unable to understand why it wouldn't fasten, and grimacing at her own foolishness when she finally worked it out.

'On your own?' a woman next to her had asked. She was about thirty; beside her sat a small boy.

'Yes,' Kate said.

'A late holiday?'

'Yes.'

'We always treat ourselves at half term,' the woman confided, deftly opening the in-flight entertainment pack for the child. 'Mel's a farmer; can't get away in the summer.'

She talked non-stop; through drinks, through lunch, switching between Kate and her husband on the seat across the aisle.

'In a hotel?' she asked, as the flight began to circle to land.

'No. A villa.'

The woman's eyes had widened. 'On your own, in a *villa*?'

Kate's grip had tightened on the armrest. 'Yes. Just a small one.' She named the resort.

'Oh, I couldn't do that. Could I, Mel?' she asked her husband. 'Not on my own, miles from anywhere, alone in a house, when you never know who might break in . . .'

Kate focused on the woman's beaming, complacent features. She felt like slapping her. Instead, she turned her face away and closed her eyes.

She had had hardly any sleep at Isabelle's; and last night she had been restless, too. A sensation of being crowded, even in her spartan room, had made her get up and open the windows.

Resting her elbows on the sill, and gazing out into the damp blackness of the drive and the fields that surrounded it, she had drawn deep breaths, trying to calm the pressure, let the thing go. The airlessness of the villa struck her now, a repetition of the night before. She tried to open one of the kitchen windows, but it was jammed. Going back into the living room, she pulled the curtains, and opened the patio doors.

Cool air rushed in, blown from the sea. She walked out into the garden. The villa was set on a short slope; the garden ended a few yards away in the same ringed stone wall as the front. Beyond it was the beach.

She went to the gate. It opened on to a path that ran parallel to the beach, on a rocky shelf. She stepped out, standing at the edge of the rocks, seeing a drop of perhaps ten feet to the sand below. Looking to the right, she noticed a small hotel about two hundred yards away. To her left there was nothing but the beach and the sea.

She shivered; she was wearing only a shirt and jeans. She went back into the house, opened her suitcase and pulled out a sweater. In the kitchen, the kettle had boiled, but she made no move towards it. Instead, her feet dragging with a sudden weariness, she went up the stairs, lay on the bed, pulled the bedspread across her, and, in no more than a minute or two, fell soundly asleep.

It was late afternoon when she woke up.

She sat up suddenly, totally disorientated, realising where she was only when she glanced to the window and the view of the sea. She couldn't remember having dreamed at all, and yet her heart was thumping, her skin clammy.

She got out of bed, went to the bathroom, and turned on the

shower. The water was hot, at least. She peeled off her clothes where she stood, letting them drop to the floor, and then stepped under the comforting flow of water.

She stood for some time, letting it drain down over her body while she remained motionless underneath it. Then, slowly, she soaped herself. She shampooed her hair, and let the hot water flood her face. Lowering her head and opening her eyes, she looked down at herself, at a body she had not shared with anyone for years.

There had been a couple of men after Richard. Two bleak couplings that could never have had the title of a relationship. She couldn't even remember their faces now. They were just reactions, results of drink. She had formed few friendships, and had no romances. Her heart was turned off. She thought of it like something paralysed inside her: barely functioning, it would occasionally falter into life, to make her cry at a film, or at pictures on the news of yet another senseless war. But that was very rare. Mostly it stayed warped, still, disabled.

She had become another person since the time she and Richard had been together.

Last night, as she had packed, a conviction had come over her that she must talk to him. Perhaps, she thought now, if she were honest, there was the merest seed of suspicion that Richard could have sent the letters. The seed planted there by Jonathan Reeve. But she had thought, if she could just hear Richard's voice again, even for a second, she would know whether that were true or not.

And so she had got out her old address book, and found the barely touched page where she had written Richard's address in Cumbria nine years ago. The last address he had given her after the divorce.

Not very likely that he would still be there. But she rang the number just the same.

A woman's voice had answered. It had been about eight o'clock in the evening, and, in the background, Kate could clearly hear the television, and two or three other voices.

'Hello?'

'Hello,' Kate had replied. 'Is that . . .' She had repeated the number.

'Yes, that's right.' The voice was light, humorous, friendly. 'Excuse me a sec,' she had said. Then, evidently, turned away from the receiver.

'Will you lot be quiet for two minutes put together?' she shouted. She had come back to the phone, laughing. 'Horrors!' she had exclaimed. 'I'm sorry. Maybe I can hear myself think now. Who is it calling?'

'My name is . . .' Kate had hesitated. If this was Richard's wife, if he had married again, and had . . . her heart had skipped a couple of beats . . . if he had had a family, it was not very welcome to get a call from his previous wife. 'My name's Evans,' Kate had lied. 'Is Mr Lydiatt in?'

'No,' came the reply.

So it was his home. Still.

'This is Karen Lydiatt,' the woman went on. 'Can I take a message?'

'Are you expecting him home soon?'

The woman laughed. 'Hardly. He's on a research project in Sumatra. Ten weeks gone and six to go.'

Kate had relaxed back into the chair. On the other side of the world, Richard could not have sent the letters.

'No,' she said. 'I . . . it's fine. Nothing urgent. In fact, I must have got my wires crossed. Sorry to have disturbed you.'

She had put the phone down, guilty at cutting across the other woman's still-voiced questions.

Richard had children. Was married.

And happy.

She got out now, trying to shut the train of thought down. She towelled herself dry, and, wrapped in a towel, went downstairs. Taking a bottle of Calvados from the duty-free carrier, she sat down in front of the fireplace, and made up a fire out of the half-dozen logs that had been left there.

In ten minutes there was a comfortable glow. She watched it, nursing her drink in both hands. The afternoon light was fading. It was almost seven o'clock.

It was a long time since she had sat in front of an open fire. She and Richard had had one in London; a bone of contention between them since it was always she who had the job of making it.

On the night that James had first come home, they had sat in front of a fire just like this one. Music had been playing softly; James lay in her arms, asleep.

'What do you see?' Richard had asked.

She had listened. The shapes were already in her mind; she did not conjure them or imagine them.

'Three lines. Smooth, like polished wood.'

'That's the violin?'

'Yes . . .'

It had been Bach's Concerto in D minor. Two sets of strings swept past each other. Two birds describing a complicated flight, turning back, turning away, wings touching; two voices gently arguing in the firelight.

'The lower one is wood, with a . . . slippery, shiny feel . . .'

She paused, savouring the sensual delight of the surface that ran through her hands. 'It stretches a long way, turning, turning, like a smooth coil, but warm . . .'

'And the second?'

It was hard to drag herself away from the almost sexual delight of the first violin. 'This one is flatter, metallic. Two strands, the upper one thinner.'

She had opened her eyes, to see him smiling at her. 'I wish I could feel it,' he said.

Richard was the only person who knew about Kate's curious sixth sense. It was called synaesthesia. She was six when it had dawned on her that other people didn't possess this wonderful expansion of the mind, the ability to touch sounds. She had been in the school playground when a girl had come out of a higher class playing a recorder. Kate had clapped her hands to her ears, saying, 'Oh, the sharp!' She had not meant sharps or flats. She had meant that the off-key noise was itself sharp, edged like a blade, making cutting sensations across the tips of her fingers.

She had jumped about, shaking her hands, then pressing them to the ground in an effort to rid herself of the discomfort. Only when the girl had passed, and she was able to stand up did she see the bemused expressions on the faces of her friends.

She learned very quickly not to say what the sounds meant to her. Not to savour the long, fluid ribbons of a Christmas carol too much. Not to turn to look at the green, round drops of song from the bird outside the window.

One in ten million had the same trait. But the sense might be altered slightly so that others tasted sound or felt taste. She had read a book in which a man described the taste of chocolate as a fur coat, the fur deeper and thicker than any ordinary fabric.

It was an extraordinary alliance.

Richard had loved it, and envied it. He was always asking her to translate sounds to textures for him, trying to understand her curious language.

Music moved her most.

It was multiplied if she drank alcohol.

Here, in this other firelight, she remembered the neatly woven Bach, the wood and the coils and the plaited sensation like wings.

She had been able to feed James herself then. She had done so while they sat in front of the fire, and the concerto finished. Yet only a few days later, she had come down with flu, and her milk supply had waned. It was about then that James began his agonising wailing and screaming. She had felt a failure, as though she had betrayed him.

Richard brought James to her, but the baby wrenched his face away from her breast. They had to make do with bottles, Richard sitting on the edge of the bed, holding James in his arms.

The fire was burning low. Kate reached forward, and put the final log into the flames. She took a last, long drink of the brandy. The note played by air blowing through the trees closest to the window was light, like a blade of grass brushing her palm.

There was a flash of light, and then, almost immediately, a crack of thunder that shattered the palm blade into a hundred pieces.

She got up, frightened, in time to see the first splashes of rain against the glass. Far out on the horizon, sheet lightning illuminated the sea and sky, and the banked mountains of cloud.

'*What is thunder?*'

'*Oh, hell! That's a hard one. Stone . . .*'

'Lord,' she muttered, under her breath. She hated storms. Always had, even as a child.

'*And rain?*'

'*Rain has nothing. No shape at all.*'

Richard had laughed. It had been their fourth, maybe fifth date. She had felt close to him since the first meeting, able to tell him the carefully guarded secret of the synaesthesia, knowing instinctively that he would never make her feel like a freak. It had been raining that night as they stepped outside the restaurant. Pouring in a curtain.

Smiling, he had kissed her. They had gone to his flat, making love before they were barely over the threshold. Afterwards in bed, before sleeping. Waking again in the night. Again that evening, the next, the next. The world was fresh and full of promise.

She had never gone back to her own flat. They had done all the things they ought not to have done, all the things advised against. Made love too soon, moved in too soon, married too soon. It was only six short weeks between the first date and the wedding.

The fire was now reduced to a fringe of red ember. Kate kneeled before it, trying to keep the warmth going. She did not want to be in the dark. A long time, since the restaurant and the rain. She hadn't thought of that evening in . . . how long? Really *thought* of it. Really recalled his face, the sight of that opaque downpour beyond the warmth of the doors. Really allowed herself to remember, through all that subsequent terrible dark . . .

And, as if her thoughts had been read, the light suddenly went off. 'Oh no,' she whispered.

She stood up, stretched her hands, felt her way to the kitchen. Working her way around the walls, she tried to find the fuse box. All the time, the rain howled and drummed on the doors, the windows. She could even hear it on the sloping roof upstairs. She stopped by the back door, looking through the pane of glass at a landscape dancing with the cloudburst. Sand ran in an ochre river under the shrubs just beyond the door; the drops leaped from the stone of the small patio.

She went back through the living room, stubbing her feet in the dark, cursing softly. She opened the front door, finding the white box in the porch that she had noticed then forgotten as she came in. It must surely be the meters and the fuses, she told herself. Dodging the rain slanting in under the narrow shelter, she realised that the door to the box was locked. Her hands slid over its surface in vain.

Water drenched her face and shoulders. She slammed the door

shut, coming back into the room, and looked through the gloom at the dying fire.

She began to shake, from cold, from disorientation, from weariness. She started to make her way back towards the stairs. The drops of cold rain ran down her arms.

An enormous clap of thunder boomed directly overhead; the windows shook. She heard the rain explode into a frenzy, a thousand hammering hands on the roof and windows. The noise was so intense that it was physical, vibrating inside her. She dropped down, crouching close to the floor. Through the open curtains, she saw the garden and the sea lit up for seconds at a time, in a brilliant, phosphorescent bluish gleam. When the lightning faded the darkness was complete: crushing, claustrophobic.

She stood up, and ran upstairs. Here, in the dark, she fumbled for her clothes, dragging them on. She didn't bother to comb her still-damp hair.

She rushed from the room, and down the stairs, and flung open the door to the street. The palms that bordered the road thrashed in the rain. She felt for her purse in her pocket, took the keys from the lock, and slammed the door shut behind her as she left.

In the hotel foyer, the Reception staff looked at her as if she were a madwoman.

She ran up to the desk, aware that she was dripping wet; that the rain was actually running down her face. They had candles spread along the length of Reception, and, along the corridors leading to the stairs and restaurant, little red discs of emergency lighting at floor level.

'Señora?' asked the clerk.

'Do you have a telephone? An International phone?'

'Of course.'

'They're still working?'

'Yes.'

'Can I make a call to England?'

'Please . . .' He took her a little way along the corridor, to the telephone booth. It was intimate and strange, this escorted walk through the barely punctuated gloom. She wrote down the name and number that she wanted, standing close to a candle perched on a coffee table. He smiled, still looking at her warily.

She shut the door. Alone in the black wooden cubicle, she waited for the phone to ring.

Please put the lights back on.

'Señora? You are through to the number . . .'

She pressed the receiver to her ear. Far away, Isabelle's phone rang. Three times, four . . . eight, nine . . .

'Oh, please,' Kate whispered.

Fourteen . . . maybe Isabelle would come out and stay with her. She ought never to have come here alone. She wouldn't be able to stand this, seven days, a week alone, in this bloody dark . . .

'There is no reply,' said the operator.

'Please let it ring a bit more.'

Twenty . . . twenty-five. It was only nine o'clock in England. Isabelle rarely went out in the evenings. She must be in, not just forgotten to switch on the answerphone. Isabelle would come. She would arrive and take charge, tell her how stupid she was, how things could be improved. Isabelle would know what to do; she was so sane, so fixed . . .

'No reply.'

Christ, this suffocation. Make them put the lights on.

'Can you . . . can you try another?'

'Certainly.'

She gave it.

Another distant ringing, then a click.

'This is Jack Seward. Can't speak just now. Leave a message after the tone . . .'

She slammed the phone down.

'Oh God,' she murmured. She had no idea why she was ringing Jack anyway. She was going crazy. *Crazy* . . .

The dark enfolded her. There was a small glass window in the cubicle door, and, beyond that, a window with a view of the sea. It was a Goya landscape of black, white and red. Every so often, the lightning showed the hotel balconies, the tightly closed shutters to the rooms, the terracotta tiled roof on the little bar by the pool. She could hear voices, but could see no one.

I know where . . .

The phone rang. She leaped in fright; she had momentarily forgotten where she was, what she was waiting for. She picked it up.

'Yes?'

'Señora, you wish any other call?'

The voices came nearer.

A family passed the cubicle, feeling their way along the corridor with assorted groans and laughter. It was a large group—grandparents, parents, and three small children, one in a pushchair, and the others carried. As the next crack of thunder came, the grandmother raised her hands to her ears, and one of the children began to cry.

Their language was a torrent of Spanish; the crying child was passed from one set of arms to another, the smiling adults pressing their faces against the little girl's, smoothing her with their hands, hushing her with little laughing moans.

'Señora . . . ?'

She should have picked him up, like that.

She ought to have taken him with her, no matter if he had begun crying, no matter if he had woken up. She ought never to have left him in the car. He was so very small, and he depended upon her, upon her . . .

I know . . .

'Señora?'

'Yes . . .'

'You have any other number?'

'I . . . yes . . .'

'You wish me to ring for you?'

'Yes, but . . . I don't know the number only the name and the address . . .'

'OK. You give me the name, I find you International Enquiries.'

She leaned on the wall, and rested her head on her forearm. The phone dropped slightly away from her face.

'It's my fault,' she whispered.

'The name?'

She pressed her free hand to her eyes.

'Reeve,' she said. 'Jonathan Reeve . . .'

TWENTY-TWO

'KATE, WHAT DO YOU DREAM ABOUT?'

'I don't dream.'

'Yes, you dream. Everyone dreams. What did you dream about last night?'

A protracted silence. Then, Kate laughs softly. 'I dreamed there were a lot of people, in a restaurant . . .' She stops. 'It's ridiculous. It only lasted a moment.'

'What were you doing?'

'Serving. Taking the orders.'

'And what happened?'

'Nothing in particular. They all wanted different things, and the kitchen was closing. That's all. It's all there was.'

'Did it wake you up?'

'It was time to wake up. It was light.'

'What else do you dream about?'

She looked at him. Jonathan was sitting opposite her in the room in the villa, his back to the light; she could hardly make out his face. Behind him, the landscape, in contrast to two days ago, was a bright palette of blue and yellow.

Hard to believe that he had actually come here. She hadn't asked him to; she had hardly been able to get a coherent sentence out when she finally reached him by phone. He had told her to ring him again in the morning, and then, when she had done so, dropped the bombshell that he had already booked a flight.

She asked him the question that had been on her mind since then.

'Why did you come here?'

He smiled. 'To help you.'

'I can't afford to pay for your flight, Jonathan.'

'I didn't ask you to.'

'Did you think I was that urgent?'

He shook his head. 'I'm asking the questions.'

'I'm sorry. I find it hard to take them seriously.'

'Why?'

'Dreams . . .' She waved her hand dismissively.

'All right. Then it's no big deal to tell me about them. Tell me about your dreams.'

'I dream . . .' She looked down at the floor. 'I dream about Jamie. He's crying in a house. A dark house, with huge staircases. I can never get to him.'

'Why not?'

'Because it's too big. I try . . .'

'You try to get to him, but you never reach him?'

'Right.'

'What would happen if you reached him?'

She stared at him, wide-eyed. 'I'd . . . pick him up, carry him out, of course . . .'

'He would be alive?'

'Yes.' She stopped. 'Ah. I see.'

'See what?'

'I'm telling myself that he's alive.'

'Perhaps.'

'Perhaps? You're not going to tell me that I'm right?'

'Only you can say that.'

She twisted her hands in her lap. 'I see. So I believe that he's alive, and I have the dreams because I won't allow myself to believe that?'

'Perhaps.'

She slammed one hand on to her thigh. 'Is that supposed to help me? Perhaps . . . perhaps!'

He began to smile. She held up the same hand, palm facing him. 'Don't say *perhaps!*'

'What other dreams?' he said. 'What did you dream about before Jamie disappeared? As a child? Anything recurrent?'

'No.'

'Try to think.'

'Why don't you take my word for it?'

'Why don't you want to think?'

'You've got a pat answer for everything, haven't you?'

'Any recurrent dreams?'

They looked at each other steadfastly. His expression was level, unclouded; hers, sardonic.

'I used to dream that my teeth were falling out.' She laughed, expecting him to do so. He merely wrote on the sheet of paper balanced on his lap. 'You don't think that's funny?'

'It's very common.'

'Oh.'

'Painful?'

'No. I'd be speaking, and my teeth would be in pieces, filling my whole mouth. They wouldn't be sharp, but soft, like pieces of cardboard.' She sighed. 'I was only ever bothered that the person I was talking to would notice. There would be this incredibly surreptitious effort to organise the broken teeth in my mouth so that this person wouldn't notice.'

He nodded.

'You see how stupid this all is?' she asked.

'Did you have the same dream after meeting Richard?'

'I can't remember.'

'OK. Ever had it recently?'

'No. Not the same as that.'

'In what way different?'

She paused. 'More violent, I suppose.'

'How?'

119

'Well, I . . . dream about things on the news, superimpose those things on to work, or where I live . . .'

'What would be the scene, at work?'

'I dream that . . . the building is falling to pieces, the desks crumple when you touch them. I dream that . . .'

'Go on.'

She made a tremendous, visible effort. 'I dream that the building begins to fall . . . or I'm in the street, and the buildings fall.'

'An earthquake?'

'Yes.'

'Out of your control?'

'I feel responsible.'

'Why?'

'Because there's this feeling, I should have seen it coming. I knew, and I didn't warn anyone.'

'How could you know about an earthquake?'

'I don't know. It's always something very small. I've done something ordinary, and it has terrible consequences . . .'

'Like what?'

Kate feels her temperature rise. The room becomes stuffy, uncomfortable. 'I just do something perfectly ordinary . . .' Her voice is higher. She looks at him. He seems interested. More than interested. Animated. Flushed.

'All right,' he says. 'But not to hurt anyone.'

'Yes. Not to hurt anyone. Just turning a door key, or signalling in the car, pressing the indicator switch. And the thing is, no one *notices*. No one complains. They are about to be crushed, to be killed, and they just carry on, looking at me, knowing I've caused it, but they just glance over me, they never ask for help . . .'

'And you feel that you've caused this catastrophe?'

'Yes. People under rocks, stones . . . the ground cracks . . .'

'OK. And why is it your fault?'

'I don't know. I just did one ordinary thing, just something anyone would do, and this . . . terrible . . .'

She began to cry.

He let her for some time. She got up, moved to the kitchen, tore off a strip of kitchen paper and blew her nose. After a minute or more, he got up too and moved to join her, putting his hand on her arm.

'I can't bear it,' she said very quietly. She still did not look at him but out, through the window. 'I simply can't stand it. All this talking.'

'OK.'

'I *can't*. It's just dredging things up.'

He left the kitchen, and returned, holding her coat in his hands. The high colour that his face had had a few moments ago had vanished. 'Come for a walk with me,' he said.

They went out of the house and down on to the beach.

The day was warm enough for a few families to brave the sea; as Kate walked alongside Jonathan, she kept looking sideways at him. His obvious relaxation intrigued her: he gave off no sense of urgency. He must have cancelled appointments, made provision for being away—the whole exercise must have turned his life, if only temporarily, upside down.

And yet he behaved as if he had planned, and was enjoying this. He had taken off his shoes, and walked barefoot, carrying them loosely in one hand, his jacket slung across his shoulder. He smiled at children dashing in and out of the waves. While she, in contrast, walked with her arms folded across her, shoulders hunched.

They came to the end of the bay. There was a small promontory of rocks. He climbed them, reaching back to offer Kate his hand. They picked their way up, and he sat down on a flat stone, looking backwards, the way that they had come.

She stood above him.

'I want to know why,' she said.

He glanced up, smiling. 'Why what?'

'Why you came here.'

'Because I was concerned for you.'

She shook her head.

'You find that difficult to believe?'

'No. I believe that you're concerned,' she said. 'But I can't believe that you would just drop everything like that.'

'Just for you, you mean?' He was still smiling; she glared at him.

'Yes, that's what I mean.'

'Sit down. You look uncomfortable standing there.'

'I'm fine.'

He sighed. As he spoke, he picked stones from beside him, weighing them briefly in his hand before skimming them towards the sea. 'There really isn't any great drama about it, Kate,' he told her. 'As luck would have it, I had this week booked to go to a conference. I'd paid for it eight months ago, without giving it a lot of thought, and in the last few weeks was beginning to regret it. So when you rang—'

'It was a good excuse to cancel.'

He laughed. 'There you have it.' He put down the last stone, and turned to face her. 'My confession. I wanted a holiday as much as you wanted to speak to me.'

She watched him for a few seconds.

'Does that make you feel better?' he asked.

She relented, sat down at his side. 'Yes, that makes me feel better.'

Together, they watched the beach in silence for some time. Then, 'Is this the kind of place you always come to?' he asked.

She shook her head. 'I don't go on holiday at all.'

He looked at her. 'What, never?'

'No.'

'Why is that?'

'I don't enjoy them.'

'Why not?'

'They waste money.'

'Ah . . . yes. That's true. Everything costs a lot of money,' he observed rather acidly. 'Where did you used to go as a child?'

'We travelled. So it was always a kind of holiday.'

'Really? What did your parents do?'

'I don't know what my father did. I never knew him.'

'Your mother, then?'

'She was crazy.'

He looked hard at her, interested. She avoided his gaze for some time, then gave an exasperated, breathy laugh. 'We're not going into my mother, surely?'

'Not if you don't want to. You mean she was clinically disturbed?'

'No, no . . .' Kate put her hands behind her, rested on them, tipping her face upwards to the sun, and closing her eyes. 'No, she was reliable enough, normal enough. She just didn't obey any rules. She was unlike any kind of mother to look at. She was sixteen when she had me. It was 1965 . . .'

'Flower power.'

Kate opened her eyes. She was smiling faintly. 'Yes, all that.'

'And you travelled about?'

'Yes. But we didn't live on the road. It was a succession of houses. Some were communes, I suppose. Others belonged to men she lived with.'

'A completely unconventional childhood.'

'Well, until I was seven.'

'What happened then?'

'She caught hepatitis, and her brother came to fetch me. He was married. Childless. I went to school for the first time. I lived with them for six years.'

'Did your mother recover?'

'Yes. She went to live in Greece, then came back here. She bought a house in London, and began teaching.'

'And you went back to her?'

'Yes.'

'That must have been difficult for your uncle and his wife.'

'I chose to go.'

'How old were you?'

'Thirteen.'

He sat with his hands folded one over the other, resting his chin on the closed fists, looking at her intently. She leaned forward.

'You can't make a trauma out of this, because it wasn't traumatic. They were kind, but they weren't her. I was overjoyed to see Mum again.'

'I see.'

'Now you're going to tell me that I was cruel to leave them.'

'Not at all.'

'She was my mother. She wanted me with her. And she was a lovely person. Cheerful, clever, funny . . .'

'OK.'

'She loved me. And I loved her.'

'OK.'

'People say that they love their parents. But they mean that they owe them a debt, or they're afraid of them, or they can't wriggle free of them. But I truly did love my mother. She was a wonderful person. And she had changed.'

'In what way?'

'Well, she earned her living. She didn't have many boyfriends any more. And those she *did* have were almost staid.'

'Is she still alive?'

'No,' Kate said. 'She died when I was nineteen. I had just met Richard.'

'How did she die?'

'Heart attack.'

Jonathan raised his eyebrows in surprise. 'In her thirties?'

'She was thirty-five,' Kate said. 'They did a postmortem and said it was a congenital abnormality. That she could have died at any time from her teenage years.'

'Did you find her?'

'No, no. She died on a bus journey to work. They thought she had fallen asleep.'

'And that left you alone, in a London house. But you had Richard.'

'Yes,' Kate said.

'And then . . .'

Abruptly, she stood up.

'It's getting cold,' she said. 'Shall we go back?'

They reached the villa as the afternoon sun began to wane. The tide was high on the beach.

At the door, to Kate's surprise, Jonathan shook her hand, then, after almost releasing it, held on to it for a second.

'I'm going back to my hotel,' he said.

'OK.' She looked down, rather embarrassed, at their linked hands.

'Would you like to go somewhere to eat tonight?'

She finally got her hand free, smiling. He made a gesture, recognising her discomfort, a backing-off movement. 'Yes,' she said. 'If you like.'

'Fine. I'll come and collect you at eight. Is that all right?'

'Yes . . . OK.'

He stayed another moment on the doorstep, regarding her closely. 'Is it getting any easier to talk to me?' he asked.

She paused, then smiled. 'Perhaps.'

'That word!' he laughed. Stepped back, began to walk along the path.

At the gate, he looked back at her.

'Goodbye,' she called. 'See you later.'

He raised his hand.

TWENTY-THREE

*J*ACK SAT IN THE PARKED CAR and watched the woman in the white Volvo.

She got out hurriedly. She had a coat flung over a green uniform, and, as she locked the car's door, she undid the ponytail tied at the nape of her neck, and walked towards the school gates, fluffing out her brown hair with a free hand.

It was a dull, drizzly afternoon. The small county town had lain almost obscured in its valley as Jack had driven down through green country from the motorway. Surrounded by hills, and built in the comfortable golden stone, it looked idyllic; an old town deep in the English countryside.

They must have been sure they were safe here.

He had lost the woman for a moment in the crowds. He glanced at his watch. It was three fifteen, and the middle school forecourt would soon become a mass of children. Jack leaned forward, scanning the pavement.

He saw her at last, talking to another woman. They were laughing, looking down at a piece of paper. Most of the women waiting had another child with them, either holding their hands, or sitting in a pushchair. As far as he could see, Anita Warburgh was the only one on her own.

The children started to emerge.

Jack realised that his heart had begun a small, insistent dance. The scene was a jigsaw of constantly moving bodies: dark heads, blond heads.

He saw the child open the door, and come out alone.

The boy was about five feet tall, and very fair. He had a pale face, and rather ascetic features; he almost looked ill, if it had not been for the broad smile on his face. He walked straight to Anita, and she took his bag from him, and put her arm around his shoulders.

Jack snatched up the picture of Kate McCaulay from the seat. He propped it on the dashboard, and, above it, the two figures walked towards him, framed by the windscreen.

The ten-year-old boy had Kate's look. He rounded his shoulders in the same way; he took the large, rather awkward strides that Jack had become so familiar with. A sick, pounding feeling rose in Jack's throat.

They got into the car, and Anita Warburgh reversed, almost until her back bumper was touching Jack's car. He saw her stare questioningly at him for a second, then shrug, pulling hard on the wheel.

He let her drive off. He almost let her disappear behind the high hedges at the edge of the school grounds.

Then, he followed her.

TWENTY-FOUR

*G*EORGE HAD HAD A CUSTOMER LATE THAT NIGHT.

He had been ready to close—it was nearly six—when the car had pulled into the drive. A man had got out, plainly annoyed, and more plainly still in a hurry. He had run, head down, for the doorway, where George stood, one hand already on the alarm, which he had been about to set.

The man had come in, shaking rain from his coat.

'Bloody awful, isn't it?' he had said, smiling just once at George and then looking distractedly around.

'Bloody awful,' George had agreed.

The man had strode forward, glancing to left and right. At a desk, he picked up a plate, turned it over, squinted at its mark, and put it down again. George sighed, looked out resignedly at the dark drive-way, and the ruts in the gravel that the car had caused as it slewed to a halt.

'Looking for anything in particular?' he had asked.

The man had run his hand through his hair.

'Anniversary,' he had said. 'I forgot the anniversary. Can't go home without something. She'd fucking well castrate me.'

George walked after him. 'I see,' he said. 'And what does she like?'

'I don't know what it's called.'

'Jewellery . . . ?'

'No, no. They're pots. Green things.'

'Green porcelain?'

'I don't know. It's green. Greenish blue stuff. She's got a shelf of it.'

'Greenish blue. Carlton Ware—Vert Royale?' George took the man to a display cabinet, and handed him a plate edged with gold.

'No. What she's got—it's got twisted handles . . .'

'Ah.' Light dawned. 'Watcombe.'

'That's it! That's the bugger.'

George led the man further back. Here, he had a display of Watcombe's green-and-straw.

'Thank God for that,' the man had muttered, as George wrapped the vase. He had paid willingly and off-handedly, even though George had quietly added a fiver for being kept open at six o'clock. He let him out of the shop, watched the car slide off with more spraying of gravel. George had switched off the outside lights, set the alarm as he had originally intended, and went through to the house.

He had started cooking his supper, leaning against the draining board, peeling vegetables. China stood next to him expectantly, waiting for a piece of carrot, but George hardly registered the dog's presence. From here, he could see the back of Kate's flat, the obscure glass of her bathroom window. His gaze flickered up to it repeatedly, but there was no light.

There had not been light for two days.

Her absence made him ache unmercifully. This morning, he had gone up the stairs and listened at the landing door, in case somehow she had come home without her car, and he had missed her. But there had been no sound. In fact, standing there alone as the daylight strengthened, he could feel the emptiness of the flat behind the door. Sense its hollowness and coldness.

He stopped what he was doing now, hands resting on the stainless-steel ridge of the sink. She would be at Isabelle's, he thought. Her car had disappeared between midnight and six; he knew that. Perhaps she had not been able to sleep, and had driven to Isabelle on a whim.

This business with Maggie Spence had unnerved her. Her, and everyone . . .

He let the knife fall from his fingers.

Walking back to his living room, he picked up the phone and dialled Isabelle Browning's number.

As he waited for his connection, he chewed unconsciously on the knuckle of his thumb.

She really ought not to do this. She really ought to let him know where she was going, who she was going with. Just for the safety of the flat, if nothing else. Just so that he could make sure it was kept heated in cold weather . . .

As the number began to ring, George knew that that wasn't true. He didn't, in fact, give a damn for the flat. It was Kate, and this terrible creeping, growing attachment to her, that mattered to him. He knew it was irritating. It irritated her, and it irritated him. Like an itch it was impossible to scratch. He despised the kind of man that went for younger women—invariably the kind of dependent disfunctioning male that had never grown up. He hated that kind of man.

And he had become one. He had become fixated on this perfectly pleasant young woman . . . he blushed hard as he recalled the look on her face when he had told her about the bureau. Perhaps if he could manage to speak to her now, he told himself, he could apologise about the thing. In fact, he would move the bloody eyesore out of this room tomorrow, put it in the shop where it ought to be . . .

The trouble was, he had this plague: this persistently rankling, pinching need. She had done nothing to encourage it. But then, neither had he. He had no wish to appear foolish, but this paralysis, this irrepressible smothering desire, was in him and he carried it like a virus, angry at himself. Angry at her. It was simply an infection . . .

He realised that the phone was already ringing. He counted five, six rings. Suddenly, it stopped. There was a hitched tone, and then, Isabelle's voice.

'I'm rather busy. Do leave a message after the beep . . .'

He heard the signal.

He heard the soft, ballooning, waiting silence.

'Isabelle,' he said, 'this is George Dale . . .'

He put the phone down.

He couldn't possibly discuss Kate with her over the phone. It was too stupid. The pair of them were probably there anyway, eating dinner. Quite oblivious to the worry they were causing.

A small voice in the back of his mind told him—very faintly, very clearly—that it had nothing at all to do with him.

Nevertheless, in a fit of pique at being so ignored, George picked up his car keys.

TWENTY-FIVE

*I*T WAS ALMOST MIDNIGHT WHEN THEY LEFT.

They stepped out into an ink-black night. Jonathan had taken her not, as she had expected, to an hotel, or even to a restaurant, but to a small taverna further up the coast. It stood on a headland where a village was barely elevated from the shoreline of a bay; the white stone street ended, there was a width of sandy soil, and then the sea. From their table they had watched the coastline darken from blue to indigo to black, the final darkness only punctuated by lights on boats moored in a semi-circle a hundred yards out.

There had not been many people in the place; just a few locals at first, then one other visiting couple. Finally, now, it was just themselves.

They walked to the edge of the water.

'Thank you for the meal,' she said. 'It was lovely.'

'A pleasure,' he told her.

He was standing at her side, not looking at her but at the bay. Feeling warm, almost dazed—she had inadvertently drunk most of their bottle of wine—Kate looked at his profile. He was conventional-looking, she decided: neatly parted hair, very thick, light brown with

flecks of early grey. A white shirt, and navy-blue trousers, highly polished shoes—and a tie. He wore a tie.

Suddenly, he glanced at her. 'Something funny?' he asked.

She denied it.

The car was parked along the street. Walking to it, she stopped. 'I
want to paddle,' she said.

She knew she was drunk. He knew it, too.

'We had better get back,' he said.

'I want to go and walk in the sea,' she told him. 'You stay here. I
shan't be very long.'

He had the car keys in his hand, weighing them from one palm
to another. She smiled, turned away, and stepped on to the sand. She
took off her shoes, just as he had done earlier.

The water was surprisingly warm.

'Kate!' Jonathan called.

'I'm walking,' she murmured to herself.

The beach lay like a grey horseshoe, barely distinguishable, the
water completely dark, the sky as black as the sea. There was no one at
all about. She looked over her shoulder at the little bar and the headland of houses, glimmering, as though floating in space between two
dark bands.

Ahead of her, there were pine trees: stunted by the wind into fan-
tastic shapes. Jonathan had pointed them out earlier. He had been
knowledgeable and witty, a good companion. A good man, a nice
man . . .

She reached the pines. There was a flatbed of rock, about ten feet
high, shuffled together like a pile of solid playing cards. She leaned
down to touch the first, then climbed the little outcrop, feeling her way
more than seeing it. At the top the wind caught her hair and blew it
back from her face. She was at the edge of the bay, facing the open sea.

She sat down, drawing up her knees, holding her bare feet in her
hands, feeling the coldness, the grainy salt and sand. She had the
most curious sensation, that of being rigid, made from stone herself,
straight and unbending in the body. Abruptly, her good mood—the
relaxed, hazy mood—vanished. Something closed her throat, blocked
it like a fist. And the world buckled. Whether it was the darkness, in

which she felt herself floating . . . Her heart slammed in protest, the blood thundering in her head. She tried to draw breath. There was no air at all, and only a fierce, electric vibration in her hands to the tips of her fingers.

She tried to get up, fell, and righted herself. The rocks went down in the same uneven staircase on the far side; she heard, rather than felt, their edges as her hands scraped them. She scrambled and, more or less upright, landed on her feet in a cove of perfectly flat sand. It was no more than twenty feet across at most: on the other side a wall of rock rose up out of the water.

'Kate!'

Jonathan's voice was far away. Too far. Too far. She stood at the edge of the sea, shaking, gasping. Her body was red-hot inside, her mouth plugged by some incomprehensible obstruction.

'Kate!'

He was above her, on the rocks, standing where she had just been. She had no idea if he could see her. The idea that she had died—was not really here at all, but still there, under his feet, on the rocky plat-form—occurred to her.

'Kate—stay there,' she heard him say. 'Wait there.'

The past and the future compressed her, crushed her between them like two vast, remorseless hands. There was no way back; there was no way forward. There was no point at all in stepping forward, continuing in the same dogged, desperate path. There was no release, no answer to the only question she wanted to ask. Jamie was gone, obliterated, traceless. She stepped into the water.

Behind her, she heard Jonathan coming down the rocks.

'Kate—what are you doing?'

She was up to her knees in water, the sea plucking dreamily at the fabric of her skirt. He caught her by one arm and tried to pull her back.

'Don't,' she told him.

'Kate—'

'Don't, don't.' She slapped at his hands, now trying to encircle her. 'Leave me alone.' She was still gasping for breath. He stood behind her and closed his arms tight around her.

'Hold your breath.'

She wriggled to get free.

'For God's sake, do as you're told,' he said. 'Hold your breath.'

She took no breath; but she stopped breathing.

His fists tightened under her rib cage. 'Now, when I tell you, breathe from here.' He pushed at her diaphragm. 'D'you hear me? Breathe from here. Don't gulp. Fill up your lungs. *Slowly*. Now.'

She obeyed him.

'Another. More slowly. Rest your head on me. Count eight as you breathe in. Eight as you breathe out.'

She was shaking, her head resting on his shoulder. Around them, the sea whispered. The tingling in her hands stopped. She took air in small, staggering sections, the sound rasping in her throat.

'And another . . .'

Her knees sagged. He half lifted, half pulled her back to the sand, where she sat down heavily, still with him at her back, kneeling behind her.

'I'm all right,' she said.

His grip only lessened slightly.

She saw, for the first time, the startling half-moon overhead, and thickly littered stars visible through a high veil of cloud.

'I had my wish,' she said.

His reply was muffled. Close to her, his head was bowed. 'What wish is that?'

'I wanted him dead,' she told him.

He let his hands fall, and moved so that he was alongside her, sitting, his body at right angles to hers. She looked at him, at what she could make of him in the shadows.

'They say that, don't they?' she whispered. 'Don't wish too hard because it might be granted. Be careful what you wish.'

'Tell me,' he said. His breath was loud in her ear.

She put her hand to her mouth, as if she could stop the words. But they tumbled from her anyway.

'When he was born, he was underweight,' she said. 'He didn't feed very well. He cried continually. He seemed to hate any kind of noise. It was impossible, and everything we had planned fell apart . . . we were so tired . . . so tired . . .'

She stopped for a second. Her voice, when it came, was level. 'I wished he would stop. I wished he would . . . be taken away . . .'

'Everyone who looks after children feels that at some point,' he said.

She slammed her hand into the sand. 'But this wasn't like that!' she said. 'This wasn't some lapse, some—some kind of *impatience!*' She paused. 'This was . . . my answer. I prayed for him to be taken away. *I wanted him dead.* Do you see? I wanted him *dead.* I couldn't stand it. I wanted him to go, I had no feeling for him, even touching him drove me crazy . . .' She began to cry: racking sobs dredged from the depths, from a pit of despair she had covered up for so long. 'It was my fault. I left him in an unlocked car, and all the time that people were kind, and sympathetic, I wanted to tell them, *I did it, don't pity me, don't be kind to me . . .* Someone else took him away, but they were only doing what I had asked for, they answered my prayer . . . you see that? I wished him dead, I made it happen, begged God to make him *dead,* my own son . . .'

She lay face down, moaning agonisedly, pressing her mouth into the palms of both hands.

Eventually, her tears lessened and she began to wipe her face. Jonathan started to speak slowly.

'Someone stole James from you,' he said. 'That was a criminal act. There is no way you can be responsible for criminal acts.' He picked up her hand from where it lay inert on the sand alongside them. He began to stroke it rhythmically and gently. 'Wishing doesn't make things happen,' he said. 'Wishing just gathers our thoughts, pinpoints our desires.'

She rolled over slightly, on to her side.

He lifted her fingers one by one, running his own along their length. Then he stretched his hand to her hair, and smoothed it with the same soothing motion. His index finger traced the side of her face.

'I'm so very sorry that you're unhappy,' he said.

She closed her eyes. She had heard excitement in his tone, not pity. In the next moment she felt his lips on hers, with very little pressure. His hand rested on her shoulder. She raised herself on to one elbow, and he moved with her. For a second she tried to dislodge his touch, reached to pull his hand away; then, he put his arms round her. She gave herself up to the embrace, falling back on to the sand. He kissed her: lips, face, eyes, neck. All the time his hands made the same stroking, caressing movements, passing over her arms, her shoulders. She raised her own hand to his head, felt the muscles tighten across his back. Their hands linked; then she freed her own and passed it down his body.

'Kate,' he whispered.

She silenced him with a kiss that became intense. Her body arched under him, needing his warmth, needing comfort. She had never told anyone, not even Richard, what she had just told Jonathan; it was the secret that had corrosively eaten her away since the day of Jamie's disappearance.

Now it was released into his keeping.

His hand was on her thigh. She took it gladly, guiding him to her. He murmured a protest; she sat up, pushing him back a little so that she could stand. In the intimate darkness she took off her clothes, standing over him while he kneeled. She reached for his hand, pressed it to her, bore down on his fingers, moving her hips against him, her head thrown back.

Putting both hands on her hips, he buried his face in her; then pulled her back down. She lay back and, in the next moment, he plunged into her, knocking the breath from her. All his previous gentleness fell away; he kneeled, lifting her hips and legs from the ground.

Under her, darkness.

Above her, darkness.

TWENTY-SIX

*F*OR A MOMENT, when Jack was slammed back against the wall, everything went black. He could hear the woman scream, feel her hands plucking at his shoulder and the man's arm that wedged him there; then light swam back, and he found himself face to face with Anita Warburgh's husband.

'Tony—don't,' Anita was saying. High-pitched. 'I'll call the police.'

The man ignored her. 'Suppose you tell me,' he said to Jack, 'exactly what you're doing following my wife.'

It wasn't going exactly as Jack had intended.

He had watched the man go out with the boy at ten to six; giving them another five minutes to get away, he had knocked on the door of the house.

The woman did a rapid double-take when she opened the door; her face paled and she began to shut the door again almost at once.

'Mrs Warburgh?' Jack jammed his foot in the opening.

'Go away,' she said, shoving.

'Mrs Warburgh, I'm an investigator—' One little lie. In his experience, investigators came marginally above reporters at the bottom of

138

the pile. 'I'm trying to trace Jamie Lydiatt. You lived in the same street as the family when he was abducted . . .'

She narrowed her eyes.

'I'm working for his mother, Kate.' Another slight exaggeration.

'Kate Lydiatt?'

'She's called Kate McCaulay now. She and Richard were divorced.'

'I . . .'

They never got any further with that particular branch of the conversation. Tony Warburgh had come back, stealthily walking up the path at Jack's back. He had pushed Jack into the hallway of the house, got one arm behind his back, shoved his elbow under his chin, and slammed Jack's head against the wall, all in a couple of seconds. He was fitter than Jack too. And had the advantage of surprise.

Jack tried, now, to take a breath.

'If you could just let me explain, if you could just—'

Tony Warburgh glanced over his shoulder at his wife. 'It's the same one?'

She nodded. 'He was the one in the car at the school. I'm sure of it.'

Tony looked back at Jack, who tried to nod in agreement. 'Yes, look . . . I was at the school, but—'

'He says he's looking for Jamie Lydiatt. The baby,' Anita said.

'Lydiatt?' Tony asked.

'You remember, when we were in London . . .'

The grip on Jack's neck slackened, then dropped.

'You lived at number 30,' Jack said. 'The Lydiatts were at 18. Jamie Lydiatt was taken from Kate Lydiatt's car in a motorway service area when Jamie was eight weeks old.'

Anita Warburgh had taken a couple of steps back, and was leaning against the door to the kitchen. 'You mean they never found him?' she asked.

'Didn't you know?'

Tony was looking Jack up and down warily. 'We moved house,' he said.

Jack was breathing easier. 'I spoke to Mrs Renfrew,' he said. 'Do you remember the old lady who lived at the end of the road? She must have been seventy then. She's still there. I went to see her last week. She remembered you. She remembered who you worked for.'

The couple stared at him, weighing him up.

'Please help me,' Jack said.

They didn't offer him tea, but at least they let him sit down.

Jack rapidly took in the furnishings of the living room; a mixture of expensive pieces, rather out of style, and cheaper, chainstore additions. The carpet, nylon, stuck to his shoes. There were no ornaments except for a framed photograph of the boy, probably taken two or three years previously.

'Nice-looking lad,' Jack said.

'That's Ian,' Anita Warburgh said. 'Our son.'

Tony said nothing. While Jack eased himself back into the chair, the husband sat on the edge of the couch, as though ready to spring up again at any moment. 'You haven't answered my question,' he said. 'Why you were following my wife.'

'I wanted to make sure that I had the right person.'

'But how did you find out what I looked like?' Anita asked.

Jack smiled. It had actually been much easier than it might have been, courtesy of a particularly nice—nice, talkative, unsuspecting—girl at Tony's old firm. It had been relatively easy finding, from the major company in London, that Tony had been transferred to Wiltshire; then, when he rang the provincial branch, another cheerful junior in Tony's office had told him that yes, Anita was still working up at the hospital . . .

Light dawned on Anita Warburgh's face. 'You were the one asking about my car parking space,' she murmured.

'I'm sorry,' Jack said.

'And asking about Ian.'

'That was a fluke,' he admitted. 'You had just gone to take him to the dentist.'

Anita half-laughed, then stopped. 'I couldn't make out who you were—this medical rep I'd never heard of.'

Tony had edged even further forward. 'This is about Ian,' he said.

Jack saw absolute defensiveness in his eyes; at his side, Anita, hearing her husband's tone of voice, jolted.

'I'm right, aren't I?' Tony insisted. Jack noticed that his hands had clenched to fists. 'You've done all this because of Ian.'

'I was looking for *you*,' Jack said. 'Anyone who had lived on that street. But, yes—'

Anita had grabbed her husband's hand. 'Ian's picture is on my desk at work,' she said.

Pure horror immediately crossed both faces. Neither moved.

'What do you want?' Tony asked.

Anita began shaking her head.

'I just want to talk about Jamie Lydiatt.'

'He's lying,' Anita whispered.

'You don't have any right,' Tony said. He had got to his feet.

'There's a misunderstanding here—' Jack protested.

'Who the hell are you?' Tony demanded.

Anita gripped her husband's arm, her voice low and urgent. 'An investigator. I knew they would! I *knew* they would!'

''Nita,' Tony Warburgh said. 'They haven't any claim to him, I don't care what they say, he's legally adopted—'

'Look—' Jack interrupted.

Tony had turned to the cabinet behind him. 'I've got the papers, he's a British citizen, look at the papers.'

'I know he's British,' Jack said. 'No one's denying that. He was born in St Mary's Hospital at twelve-thirty a.m. He weighed less than six pounds. He was premature.'

Both parents stared at him. Tony's hands rested on the open drawer. There was a lull of total silence.

Then Anita Warburgh walked over to Jack and looked deep into his eyes.

'Our son was born in Romania,' she said quietly. 'He was rescued, aged two, from the most dreadful conditions in a state orphanage.' She crossed her arms while Jack looked from one to the other. 'Now, Mr Seward,' she added coldly. 'Why don't we start again, from the beginning?'

* * *

'We knew about eighteen months after we were married that we would never have children,' Anita told him.

She had relented by now; and they sat, three around the low table, each with a cup of tea. She brushed her hair back from her eyes.

'Because we were in our thirties, it was difficult to get any County Council to consider us for adoption. It was another year before we were taken on by a private agency, and, because we wanted a baby, even there our chances in England were slim.' She gave Jack a tepid smile. 'You have no idea of the heartache involved,' she said, glancing at her husband, 'of wanting a child and being told that you are too old, too *Christian* even . . . too middle class. Can you credit that? Too middle class; not the right ethnic background.'

She paused, looking down into her cup. Tony Warburgh took up the story.

'We saw those orphanages on the news. Like a thousand other people, we wanted to adopt one of those children. We didn't even stop to think about it. We went straight out there.'

Anita looked up. 'Ian was in a ward, in a bed, *tied* to the bed. He was like a skeleton. His clothes—all too big for him—were filthy. They weren't feeding him—well, hardly at all. Because he had Aids.'

Jack's expression must have dropped. They looked as if they were waiting to see that reaction—his drawing back. They exchanged a pained private smile. All Jack could think of was that the boy had survived for nine years or more. And probably would not survive, could not survive, much longer.

'We brought him out just the same,' Tony said.

'I'm sorry,' Jack told them. 'I had no intention of hounding you.' He tried not to look at them; instead, his gaze rested on the documents, proof of Ian's adoption and place of birth, that rested on the table between them.

Anita smiled. 'Don't be sorry,' she said. 'You see, when we got him back here, to a doctor, it turned out that he was ill, yes. He had a kidney infection, a chest infection. He had a small heart defect. But he *didn't* have Aids.'

Jack put his cup down.

'He still has a heart murmur; we have to watch him,' Anita went on. 'But he's fine.'

'Why did you say—when I first came in—that *they* haven't a claim to him?' Jack asked. 'Who are they?'

Tony sighed. 'The day we took him out, this couple were at the doors of the orphanage. An old couple,' he said. 'They saw us with Ian and they started screaming, yelling . . . The interpreter with us said to ignore them, that they were street people who had hit on this scam, preying on foreign couples leaving with children, pretending that they were the child's grandparents, causing all sorts of trouble in public. They would take cash, American dollars, to shut up—when all the time they had no idea who the baby was. It was just a trick to make money.'

'And you thought—'

Anita put her head in her hands. 'I've had this nightmare since we got home. I always dream that they're coming back, that they turn up here. Saying that Ian really is their family, saying that we stole him. When you admitted that you were interested in Ian—'

'I see,' Jack said. 'Yes, I see.'

Anita looked up. 'That wasn't it, though, was it?' she said. 'That wasn't the real point. You thought that Ian was Jamie Lydiatt.'

Jack shrugged. 'Like I say, I'm sorry.'

Anita nodded. 'She's still looking for him?'

'Well . . . yes.'

'My God. Poor Kate.'

'Did you know her well?'

'Oh, no. Not very,' Anita replied. 'Just to say hello to in the street. After Jamie disappeared, I did knock on the door, said that if there was anything I could do . . .' She paused. 'Of course, there wasn't. Silly of me, really.'

Tony put his hand on her knee.

'You remember that time quite clearly?' Jack asked.

'Oh yes. I remember thinking, seeing her bring that baby home: *If only that were me.*'

'You didn't know he was never recovered?'

143

'No—we were abroad for a while.'

'And we moved house later that year,' Tony added.

'I don't think I ever spoke to Kate when we came back,' Anita said.

They all looked, as if by mutual accord, at Ian's photograph on the shelf.

'Jamie would be just a little older, wouldn't he?' Anita asked thoughtfully. 'And the colouring . . . Kate and Richard were both fair. He would look very much the same.' She turned back to Jack. 'I can see how you leaped to that conclusion.'

Tony stirred in his seat, making a move to get up. 'Chess club finishes in a quarter of an hour,' he said. 'I'd better go for him.'

Jack and Anita rose, all three walking to the front door.

'I'm sorry to have disturbed you,' Jack said.

Anita smiled. 'It must be costing her a hell of a lot of money, looking for him like this,' she said. 'Still, I suppose she can afford it. She must be quite a high-flyer by now.'

Jack paused, putting on his gloves. 'As a matter of fact,' he said, 'she isn't. Not unless you call a local rag high-flying. She left London nine years ago. As for money, I doubt it. But then she isn't paying me.'

Anita and Tony looked at each other, then back at him. 'You mean you're doing all this for nothing?'

'That's right. In fact, she doesn't even know that I'm doing it,' he admitted.

'But why?'

'She's started to get letters. One sentence. All it says is, *I know where he is.*'

'Jesus,' Tony muttered.

'She must be frantic,' Anita said.

'She . . .' Jack tried to find the words to describe Kate, 'she keeps things pretty much to herself.' He smiled, trying to shake off the sudden atmosphere of gloom that had descended around them. 'Still, it's great that everything worked out for you. That's good.'

Anita opened the door to the damp, misty evening. 'I don't think I'll ever forget that time,' she commented. 'Years of worry, before and after. I was really jealous of Kate Lydiatt. Nice husband, beautiful house, good looks, glamorous job, then a child. She was like the fairy princess. I could have killed her.' She began to laugh, then, sensing the inappropriateness of the phrase, rapidly became serious. 'The day she brought Jamie home—well, she and Richard—I was standing at our window with a girl who was registered with the adoption agency we'd joined, and we saw her come home with that baby in the Moses basket . . . my God, it broke my heart. I know I ought to have been glad for her, but I wasn't. It was as if someone had put a knife through me. Her husband kissed her as she got out, they were laughing . . .'

Anita looked at her feet. 'Shameful, really. But Merry and I just stood there, hating her, really hating her, and I said, "Now I know why people steal babies." For two pins, I'd have gone over there and taken that child for myself . . .'

'Merry?' asked Jack.

Anita smiled. 'Merry . . . God, what was her second name? Isn't that stupid, I can't remember her second name. And she came round a lot, didn't she, Tony? That girl married to the American?'

Tony looked at his watch. 'I've got to go.'

'She had this really strange first name.'

'Meredith?' Jack persisted.

'No, it wasn't Meredith. That's what was peculiar about it,' Anita said. 'Her mother was a singer and she had named her—after all things, if you can credit it, some people are weird, aren't they?—she'd named her after an Egyptian priestess, a singer in the temple of Amun at Karnak. Meresamun. Merrys-amun. You see? But it did suit this girl because she was very dark . . .'

Tony was pushing past them, apologising, trying to shake Jack's hand by way of goodbye.

'And she felt the same?' Jack said.

'Who?' Anita asked.

'This girl, Merry. She felt the same as you, about seeing Jamie?'

'Well yes, we both said—'

Anita's expression changed. The colour first heightened, then drained completely from her face. Her hand flew to her mouth.

'Did you see this girl again after Jamie had disappeared?' Jack asked.

'I don't know, I can't recall . . .'

'Did she come round to see you after you brought Ian home? Did she go to Romania, too?'

'No, no, she didn't . . . she didn't come . . .'

'What happened to her?'

'I . . . my God. I don't know.'

Tony had stopped on the doorstep, looking from Jack to Anita.

'Would the agency know?' Jack asked. 'The adoption agency you were both registered with?'

'Yes, but it was so long ago.'

'It's worth a try.'

'Yes,' she agreed. 'It is. I've still got the papers, upstairs.' She looked back at her husband. 'See you in a minute,' she said. 'I think Jack will be staying to supper. After all, all that adoption stuff must be in the loft by now.'

They closed the door, and walked back to the living room.

In the doorway, Anita took hold of Jack's arm.

'Kate's not paying you, and she doesn't know you're doing all this?' she asked.

'That's right.'

She looked at him, her head cocked to one side, a small smile on her lips. 'You must love her very much,' she said.

It took him no time at all to reply. He didn't even have to think about it.

'That's right,' he told her. 'I do.'

TWENTY-SEVEN

K ATE LAY AWAKE. Bright sunlight streamed over the bed.

She watched as Jonathan moved around in the bathroom opposite the bed. His actions were measured, almost slow, and rather precise, like a doctor preparing for a surgical procedure. He was very careful and controlled, washing his hands in the sink, looking at himself in the mirror. She had never seen anyone wash that way, almost rhythmically, with delicacy.

She considered his profile. Even his features were regular and even. The thick hair was combed to a straight line. He sang as he washed, low down in his throat, a continuous unstructured murmur, almost a lullaby.

He suddenly realised that she was watching him.

He smiled, dried his hands on the towel, walked into the room, and sat down on the edge of the bed. 'You're awake. Good morning.'

'Good morning,' she said.

'How are you feeling?'

'Fine. What time is it?'

'Midday.'

She sat up in the bed, wide-eyed. 'You're joking.'

'You must have been exhausted. How much have you slept recently?'

'Oh . . . God knows. I suppose four or five hours a night.'

He made a tut-tutting noise of disapproval. 'No wonder, then.'

She tried to swing her legs out of bed.

'No, no.'

'But I want to get up!'

'Stay right there. I'll get you breakfast.'

She took his hand. 'Jonathan, I don't like eating breakfast in bed. It's the most uncomfortable feeling in the world.' She kissed his fingers, held his palm against her face. He let it rest there for a second, then moved to get up.

'Come back to bed,' she said.

He smiled. 'No. Rest, and I'll get you breakfast. It's an order.'

'But—'

He pressed his index finger against her lips softly. 'Listen,' he told her. 'From now on, we do everything together. You don't have to think about anything. Not a single thing. You just have to listen to me. I'll take care of it.' He smiled, bent down, and kissed her on the forehead. 'Do as you're told for a change. All right?'

She hesitated, looking up into his eyes, enveloped by his warmth, drawn to the nearness of him, the scent of his body, his lingering touch. In truth, she had not really heard all that he was saying. His voice was whispering, dreamlike. And the sensation of being soothed, stroked, loved—after all this empty time—was centre stage, blocking out any other scene.

She leaned back, sighing, against the pillows.

'All right,' she murmured. 'Whatever you say. All right.'

TWENTY-EIGHT

$\mathcal{I}$T WAS RAINING HEAVILY, threatening to turn to snow. George drove with his foot down, the needle nudging eighty as the car negotiated the long incline.

He passed two lorries, other cars. The driver of the last one flashed him, headlights blinding in his mirror, a warning to slow up on the bend ahead. Visibility was down to no more than fifty yards.

He only vaguely registered the lights, the bend, the fog.

He changed down, and the car leaped twice as he took the corner, skittering on the striped central curve. Black-and-white signs bordered the road and the drop beyond. What was normally a broad, sweeping landscape of hills and valleys had become a white vault.

He corrected the steering and slowed. He was coming to the village. He caught sight of himself in the mirror, seeing just the left-hand side of his face, a yellowish plane, eyes full of water. He looked away.

If there were diversion signs, he missed them.

The next thing he knew, he was coming to a barrier. Vans and cars were parked across the street, red lights periodically dotting through the rain. Only then did he see it. There was a Road Closed red sign. Behind the barrier, he could see a crane and a JCB jolting in the mud.

He sat transfixed, trying to understand.

After a minute, a man in a fluorescent yellow jacket walked towards the car. He knocked on the driver's window.

George looked out at him—a face made filmy by the pouring rain, rain mixed with sleet now. He could hear it scratching on the windscreen.

The man knocked again, saying something. George pressed the window control and the glass slid down. Icy air rushed in.

'Road closed, mate.'

'Yes . . . yes, I see.'

'Not catch the signs back there?'

'No . . .'

'Closed for two weeks. We've got signs out back ten mile. Not seen 'em?'

George could not reply.

'Not see traffic going right at that last roundabout?' The man leaned on the roof of the car, grinning. 'Here, look. You back up, take the turn by the post office. Space to turn there, right?'

'Right.'

The man was looking hard at him, weighing him up. 'Where you heading, mate?'

'Fetterstock.'

'Fetterstock? You're on the wrong side of the Rideway, en't yer?'

'Yes. Yes, indeed. I took a wrong turn.'

'Ten mile out. You'll have to go up at Minter.'

'Yes, I know.'

'Back along, turn right, round here'm . . .'

George wound up the window.

The man, still talking and trying to direct him, gave a backwards step of surprise. He knocked again. George put the car in reverse, jammed it, declutched. Tried again. The man hammered on the window.

'You don't want to be driving in your condition,' he shouted. He pounded a lazy fist, not enough to make a mark, on the roof. 'Take more water with it. 'Az my advice . . .'

George got reverse. He swivelled erratically down the street, back to the post office, turned right, vacantly cut up the drivers behind him, and took the Minter road.

He got to the sale very late.

It was a country house, isolated in a great grey parkland of grass. Run-down, the stone dirty, the outbuildings' rubbish spilling on to the drive, the front steps littered, the windows uncurtained. The place was the embodiment, the spectre, of decay.

He pulled in amongst the cars, and went inside with his catalogue in his hand. His feet dragged, like a boy on the first day at school, miserable, weighed down. There was a crowd packed into the main hallway, and the smell of them was overpowering—wet coats and shoes, cigarettes, wet paper. The auctioneer was in a bad position, with an enormous stairway window at his back, so that he stood out in silhouette. George peered at him, at the catalogue, at the people ahead.

Nothing at all made any sense.

He looked down at the page, trying to listen. Trying to remember what he had come here for.

Then the sickness welled up. Abruptly and without warning, he knew that he had to get out. Bile rose in his throat, choking him as he blundered backwards, back down the steps, out into the driveway. His stomach was twisting in the grip of some unseen hand, wrenching in a vice. He ran to the hedge, and was immediately sick. He bent over at the waist, weeping as he was in the spasm, moaning helplessly to himself.

At last, when he could straighten up, he went around the side of the house. He found himself in a garden of low box hedges. Once clipped and neat, they were now growing out of shape, splayed fingers spreading up out of once-pruned lower branches.

The rain lashed at him as he leaned on the enormous side wall of the house. He turned his face up to meet it, rain mingling with tears.

He couldn't get the picture out of his mind. That was the trouble, the trouble. The worst of it. It would never go . . . never.

He would see her, eyes fixed on him, blood at the corner of her mouth, for the rest of his life.

'Oh God,' he whispered, closing his eyes. 'I didn't mean it, please God, I didn't mean it . . .'

TWENTY-NINE

*K*EN BARTLETT FROWNED as he parked his car in front of the small terraced house.

It was almost midday, but the curtains were all drawn. Setting his face, he walked through the gateway—the gate was propped, off its hinges, against the wall—and knocked loudly on the door.

As expected, the answer was slow in coming. Eventually, he heard Jack Seward coming down the stairs. Jack opened the door and stared at him for a second, then stepped back to let him in.

Ken walked through to the back room. He wrinkled his nose in distaste at the mess.

'You woke me up,' Jack said, rubbing his face.

'It's midday.'

'Is it? Shit.' Jack moved to the galley kitchen, filled the kettle with water. 'I got back late last night. D'you want some tea?'

'No. Where have you been the last two days?'

'About.'

'Not in work.'

'No . . . not *in* work. At work.'

'Doing what?'

Jack eyed him wearily. 'Look—sit down, for Christ's sake. You look like a bloody inquisitor.'

'I don't want to sit down. I just want to know where you've been.'

'*Christ*,' Jack muttered under his breath. 'Wiltshire.'

'Oh?'

'It's a story.'

'Not on the developer?'

Jack was working on land that had been sold below market price in three different locations within the county to the same man. 'No,' he admitted. 'Well, yes and no. I talked to some people in Somerset, and—'

'What's on paper?'

'Nothing, yet.'

Bartlett looked at him steadily. There was no love lost between the two of them, but his expression now was of more than that: it spelled mistrust, dislike.

Jack went to make the tea. He brought back his cup, and began to heap sugar into it.

'Do you know where Kate is?' Bartlett asked.

'No. Why?'

'She hasn't been seen for a few days.'

'You've tried her flat?'

'The landlord hasn't seen her either.'

'I thought she resigned. What's the problem?'

'She didn't resign. I didn't accept it.'

Jack shook his head. 'Can't make her work, Ken.'

'It seems I can't make either of you work.'

'That's not fair.'

'Isn't it? How about you resign, Jack? Resign and I'll take you on as freelance. I'll pay you what you deliver.' Jack straightened, putting down his cup. Bartlett turned away, walking to the window. 'I can't afford to keep staff on that don't come in.'

'If you want someone to punch a clock, ask one of the juniors.'

Bartlett began to laugh. He turned back to face him. 'You've got a very twisted idea of what it is you do, Jack,' he said. 'This is a provincial paper. We sink or swim every week. I can't have slack. I can't waste money.'

Jack strode up to him, irritation climbing to anger. 'I can't find stories sitting at a desk. I'm not an accountant like you.'

Bartlett smiled. 'You aren't Woodward or Bernstein, and this isn't the *Washington Post* either,' he said. 'If you don't like it, fuck off.' It was delivered with an even, icy tone. Jack remained where he was, staring belligerently into Bartlett's face.

'I've been *working*,' he said.

'Tell me what.'

'OK, OK. I'll tell you what. I'm working on a story about Kate.'

Bartlett, at last, registered interest. Even, to Jack's surprise, apprehension. 'Kate?'

'That's right. She's Kate Lydiatt. You remember the Lydiatts? Ten years ago, the child abduction?'

Bartlett's eyes narrowed. 'So?'

'Lydiatt—she's Kate *Lydiatt*.'

'I know that.'

Jack paused. 'You know? Since when?'

'Since I hired her.'

'Since . . .' Jack stepped back. He walked round the table, then laughed. 'Well, thanks for telling me.'

'Why should I tell you? It was none of your business. I can't see what business it is of yours now either.'

'I'm looking for Jamie. The child.'

Bartlett frowned. He looked jolted off course for a second, then irritated. 'This was Wiltshire?'

'That's right.'

'And?'

'I've got a couple who lived in the same street, and a lead to a girl they knew, trying to adopt, who disappeared around the same time.'

'Sounds thin. Expensive, and thin.'

'It's a good lead.'

'Only if you find him.'

'I will.'

Bartlett looked hard at him, his eyes ranging all over Jack's face. 'Is that where Kate is? Wiltshire?'

'No. I don't know where she is.'

'You must have spoken to her.'

'No. I haven't told her. I haven't told her that I'm even looking.'

Bartlett's head rose. Jack saw something strange—relief—pass over the older man's face. Then another look that he recognised at once: whenever it came, it was a sign of drawing back, of denial. He habitually used it just prior to spiking a story, or tearing up an expenses sheet, as if a particularly vile smell had offended him.

'Look,' Jack said, 'she's been getting these letters . . .'

Bartlett raised his hand, to stop him. 'I don't want to know.'

'But it's—'

'It's nothing. Drop it. Get your backside into the office this afternoon.'

'Anonymous letters. That's nothing?'

'I don't care. Leave Kate alone.'

'I don't want paying for what I've done. I'll bear the cost so far.'

'Damn right you will. I'm not interested.'

Jack slammed his fist on to the table. Plates and milk bottles, abandoned there amongst the heap of newspaper, rattled. 'You always bloody do this—you always do it,' he shouted. 'This is a great lead, a great story, if I find him—'

'*If*,' Bartlett retaliated. 'If. That's the key word, Jack. You've hit the nail on the head. The police couldn't find him. The family couldn't find him. They had publicity for weeks. Dead trail. Vanished. Kate doesn't want to pursue it, so leave the thing alone. It's ten years ago. Nobody cares. Leave it.'

Jack leaned on the table, both hands down, staring in front of him. 'I can't do that,' he said finally.

Bartlett looked at him for some time, willing him to glance up and meet his gaze. 'All right,' he said. 'Then leave. I don't carry dead weight. Go off and chase it on your own.'

Jack said nothing.

'Do you hear me?'

At last, Jack stood up. 'You can't fire me. I can't be dismissed.'

Bartlett smiled grimly. He took a last look around the room, took his gloves from his pocket. 'I just did it,' he said. And he walked away.

Jack followed him to the door. 'I'll go to Tribunal,' he said.

Bartlett laughed. 'I'm terrified,' he retorted. 'You're hounding a woman who wants nothing to do with you. That should look good in public.'

On the doorstep, Jack grabbed his arm, pulling the older man so that he faced him. Bartlett's expression was more extreme now: the thin smile was one of superior loathing.

'What's it to you?' Jack asked. Bartlett looked pointedly down at his sleeve, bunched in Jack's grasp. 'What's it matter to you how she feels about it?' Jack repeated.

Bartlett pulled his arm free. He walked away almost leisurely, opened the door of his car, and got in.

Jack watched the BMW draw away.

'What's it to you?' he wondered softly to himself.

THIRTY

*T*HE SUN WAS GOING DOWN; Kate and Jonathan sat in a bar overlooking the beach. The place was no more than a corrugated iron roof over a few tables, complemented by rickety iron chairs, just above the path. They had walked round the headland from the villa, and been rewarded by a fine sand bay fringed with fields that ran almost to the edge of the water.

They sat in the warmth of the evening, watching the sun rapidly slide to the sea, turning the water through shades of blue down to its present reflected copper. There was hardly any breeze.

Kate looked sideways at Jonathan, thinking how often she saw his face turned half away like that, his eyes resting on some distant point. He was very undemonstrative; or, rather, he displayed that same smiling face to everything. The fact that they had become lovers seemed not to have altered his usual demeanour. It puzzled her. The only true yardstick she had to compare him with was Richard, and his had been a totally different personality. Richard had been affectionate to the point of smothering at times; childlike, he had taken their split to heart, as much as he had taken her to heart. Their separation had wounded him to the point where he could not bear to speak to her. He had taken himself away and never contacted her.

She had the feeling that, if she told Jonathan that their relationship was over, he would simply smile in that infuriatingly calm way of his and tell her that she was wrong. The relationship would not be over until he told her so. And it was this—this unruffled surface that masked something else—something compacted, immovable—that made her search his expression for answers.

'What are you thinking?' she asked.

He turned back to her immediately, smiling and putting his hand over hers on the edge of the table. 'I'm supposed to be asking you that,' he said. He drank a little of his wine. 'I was thinking of when we go back.'

She did not comment. She had been quite content to let the days slide past. Home was associated with the letters more than anything else.

'How much do you pay for your flat?' he asked.

The question surprised her. 'Not much.'

'How much is not much?'

'Well . . . thirty pounds a week.'

'Why is that?'

'Because I work in the shop for nothing.'

'I see.'

He paused, looking down.

'What is it?' she said.

'George,' he murmured.

'What about George?'

'Well, let's face it. He'll have trouble finding anyone so accommodating.'

'What do you mean?'

'When you don't live there any more.' He glanced at her. 'You're not with me, are you?' he asked.

'No, I'm not.'

'It's like all the other things that have to change.'

She put her hand to her head. 'I'm sorry, Jonathan. No doubt I'm being incredibly stupid, but I don't see what you're talking about. What change? What things?'

'Well,' he said easily. 'You can't live there when we're married, can you?'

She looked at him steadily. Behind the bar, the waiter was filling the ice machine, whistling loudly. The clattering and occasional singing pierced their conversation.

'Are you asking me to marry you?' she said.

He lifted her hand, and kissed it softly. 'Do I need to? Surely it's understood.'

She watched her hand beneath his lingering lips; watched still as he replaced it on the table, as if it were some soft, yielding, inanimate object.

'Do I have any say at all in this?' she said.

He started to laugh. 'None at all.'

She stared at him. His face was so open. He looked—she tried to find a phrase for it—he looked like the kind of boy that any mother would like for her daughter. Clean, wholesome-looking. Charming, direct, kind.

'I want you to move out of that terrible flat of yours, stop flogging yourself to death at the paper, stop running yourself ragged for George—'

'Jon, I *don't* run myself ragged.'

'But you only finished telling me this morning what a pain George was.'

'Well, yes, he can be—'

'Why put up with it?' he asked. 'Why should you? Why not be good to yourself?'

She hesitated. She hadn't thought that the arrangement with the flat and the job was in any way harming her. In fact, she had always rather congratulated herself on such an easy exchange. Her hours in the shop could actually be quite pleasant; she looked forward to it.

Jonathan leaned forward. He pushed their two glasses to one side. He kissed her on her neck, his lips brushing her skin delicately, sensitively.

'Be good to yourself,' he repeated.

She turned her face and kissed him back. Just beyond them, the sea whispered and turned on the sand. Under the table, he ran one hand over her thighs, working his way slowly under the thin fabric of her dress. Her legs parted instantly to the insistence of his touch.

Above the table top, he looked directly into her eyes while his fingers, below, aroused her.

'Don't you know how valuable you are?' he asked. 'Don't you know how you must be treated?'

She didn't care whether anyone could see them, whether the man behind the bar might be watching. Closing her eyes, she gave herself up to the exploration of his hand. He began to whisper to her, softly, incessantly, about what they would do, what he would do, when they were alone, when they were together, when they were married and together . . .

He dropped his hand, and pushed back his chair. They stood up slowly, and stepped back from the table. As Jonathan walked to the bar and paid the bill, she smoothed down her dress as unobtrusively as she could. Then, linking hands, they went down the few steps from the bar and on to the beach.

They walked quickly, without saying a word, the half-mile back to the villa. There, in the darkness of the doorway, he took her key. They found their way in without light.

Once inside, he took off her dress, pulling it from her in such a hurry that she heard the seam tear on the shoulder. She ran her hands over his face, his neck, his back, pressing her bare skin to his still-clothed body.

He ran his hand through her hair and grasped her suddenly at the back of her head. With his other hand, he pushed hard on her shoulder.

'This. Now,' he said.

She was forced down, to her knees.

THIRTY-ONE

$\mathcal{T}$HE VICAR OF LOVATT WAS IN A HURRY THAT MORNING. Responsible for three parishes, he was booked to talk to the first school in a neighbouring village in their lunchtime assembly. He had only come to the church vestry to pick up a timetable of services.

But, as he walked into the church, he knew at once that he was not likely to get away that easily.

Pat French was at the altar rail; strewn about her in a fan shape on the floor were the flowers for the weekend. She was halfway through a display. Hearing him, she turned immediately.

'Oh—Brian,' she called. 'A word.'

He walked up to her. Actually, he didn't mind Mrs French. She was a capable, no-nonsense woman who only occasionally became fond of her own voice.

'How are you?' he said.

'Fairly well. The arthritis is a bugbear, of course.'

'I'm sorry.'

'Don't be, dear. It isn't your fault. Look—' She put down the spray of winter jasmine that she was holding, and placed her hand on his arm. 'Have you seen Isabelle lately?'

161

He thought. 'No.'

'Not since the beginning of the week.'

'Ah. Well, perhaps she's away.' He glanced at his watch. 'Look, Pat, I have to be in Durmston at twelve thirty . . .'

'She's not away. The car is parked on the street. The cats are about. There is a light on upstairs in the house.' Pat wrung her hands a little. 'I know you're busy, dear, and I wouldn't ask you if I weren't concerned.'

Brian Hemston knew his parishioners well; Isabelle liked her privacy, but she was a fairly constant figure on the village street or driving her decaying car through the lanes.

'If you're worried we shall go and see,' he said.

They made their way out of the church, through the graveyard, and, by a wooden gate, across a grass path and into Isabelle's back garden.

Winter hung heavy on the trees; drops of moisture lacing each branch with seemingly perfect symmetry. The stones were greasy with wet moss; the shrubs drooped, brushing the visitors' shoulders as they passed. They came through the stone archway into the rose garden.

Isabelle's rigorous care showed everywhere they looked: manure piled on the beds, the rose bushes pruned back. They looked up at the house; every window was firmly shut, but the light was certainly on in an upstairs room.

'That's her bedroom, you know,' Pat murmured.

Brian Hemston knocked on the door. They heard the sound echo along the stone-flagged kitchen and hallway. They waited for several minutes. At their side, running water trickled slowly into the drain.

'Does anyone have a key?' Brian asked.

'Yes, I do.'

He looked at her, eyebrows raised.

'Well, I don't like to go in,' Pat objected. 'You know how fierce she is about being disturbed. I only have the key to see to the cats if she's away. And I—' Her eyes trailed upwards, to the lit window. 'I don't like to go in alone, Brian.'

'Do you have the key with you?'

'Yes.'

'I think we should try it.'

They did so. It worked the old lock quite smoothly. They stood in the dark hall, looking around them.

'Isabelle?' Pat called.

There was no reply. Pat walked through to the kitchen and the living room, then came back to him with a worried expression. 'Nothing. I found a tap running and turned it off.'

Brian made his way upstairs.

He stopped at her door, knowing already what he would find. Isabelle Browning was, after all, in old age. A dozen things could claim her. Only last month he had found another elderly parishioner quite dead in his chair, a fire burned down and cold in front of him, the television blaring.

He opened the door.

The covers to the bed were thrown back; the sheets were wrinkled. The light burned on the bedside table, next to an open book and a glass of water. The curtains were not drawn. The alarm clock was not ticking; picking it up, he saw that it had wound down. There was no sign of Isabelle.

Brian Hemston switched off the light.

'Is she there?' Pat French called.

'No,' he said. He walked out on to the landing where she was waiting.

'She isn't in the bathroom or the other two bedrooms,' Pat told him. 'The bed isn't made. It looks as if she has just got out of it.'

Pat looked around her. 'Well, where is she?'

Brian frowned. 'What was it like in the kitchen?'

'Tidy.'

'No note anywhere?'

'No, nothing.'

'Strange.'

'Yes, it is . . .'

They both looked back into the bedroom. For the first time, a glint of light on the floor, close to the window, caught Brian Hemston's eye. He walked forward, and saw that there was a piece of costume jewellery on the floor, half under the small table.

He leaned down and picked it up.

'What is it?' Pat asked.

He showed her, holding it flat in his hand.

It was very unusual: green octagonal stones in a gold setting.

'That isn't Isabelle's,' Pat said. They considered it a moment; then Brian placed it carefully on the table.

'I don't like this one little bit,' Pat added. 'I think I will ring the police.'

He followed her downstairs; she stood in the light shed from the small window in the front door, glancing up at him as he descended. He walked around her, listening as she recounted the details into the telephone.

The hallway was narrow, decorated in a severe striped wallpaper. An occasional table bore a vase of dried flowers and beech leaves. Next to the telephone, a notepad, pencil and the directories were carefully aligned. Brian leaned back against the stairs, wondering why someone so obviously organised should leave such an untidy loose end as her own disappearance. She had been disturbed, it seemed to him: the tap, the turned-back bed, the light burning, all bore testimony to that. And yet there was no forced entry. Isabelle Browning had not disturbed an intruder, for instance. Or even, it seemed, left the house. Through the tiny porthole in the front door, he could see the bonnet of the Mercedes.

He looked up and down the hall. Absently, he reached forward to close the door of the understairs cupboard, open the merest fraction of an inch.

The door resisted him. He stepped up to it and pushed hard. Then realised that something was blocking it from the other side.

He opened the door, bending down, squinting into the darkness, feeling forward with one hand.

His fingers closed on Isabelle Browning's cold flesh.

THIRTY-TWO

$\mathscr{I}$T WAS SATURDAY LUNCHTIME when Kate and Jonathan returned from the airport and drove into the lane that led to the Gallery.

Kate was in a good mood, singing along to the radio, watching Jonathan's car through her driver's mirror. He followed her closely, never letting the gap widen so that any other car could cut in. She waved to him at junctions, at traffic lights, all the way home. He rewarded her with his smile.

As they drew up to the Gallery, Kate saw that there were already two other cars parked in the drive. She got out and walked to the door of the shop. It was locked. Puzzled, she looked through the glass and saw that the lights were down to dim.

Jonathan had walked up behind her.

'I'll just knock on the cottage door,' she said.

George came to the door grey-faced. Kate's opening greeting floundered. He stared, first at her, taking in her tanned face, her lightweight clothes with her jacket slung across them, and then Jonathan, who stood directly behind her.

'George,' she said. 'What's the matter?'

'Where have you been?' he asked.

'Well . . .' She glanced back at Jonathan. 'I've been on holiday.'

'You didn't tell me,' he said.

She tore her eyes from George's hand, white-knuckled, on the doorframe 'Are you ill?' she asked.

'I've got visitors.'

'Oh. I'm sorry. I'll call round a bit later.'

'No—' He stepped forward, grasped at the loose sleeve of her jacket. 'No, Kate. Come in.'

She looked again at both men. 'This is Jonathan Reeve,' she told George.

'Yes,' George said. He appeared distracted, to say the least. He narrowed his eyes as he looked again at the younger man. 'I know you, don't I?' he asked.

'I don't think so,' Jonathan said.

'From the Cothem sales?'

'No,' Jonathan told him.

George shrugged. He stepped back, letting them both come in, his gaze lowered to the floor. When he had closed the door, he walked past them. 'Come into the living room.'

They saw that two men were there.

'This is Detective Inspector Harris,' George said. 'And Detective Constable . . .'

'Rossiter.'

'Yes. Rossiter.'

Kate and Jonathan nodded at them.

'Is something the matter?' she asked. The thought crossed her mind that George had been burgled. 'Is it the shop?'

'No,' George said. His voice was utterly dull, drained of any emotion. 'No, Kate. It's Isabelle.'

'Isabelle?' Kate, frowning, looked from the police to George and back again. 'What's happened?'

'I'm afraid . . .' DI Harris began.

'She's dead,' George said.

There was a split second of silence. Jonathan moved to put his hand on her arm.

'How?' Kate asked.

'She was found at her home,' the policeman continued.

Peculiarly, Kate did not feel shocked or surprised. She didn't feel anything at all; rather, it was as if she were suspended, lightweight, in space.

'Sit down,' Jonathan said. He was pushing her gently in the direction of the couch.

She resisted him. 'Isabelle,' she murmured.

'Her body was discovered by a neighbour and the local vicar yesterday morning. I'm afraid it seems that she may have been murdered.'

'Murdered!'

'Yes. There is a post-mortem this afternoon.'

'My God. But that's . . . that's so . . . it's not possible.' Kate simply could not connect Isabelle—vivid, determined, opinionated—with death; let alone a death in which she had been at the mercy of anyone else. Kate pressed her hand momentarily to her face. 'I just don't understand this,' she said. 'Who would kill her? Did they break in or something?'

'There was no sign of forced entry, no.'

'You mean she *answered the door* to whoever it was . . . ?'

She glanced up again at George.

'We've been looking all over for you to tell you,' he said. His tone was petulant; wounded. Kate saw a glance pass between the two policemen.

She turned to them. 'I've been on holiday. It was spur of the moment. I'm sorry if you've wanted to contact me.' She could feel George's gaze fixed on her, boring a hole in the side of her skull.

'It's the bracelet,' George said.

'What bracelet?'

'The one I gave you.'

'Sorry?' Kate said.

The constable stepped forward. He brought a transparent bag from his pocket and showed it to her. 'Do you recognise this?'

It was the chrysoprase bracelet, set in gold, that George had tried to give her for her birthday.

'Yes,' she said. 'Mr Dale gave it to me. But I didn't accept it.'

'When was this?'

'About ten days ago.'

'You gave it back?'

'Yes, I—' She stopped dead. Yes, she had fully intended to give it back. On that morning, George, refusing to acknowledge it at all, hadn't taken it from her. But she had, surely, returned it to the shop. 'I think so,' she murmured.

'You're not sure?'

She frowned, trying to remember. 'I took it with me that morning in the car, I would have brought it back in the afternoon . . . it had a blue case. I'm sure I left it in the shop.'

'You did not,' George said. 'You *never* gave it back!'

She recoiled a little at his tone. His face, so pale before, now became suffused with a dark red. He was trembling, she saw—trembling, his feet moving slightly, as though he were shuffling faintly to a beat, a tune. 'George, I can't really remember,' she admitted. 'I intended to leave it in the shop that afternoon. I thought I had.' She looked back at the policeman. 'It was never in the flat. I know that.'

'Is it possible you mislaid it?'

She tried to think. 'I can't believe I'd be so careless,' she said. 'I was sure I put it back in the shop.'

'You didn't give it back to Mr Dale, though? You didn't hand it to him?'

'No,' she said.

George was breathing audibly, taking small, staccato gasps of air. 'You never gave it back,' he repeated.

Kate dragged her gaze from him. 'Why is it so important?' she asked.

The constable folded the bag carefully. 'It was found in Mrs Browning's bedroom.'

Kate was astonished. She looked from the bracelet to the police, and then to George. 'But how on earth did it get there?'

'That's what we're trying to establish.'

All three of them looked at George with apparently the same thought.

'I didn't leave it!' he retorted. 'I didn't go in the place—she didn't answer—I knocked but she didn't answer!'

Kate looked at the Detective Inspector.

'Mr Dale went to Mrs Browning's house during the week.'

'But I didn't get *in* . . .'

'There was an answerphone message—'

'Yes, yes—' George was as near to hysteria as Kate had ever seen him. All his usual good humour, the throwaway attitude he had when speaking, had vanished. He looked cornered. 'Yes, I went there. I was looking for Miss McCaulay.'

'Why?' Kate asked.

'Because . . .' George's eyes flickered towards Jonathan. 'I just wanted to know if you were there. You hadn't been home for days. I was worried.'

Kate said nothing. Slowly, Jonathan took her hand.

'I never went inside,' George whispered. 'I swear. I knocked, and there was no reply. I just hung around a while, just perhaps five minutes, I knocked again . . . I came home . . . I heard nothing in the house . . .'

'You were seen entering the alley at the side of the house, and opening the door that led to the rear, Mr Dale,' the DI told him.

'Yes, all right. Yes, I went round to the back. Yes, I . . .'

'Oh God,' Kate murmured.

'You won't find anything of me in that house,' George said.

'Except the bracelet,' the DI replied.

George slammed one hand to his head, a gesture of total exasperation. 'No, no. I hadn't seen the bracelet since I talked to Kate about it on her birthday. The last time that I saw it, she had it in her hand.' He wheeled towards Kate, a mixture of emotions on his face. 'I'm sorry, Kate,' he said. 'I don't mean to tell tales, or say anything about you, but I have to show that I didn't take that bracelet there. You understand— you see? I went to the house, but I didn't get in, and I didn't have that bracelet with me—'

Kate stared at him. 'You're surely not trying to say *I* had anything to do with it?'

George looked around him with the air of a drowning man trying to grasp any straw that might pass him. 'I don't know, I don't know . . .' he said. 'No, of course you couldn't have, I know that.'

In the pause that followed, Kate's face went very white. She stepped backwards into Jonathan's grasp, and sank immediately to the sofa. Jonathan, still standing, turned to the police.

'My fiancée has not been well,' he told them. He reached into his jacket and took out a business card. 'This is my name—telephone number—address,' he said. 'I've been caring for Miss McCaulay. She has been subjected to a shock recently. She has been the subject of a hate campaign through the mail.'

They looked at the card. 'Oh?'

'Jonathan, please,' Kate said.

'She has received letters referring to an event in her past—a very traumatic event. Anonymous letters.'

'What?' George said.

'No, I—' Kate was still faintly objecting.

'They have put her under a great deal of strain. With Margaret Spence's death, and now this . . .' Jonathan looked hard at George. 'I really don't want her disturbed any more than is absolutely necessary.'

'I see,' said the DI. 'Have these letters been reported?'

'No.'

'Why is that?'

'I don't want to have them—looked at—I don't want . . .' Kate's voice trailed away. She kept glancing back to George.

George was glaring at her, unblinking. He had all the appearance of someone in pain: a real physical pain centred in his chest. His hand plucked at his shirt front. For a second, Kate was convinced that he was actually in the throes of collapse. He swayed, then raised the same hand, palm downwards. An invitation to hold it, directed at her. It was so absurd, so out of place, that it was chilling.

'Tell them I didn't leave that bracelet there,' he pleaded.

'I can't,' she told him. 'I can't, George. Because I just don't remember.'

He advanced on her. 'Did you give it to me—give it to me, in my hand, put it in my *hand*?'

She couldn't think.

'You didn't,' he insisted. 'For God's sake, Kate. Help me out here.'

'No. You're right. I don't think I gave it to you. I think I put it in the shop.'

'No!' he responded. 'Not the shop, not in my hand—*you never gave it back*. Think!'

'I can't . . . I don't know!'

Kate leaned back, away from him. She read panic, even derangement, in his face; the old and familiar and safe George was dropping steadily away, revealing a stranger beneath. Jonathan stepped between them.

'That's enough,' he said.

George was frantic, wild in expression, sweating. His head swivelled from face to face. 'I couldn't have left it there,' he insisted. 'I was only upstairs for a minute.'

The significance of what he had said hit them all at the same time. George, too. His face crumpled. His hand leaped towards his face, then fell at his side.

'Oh, George . . .' Kate whispered. 'What have you done?'

The police stepped forward, taking George by the arm.

'No,' George cried. 'This is wrong. You have to understand me. Listen, I . . .'

Jonathan turned away from him.

'Listen,' George wailed. 'Listen. Please, this is all wrong, all wrong . . .'

THIRTY-THREE

$\mathcal{K}$ATE AND JONATHAN REACHED KILCOT DOWN HOUSE at two o'clock.

There was nothing left of Kate's earlier good mood. She kept seeing George's face as he was taken out to the police car: protesting, bewildered, flushed. She kept thinking, agonised, of Isabelle.

As they drew into the drive of Jonathan's home, she noticed another car already there; an old blue Proton, spattered by mud. A woman of about fifty got out as Jonathan parked, and came running up to him. Kate watched as he opened his car door, and spoke to her. She saw his restraining hand on her arm.

Kate got out, and Jonathan walked back to her.

'A client,' he told her. 'A bit of a crisis.'

'Oh. Shall I go?'

'No, no.' He laughed. 'Kate, this is your house now. Come inside.'

She picked up her suitcase and walked forward, nodding to the woman briefly. Jonathan let them in, switching on the lights, and picking mail from the mat inside the door. He ushered the woman into his consulting room, and took Kate down the hallway, showing her into a large kitchen.

'Make yourself at home,' he said. 'I'll try to be as quick as I can.'

'It doesn't matter,' she told him.

He kissed her on the cheek, and went back up the hall, closing the door of his room firmly behind him.

She stood for a moment, trying to get her bearings. The kitchen was lovely; bright and fresh-looking. She guessed that it was an extension to the house, and had been custom-made. The fittings—the ovens, the marble-topped table, the sinks, and units—were immaculate. Pale wood doors were rag-rolled with green paint; the floor was a mixture of pale brown and terracotta tiles. Pasta and rice and dry foods were stacked in high glass jars; there were racks of spices, fresh herbs. Crystallised ginger. White china plates stacked in a Victorian plate rack. Good claret in the wine rack. It looked like the kitchen of a master cook, or an interior designer.

In fact, she thought, looking round, that was exactly what it reminded her of: those impossibly chic rooms, untouched by sticky hands, spills, or newspapers and letters, that featured in the pages of home design magazines. She smiled warily to herself: Jonathan was a perfectionist, that much was obvious. At least in that they were alike.

She took down three mugs, and arranged them on a tray. She had suggested to Jonathan that they look after China but, refusing, he had taken the dog to a neighbour in the village. Now she knew why. A dog would make for too much mess in a house like this. She sighed: boiling the kettle, she made a pot of tea. The cups squeaked under her touch: dishwasher clean.

She took the tray up the hall.

At the door, she hesitated. She was acutely aware, despite what Jonathan had said, of being a stranger in this house. A stranger to his method of working, the layout of his days. To the details of the work he did. For instance, perhaps he had some sort of light in the hall, that might indicate if he should not be disturbed. She looked about, but couldn't see one. She hated the thought that she would trespass on anything personal.

She put down the tray, and knocked softly.

There was no immediate reply. Then Jonathan came to the door.

She picked up the tray; he looked at it sharply, frowning. Then he took two mugs from her.

'Thank you,' he said.

He closed the door.

She went back through the hall, and put the tray down in the kitchen. Their suitcases were still where they had left them by the front door. She wondered if she ought to unpack, and where she ought to take her clothes. Or if she ought also to unpack *his* things.

She waited ten minutes, sitting in a straight-backed wooden chair, drumming her fingers lightly on the table. She was sure, in the silence of the house, that she could hear the woman in the consulting room crying. She got up, went out, and took the first door on the left, closing it behind her to shut out the sound.

She was in a sitting room decorated in the same sparse, clean style as the kitchen. Two cream couches were at right angles to each other; there was an open fire, a pale yellow carpet. In a white vase, a bunch of chrysanthemums were dying. In one corner of the room was a curving, open staircase.

She looked at the books on the shelves. After a second or two, she realised that there were sets rather than individual books: the complete works of Shakespeare, Milton, Byron, Shelley, Pope, all bound in the same way. Then a complete set of encyclopaedia, a complete set of Oxford Companions to Literature. She ran her finger along them. One wall was devoted to them, and they all had that never-used look.

Frowning slightly, she picked up the vase of flowers, and opened the door to the hall.

'. . . everything I have,' she heard the woman say.

'That isn't necessary,' Jonathan responded.

'I *want* to, I want to—'

Kate walked rapidly into the kitchen and shut the door tight. She looked around for a radio, found it, and switched it on. Classical music filled the room; she turned the volume low.

It was an hour since they had arrived.

She felt hungry, and, with sudden relief, realised that there was something she could be profitably doing. She took down a couple of saucepans, found the vegetable cupboard, and set about cooking.

It was about ten minutes later that she heard the consulting room door open, followed by the outside one. There was a conversation on the step; then Jonathan's footsteps along the hall. He opened the kitchen door.

'Hello,' she called, stirring the sauce mixture in front of her.

He walked up to her. 'What are you doing?'

'Cooking.' She smiled, and kissed him on the cheek. He didn't respond; she saw the expression on his face. 'What's the matter?' she asked. She followed his gaze to the saucepan. 'It's pasta. Don't say you don't like pasta.'

He looked up at her. 'I didn't ask you to do anything.'

'I thought . . .' She looked from the hob to him, confused. 'Aren't you hungry?'

He turned away.

'But—what is it? What have I done?'

'I was going to take you out to dinner.'

'Well, you still can. This is just a snack.'

There was a silence during which she tried to fathom if he were offended or not. He had taken a coin from his pocket, a Spanish peseta, and was turning it over and over in his fingers. She turned off the heat to the sauce.

'Look, tell me,' she said. 'Obviously I've annoyed you in some way.'

'I like things kept neatly.'

'It isn't untidy, Jon.'

'No, well . . .' He shrugged. 'Besides, you're not supposed to be tiring yourself,' he said. 'I wanted you to have nothing but rest.'

'But I feel fine!'

'You're not fine.' He turned back to her at last, and put his hand on her shoulder, looking deep into her eyes. 'You won't be entirely well for some time.'

She began to laugh. 'I am *fine*!'

'No, Kate.'

'What do you mean?' He began to guide her to a chair; but she stopped him forcing her to sit. She caught his arm. 'Jon, please don't smother me,' she said.

He looked terribly, almost comically, offended. 'Smother you!'

'No. Not smother. I'm sorry.'

'Do you know how you sound?'

She looked up at him. 'What?'

'Do you know how you sound? The words you use?'

'What words?'

'They are just different sides of the same coin, Kate. Watch your anger. Where is it directed? At something?'

'I don't know what you mean.'

'Of course you don't. You don't even recognise that you are angry. Think of the last week. Think of those changes. How many of them are real? What are they pointed at?'

'I don't know.'

'That's right. You don't.'

'But—'

'It recoils on you, like a gun misfiring. Remember that overload feeling? Too many unresolved conflicts.'

'Jon, I—' She put a hand to her head. She was not angry at all. She thought that *he* had been angry.

'I don't want you going down that road, experiencing those feelings without reference to me. Without talking to me,' he said.

'But I was only cooking lunch . . .'

He looked at her, paused, and then laughed very softly. He turned away and made an exasperated sound as if she had said something breathtakingly stupid.

'What have I said?' she asked. '*What?*'

He turned back to her. He spoke very slowly. 'I am not talking about cooking lunch.'

She met his gaze. 'Then I'm sorry,' she told him. 'I don't know how we got to this . . . anger, or misdirecting my feelings, or whatever it is you're saying.'

He made a slight tut-tutting sound. 'You mustn't belittle this process, Kate. You must accept that we are going through this process.'

'I don't want to be bloody processed!'

He pointed at her. 'You see? Anger.'

There was a long pause. He sat down at the table, lacing his fingers in front of him, avoiding her gaze.

'I'm sorry,' she murmured.

'It's all right,' he said.

She tried to concentrate, tried to think back to the place where she had been before this whole conversation began. She felt muddled. Finally, she sat down heavily on the chair next to which she had been standing, and rested her head on her hand.

'Can you see the pattern?' he said.

'No. I can't.'

'There is a pattern. Think. Look back.'

'What pattern?'

'In your actions.'

'*My* actions?' she repeated. 'My actions have something to do with getting anonymous letters? Or Isabelle's death—or Maggie's?' Her voice broke slightly at the mention of their names. She transferred her hand to her mouth.

'Don't you think that they do?'

'No . . . how could they?'

'How did you used to feel about your mother?'

'My *mother*?'

'Tell me.'

'I adored her. I told you.'

'No, you didn't tell me that,' he said. 'You said that you loved her, and then immediately qualified it by explaining that other people say they love their parents, but that *you really did*. Why did you say that? Why did you emphasise it in that way?'

Kate frowned, confused. 'Because I did. I really did!'

'You're using exactly the same form of words. Is that a little litany you repeated to yourself when you needed it? *I did, I really did.* Are you trying to convince me, or yourself?'

'I don't understand what you're getting at.'

He leaned forward so that he was very close to her. 'Just this,' he said. 'You protest about loving your mother, but what was she to you? Someone who abandoned you. She couldn't even give you a father, or any kind of normal home. How could you possibly love someone you didn't know? She became ill and left you. She palmed you off with relatives. She came back when it suited her to take you away from them. She gave you nothing but uncertainty. What kind of mother is that?'

'She was . . .' Kate stopped. The image she had always carried of her mother began to crack; a cherished mental picture, now suddenly run through with uncertain lines.

'What kind of mother is that?' Jonathan repeated.

'She . . .' It was no use. She couldn't think. Couldn't distinguish.

'What kind of mother is that?'

'Jonathan, please—'

'Tell me!'

'All right—OK. Not a very good one.'

'Not *good*?'

'All right. A bad mother, if you like.'

'Not if *I* like. What do *you* feel?'

'Well, I—'

'*Feel*, Kate. Don't you feel angry?'

'No. Yes. It wasn't like that—'

'No? Your mother hasn't the sense or the kindness to look after you; she leaves you for years . . .'

'Yes. Angry, then. I suppose I was angry when I first went to live with my uncle and aunt. I didn't understand.'

'You understood very well. Your mother didn't love you. How could she?'

'I don't know . . .'

'You do know, Kate. She didn't love you.'

'Maybe . . . I don't know . . . maybe . . .' She looked up at him. 'You're bullying me.'

'I'm not bullying you. See that reaction there? You're repressing that anger and twisting my motives because you can't face the question. You are angry with the question, but you don't say that you're angry, do you? You say that I'm deficient in some way.'

'I'm sorry . . . I didn't mean that . . .'

'Listen to what I'm saying. Just when you get back together with your mother, she dies. The ultimate theft. Now she's really taken from you. But never mind, here comes a replacement. Here's Richard. How long did you wait before getting married?'

Kate stared at him. 'Just a few weeks.'

'Why?'

'Because we were in love.'

'Because you were rebounding. Desperate to retain that attention you had missed all your life. Can't you see that pattern?'

'It wasn't like that.'

'It was like that. See it. Let that admission go. Free that feeling.'

She had never felt that she was repressing a feeling. But perhaps, she thought now, perhaps he was right. Perhaps she had clamped down her natural reactions all her life. Perhaps she really had been angry with her mother; really had been angry at other losses. Perhaps she had made worse things happen because of that blocked fury. She couldn't figure it; couldn't find the thread of logic.

'And what happened to Richard?' Jonathan persisted in his low, even, unremitting voice. 'When you needed him, when Jamie was missing, what did he do?'

'That wasn't his fault.'

'Leaving you? He left you, just like your mother. And your uncle and aunt didn't chase after you, or fight to keep you, did they? They left you. Richard left you. They all left you.' He stopped. 'Jamie left you.'

She covered her eyes, but he pulled her hands away.

'If none of that was their fault, whose fault was it?' he asked.

'Mine,' she murmured.

He let the word linger in the air. The single syllable seemed to fill the room, compress it, close claustrophobically around her.

'Everything was my fault,' she said.

She began to cry, worn down.

He sat beside her, watching. Then quietly he said, 'Now Maggie. Now Isabelle . . .'

'Oh God,' she whispered.

'The world is a terrible place, isn't it, Kate? Where are you in it? Where are you standing?'

'Nowhere . . .'

'Everyone has gone.'

'Yes, everyone has gone.' She sobbed desperately, the noise tearing in her throat.

'Don't you hate them for leaving you?'

'Yes, yes . . .'

'Why do people always leave you?'

She couldn't answer. She felt as if she had been torn in two; fragmented, the world swirled round her.

Finally, he put his arms about her, smoothing her hair. His touch intruded into the darkness; a warm lifeline.

'Kate, let me help you,' he said. 'But you must not resist me. Are you listening?'

'Yes.'

'Will you promise me?'

'Yes,' she said.

'Good.'

He got up, sighing. Then he put his hand on her shoulder. His fingers lingeringly caressed her neck. 'You must listen to everything I tell you,' he said.

THIRTY-FOUR

$\mathcal{T}$HE WINTER MORNING threw harsh blocks of light and shadow across the corridor; but the interview room into which George was taken was windowless. He had been brought here yesterday, but conversation had not lasted long. A doctor had been called to sedate him; he had fluctuated between long, erratic and rambling sentences, and total silence, and complained of pains in his chest.

The detectives could see at once that today would be more productive. George Dale held himself straight; he murmured a good morning to both men, nodding at them politely as he sat down.

'How are you, Mr Dale?' asked Detective Inspector Harris.

'I'm all right,' he said. 'Thank you.'

'I hear that you would like to speak to us.'

'That's right.'

Detective Constable Rossiter smiled. 'Good. Because, of course, we want to speak to you.'

The tape machine was started and Harris recorded the names of those present and the time. George fixed his eyes on the table between them.

'How long have you known Isabelle Browning, Mr Dale?' Harris asked.

'Ten years.'

'As a friend?'

'No. She was a client. She bought from me regularly.'

'How often would you see her?'

'Every couple of months.'

'And she would come to the shop?'

'Yes. Or I would see her at auctions or fairs, or sales.'

'She was a keen collector?'

'Not a collector. She liked to browse. Sometimes she bought a little piece of furniture. Or books.'

'I see. But you knew her well?'

'I knew her as a customer. It wasn't until Kate and she became friends that I saw any more of her. She would come to pick Kate up. They went to dinner or lunch together. Kate sometimes spent the weekend with her.'

'Right. This is Kate McCaulay, your tenant?'

'Yes.'

'And your relationship with Mrs Browning was no more than that?'

'No. No more.'

'Until last week. What happened then?'

George paused. He had clasped his hands together. His gaze hadn't shifted. 'Kate hadn't been back to her flat for a couple of days, and I was worried.'

'What day was this?'

'Wednesday.'

'And what happened on Wednesday?'

'I rang her.'

'Isabelle Browning?'

'Yes. I got the answerphone.'

'And what then?'

George unclasped his hands, and put one to his head, smoothing the deep crease between his brows. 'I wanted to know if Kate was there. I thought she must be there, and they had left the answerphone on because it was evening, it was about eight o'clock.'

'And you thought they didn't want to be disturbed? They were in the house, but not replying to the phone.'

'Yes.'

'What happened then?'

'I drove over there.'

'To Isabelle Browning's.'

'Yes.'

'At what time did you arrive?'

'It was . . . it was about nine at night.'

'What then?'

George's breathing became slightly more laboured. 'I knocked on the door. There was a light. I knocked three or four times.'

'Did you hear anything in the house?'

'No.'

'Was Kate McCaulay's car parked by the house?'

'No.'

'So there wasn't any reason, really, to carry on knocking. Miss McCaulay wasn't there.'

'Well, I thought perhaps her car was somewhere else. In a garage, something like that . . .'

'Go on.'

'There was no reply. I put my ear to the door, I suppose I leaned on it. And it came open.' His gaze flickered upwards to both men. 'I didn't break it open, you understand,' he said. 'I didn't intend to push the door. But it must have been just catching the latch, and it opened . . .' He stopped, ran his hand across his mouth. 'I walked inside and called Isabelle's name. I called several times. I looked in the downstairs room. I looked up the stairs and saw a light in one of the bedrooms, and I walked up.'

'Do you make a habit of walking into people's houses like this, Mr Dale?'

'No, no. But with the door coming open, and the light upstairs, I thought there must be something wrong. It wasn't like Isabelle. She was so forthright, so capable; she would have locked the door. I called again on the landing; then I went to her bedroom. But she wasn't there. The bed was turned back. I looked around the room, and felt suddenly sure that something was wrong . . .'

'Why?'

'I don't know. Just standing there, I felt there was something wrong, I couldn't quite put my finger on it—'

'*What* was wrong, exactly?'

'It looked like she had been in bed and got up hurriedly, and never come back to the room.' George's face was white now. His breathing was shallow. 'I didn't even go right into the room. I backed out and went downstairs, and I stopped at the answering machine in the hallway and pressed *Messages* . . .'

'Why?'

George frowned. 'Why what?'

'Why listen to her messages?'

'I don't know. For a clue to where she was, perhaps.'

'But you had already heard her answering message when you rang.'

'But—'

'Then why listen to her messages?'

'I don't know—'

'You weren't erasing your own message, Mr Dale?'

'No! No, I—'

'You weren't trying to erase the evidence that you had called her?'

'No . . .'

'Go on.'

'I just wanted to find Miss McCaulay.'

'Why?'

'I—just—' George's voice was high and wavering now.

'What was it to do with you?'

'I—' George dipped his head, burying it in his hands. 'I care for her.'

'Pardon?'

'I care about her. I wanted to know where she was. I was very worried.'

'Why? She's a free agent.'

'I don't—'

'Why would she leave her home? Was she frightened of staying there?'

'No. I don't think so.'

'Frightened of you, perhaps?'

George stopped dead. 'Me?' he echoed.

'Always wanting to know where she was. Intruding on her.'

There was a pause, during which George's rasping breath seemed to fill the room. Rossiter poured him a drink of water. George's hands fumbled around the pliable, disposable cup.

The Detective Inspector placed a clear plastic bag on the table between them.

'I am showing Mr Dale the piece of jewellery found in Isabelle's Browning's bedroom,' he said. He smiled thinly at George. 'Did you buy this as a gift for Miss McCaulay?'

'Yes.'

'For the tape, please.'

'Yes,' George said, louder.

'When did you last see it?'

'Ten days ago.'

'Miss McCaulay says she gave it back to you.'

'No.'

'She didn't give it back?'

'No.'

'It hasn't been in your possession since then?'

'No.'

'You didn't take it with you on Wednesday evening?'

'No.'

'You didn't pick it up, take it with you, determined to give it back to Miss McCaulay, to force her to accept it?'

'No, no . . .'

'You took the bracelet with you to force her to accept it because you were already annoyed at being refused and ignored by this attractive young woman . . .'

'No! That's not true.'

'You weren't attracted to her?'

'Yes, but—'

'You wanted her to acknowledge you. Would that be close to the mark? Wanted her to thank you. Disliked her friendship with other people. People like Isabelle Browning. You had the bracelet in your pocket when you got to the house, angry, rejected, you forced the door, and went in, and when you found that Kate McCaulay wasn't there, you lost your temper. You argued with Mrs Browning—'

'No! That's not right. That didn't happen. It didn't happen like that,' George objected.

'I think you're a jealous man, Mr Dale,' Harris said almost conversationally. 'I think you've been up to all sorts, sending letters, harrying women who don't want you, chasing them, stalking them, and this was just one rebuff too many.'

'No!'

'I think this was a breaking point,' the Detective Inspector continued. 'Wouldn't that be closer to the mark? Wealthy man like you, never had a wife, wants a wife, a companion at least, and can't make a woman interested for long enough . . .'

'No!'

'And here's Mrs Browning, probably telling you a few home truths, and you lost your temper—'

George held up his hand to stop him. It was trembling violently. 'Please,' he said. 'You're saying it wrong, all wrong.'

'Tell me the right way then. I'm listening.'

'I came downstairs,' George whispered. 'I realised that Kate had never been there. I wasn't annoyed, I was just confused and worried, and then I saw the cupboard open under the stairs, and I looked in, and she . . .' He stopped and swallowed hard. 'I looked in, and saw her in there.'

'Who?'

'Isabelle. *Isabelle.* Her eyes were open; I thought she was conscious, awake, and I pulled on her arm. There was blood on her face, on her wrist . . .' Tears welled in his eyes. He stopped for a long time, reliving the scene. 'I saw that she was dead, and I got up, and I went to the kitchen, and I tried to wash the blood off my hand . . . and then, then I . . .'

'You left the house.'

George sighed; the deep, gusting sigh of an admission. 'Yes, I left the house.'

'You didn't ring the police or an ambulance?'

'No.'

'Knock on a neighbour's door?'

'No, I didn't.'

There was a silence while the significance of this sank in.

'Why was that, Mr Dale?'

The detectives could see that George's expression had become strained. The old man's face wore a look of bafflement and pain, and—more interestingly by far—of guilt.

'Mr Dale,' Harris repeated softly, 'tell us. Why did you just leave her there?'

George began to cry. Large tears, viscous and sticky, ran down his face. His body shook silently. He made no effort to wipe the wetness from his face; probably he did not even feel it.

'Mr Dale . . .'

George made a helpless, grief-stricken sound. His eyes were fixed on the wall behind Harris's face, fixed on a point in the past that only he could see.

'I didn't mean to do it,' he whispered at last.

The detectives glanced at each other.

'I didn't ever want to kill anyone,' George said.

THIRTY-FIVE

On the Monday, Kate drove over to her flat at the Gallery. After George's arrest, she and Jonathan had left immediately. She needed to collect her clothes, to check that the flat was OK.

She made the journey slowly, careful at every junction, keeping her speed low. She didn't quite trust herself; everything felt too large, too unwieldy in her hands. When she arrived, the Gallery buildings were deserted. She looked sadly at the shop, and then went across to the flat, glancing at her watch. Jonathan had clients until one o'clock. She was supposed to meet him in town at precisely half-past one. She had offered to shop for food; he had preferred that they do it together.

She opened the outside door, and saw the week's accumulated mail. She picked it up and took it upstairs. The flat was cold, but it was comforting to see her belongings, her own bed, her own table. She ran her hands over her typewriter. Jonathan had a laptop computer. She saw how old everything in here looked: the castoffs from the shop, and things she had bought herself at sales. Jonathan had never seen this room. She wondered what he would say when he did. Her life felt second-hand under his inspection already: failed in a dozen subtle ways that he would want to repair.

She sat down on the bed and sorted through the letters. There were the usual circulars. No foolscap white envelope, thank God. But there was a letter from a market town a little north of here; turning it over, she saw that it was from a solicitor, his embossed firm name across the back.

As she was just on the point of opening it, the phone rang.

'Hello?'

'Kate. At last! It's Jack Seward.'

'Oh. Hello, Jack.'

'I've been trying to get in touch all week.'

'I've been away.'

'Right . . . right.' He sounded unsure. 'I wanted to check with you about something,' he said.

'Oh?'

He laughed embarrassedly. 'I don't know if you're going to thank me or break my neck.'

'Try me.'

'OK. It's . . . look, don't be angry, but . . .' The word *angry* ran through her like an bolt of electricity. 'I've been trying to trace Jamie.'

She looked at the floor, unmoving.

'Kate?'

'Yes. I'm still here.'

'Are you all right?'

'Yes. Go on.'

'I've found some of your neighbours. They've given me a lead. A real lead. A woman . . .' He paused. 'Look, can I come and talk to you about it?'

'I don't know, Jack. Things are . . .' Well, what were they? Strange? Busy? Fraught? Were they worse than that? All her fluency with language seemed to have deserted her. She fought off the idea, trying to assemble her thoughts in a logical line.

'Kate, I know you must be shocked about Isabelle.'

'You heard.'

'It was in the paper. Some new boy up at the *Journal* got it. I'm really sorry, Kate.'

'So am I.' She paused, her voice momentarily strangled by emotion.

She wanted to see Isabelle; wanted to talk to her. Wanted her sanity. Then, 'A new boy?' she asked.

'Yes. I've been fired.'

'But why?'

He paused. She heard him sigh. 'It's a long story. Can I come over now?'

She glanced at her watch. It was already ten to one. 'I've only popped in for a moment,' she said. 'I don't live here now. I have to meet someone at half-past.'

She listened to the prolonged silence. She could almost hear him wondering why she had moved, and where to. And with whom.

'I see,' he said.

'But look, meet me tomorrow somewhere.'

'OK. Fine.'

They arranged a place and time.

'Kate,' he said, just before he hung up, 'are you all right?'

'Yes. I'll see you tomorrow, Jack.'

'Look after yourself.'

'Thanks. I will.'

When she had put the phone down, she opened the envelope from the solicitor.

A short, businesslike paragraph asked her to ring him as soon as possible.

It concerned Isabelle Browning.

THIRTY-SIX

$\mathcal{T}$HE SOLICITOR'S OFFICE WAS IN THE MAIN STREET of a market town whose picturesque buildings, honey-coloured and winding their way up a narrow hill, were featured on postcards and calendars bought by the thousand.

Jonathan and Kate might have walked straight past the building had Kate's eye not been caught by the polished brass plate at the door-way. Andrew Manners himself came to the door after they had rung the bell, smiling as he ushered them through.

It was more of a private house than a place of business, with a comfortable Georgian sitting room, a large log fire, and a view of a court-yard garden.

'Do sit down,' he said. He stood in front of Kate, looking every inch the paternal uncle. 'And this would be . . . ?' he asked, indicating Jonathan.

'Oh, excuse me. This is Jonathan Reeve.'

The two men shook hands.

'A friend?' asked Manners.

'Yes,' Kate said.

At the same moment, Jonathan replied, 'My fiancée.'

They glanced at each other, and Kate laughed embarrassedly. 'Sorry.'

'Rather a new arrangement, I take it?' Manners asked.

'Yes,' she said.

'Are you to be married soon?'

'Yes,' Jonathan said.

Manners sat down opposite them both. 'I have been Mrs Browning's solicitor for forty years,' he said. He noted Kate's surprise. 'Quite, quite. A long time. Not that she ever gave me any work to do, of course. The purchase of the house when I had just qualified; the probate of her friend's estate in the fifties . . .'

Jonathan shifted in his chair.

'Not a great deal in recent years except, of course, for the will.' He took a file from the low table beside him. 'That is why I asked you to come here today. As the beneficiary.'

Kate did not quite hear what he had said. She was expecting to be told that Isabelle wanted her to act as an executor, or sell particular items of furniture, or some such task. The one thing that had not even entered her mind, even on the journey here today, was that she was entitled to any of Isabelle's money.

'Beneficiary?' Jonathan repeated.

Andrew Manners looked at him, then smiled. He opened the file and read the contents silently for a few seconds.

'I'm quite willing, of course, to read you the exact terms,' he said. 'But all that matters is that Mrs Browning's entire estate is left to Miss McCaulay. The house in Lovatt; the contents; the share fund in Mrs Browning's name; the residual effects from the will of Michael Chambers, which includes the small property in London; her account at the bank, some sixty thousand pounds; the car, of course . . .'

Kate sat and stared.

The Isabelle she had known was never short of money; she knew that. But—and her mind flashed immediately back to Isabelle's usual daily uniform of well-worn trousers, tattered shirts, gardening sweaters, and aged brogue shoes—she had never come across as being in any way wealthy.

Manners pressed a finger to the page in front of him. 'There are a few instructions on her burial, and funeral . . . of course, that must wait until the body is released, which may take some time . . .'

Jonathan had laid a hand on Kate's arm. He watched her, saw her total incapacity to speak, and looked across at Andrew Manners.

'How much is the estate worth?' he asked.

Manners calculated briefly. 'Hard to say. The house is listed, which has its drawbacks as well as its compensations, and makes the market value rather unspecified—'

'Roughly.'

'Roughly?' Manners repeated the word. There was a brief silence. 'The estate is *roughly* five hundred thousand pounds.' He gave Jonathan a rather lingering, disapproving glance; then he turned his attention to Kate, whose position, and expression of astonishment, had not altered.

'I think, perhaps, that a cup of tea is called for,' he murmured.

They left about half an hour later.

There was a mild winter sunshine colouring the street; people brushed past them on the narrow pavement. Kate stood in the sunlight, disorientated. Jonathan held out his arm, and she took it. He set out immediately, up the hill, with a light step.

'A half a million!' he said, after they had walked a few yards. 'Five hundred *thousand*!'

She did not look at him; he squeezed her arm. 'Well?'

'I don't know what to think,' she replied.

They had to separate for a while, to get past other pedestrians. He stood ahead, waiting for her, smiling broadly, holding out his hand. 'You're rich,' he said.

She looked at him quizzically, surprised.

'You can do anything you want,' he told her. 'Are you going to keep it?'

'Keep what?'

'The house, of course.'

'I don't know.'

'You could try it on the market, and see what interest there was. You could get a survey done; they would give you an idea.'

Kate's surprise escalated to a kind of creeping unease; she was amazed that he could discuss it so lightly. She watched his face, biting her lip. 'Isabelle loved that house. It meant a great deal to her.'

'You're keeping it?'

'I—'

'Do you want us to live there?'

'I don't know.'

'I would have to move the business, but that's no problem. Convert that front room to a consulting room.' He stepped back to allow a woman with a pushchair to get past them. 'Of course, that wouldn't be a problem. Lighten it. Do you prefer old houses?'

'I like that one.'

'OK. We'll keep it. I'll sell Kilcot.'

She put her hand on his arm. 'I don't want to talk about it now. I don't want to make any decisions.'

He smiled. In fact, she had never seen such warmth in his habitual expression. It made the other smiles look false.

'All right,' he said. He kissed her lightly on the cheek. Keeping his lips close to her, he added, 'I've got another surprise for you.'

'What?'

'Guess what it is.'

'I've no idea.'

'Come with me.'

They had reached the top of the street, where it broadened into a small square of well-proportioned houses. Tucking her arm into his, he took her across the road and down a small path. There was a house here, narrower and taller by one storey than its neighbours, and painted white. They went into its paved forecourt.

Glancing to the side, Kate could see that the front bowed window, though hung with opaque white curtains, seemed not to be a sitting room at all, but was set with a circle of chairs. There was a drawing board, facing away from them.

Jonathan pushed the door open.

'In you go, darling,' he said.

She stepped into what she could now see was a kind of shop. On a tailor's model in the corner was a magnificent—if somewhat overwhelming—gown, in magenta taffeta; on a smaller model next to it was a child's dress, equally extravagant, in tartan pinks and gold and red, with frothy white underskirts. Ranged at the feet of the dresses were matching shoes. On the shelves behind the models there were bolts of cloth, many in shades of ivory or white, others of Thai silk.

A bell had tinkled in the hallway as they came in. Now, a woman appeared from the same hall, walking towards Jonathan with her hand outstretched.

'Mr Reeve?'

'Yes. Miss Kelberman?'

'Lovely to see you.'

'We're a little early.'

'No matter, no matter. Much better early than late.' The woman was perfectly groomed, dressed in a dark green suit. She looked as if she had stepped straight from a magazine makeover. Her blonde hair was coiled in an elaborate style off her neck; her make-up was flawless.

Kate felt shabby next to her. She had dressed up a little bit, because of the appointment with Manners; but her black skirt and tan jacket felt suddenly second-hand.

'And this, of course, is Miss McCaulay.'

'Yes . . .' Kate, utterly bemused, shook the offered hand.

'Do sit down. Coffee?'

'No, thank you,' Kate said. 'I'm fine.' She turned to Jonathan. 'Jon . . .'

'I've been giving the matter some thought,' the woman said, directly at Jonathan. She inclined her head in Kate's direction. 'Your description of colouring is just a *little* out. I would say Miss McCaulay has just a faint touch of a darker note than fair in her complexion. Very striking. You know, there can be an absolute difference between light fair and dark fair. You will find that one takes ivory and one doesn't.' At last she smiled directly at Kate. 'Men are usually quite bereft of colour sense,' she said. 'Your husband has *almost* got you. But not quite!'

'Do you have anything that we could look at now?' Jonathan asked.

'Oh yes. Masses. I can show you things I have done for other weddings, of course. I have a book of those. I can show you one or two orders I am making up now.'

'Excuse me,' Kate said.

'Yes?' asked Miss Kelberman.

'Would—' Kate looked to Jonathan, and then back. 'Would you please tell me what's going on?'

Miss Kelberman smiled. Jonathan put his arm around Kate's shoulder.

'It's my surprise,' he said.

'I don't understand,' Kate told him.

'My surprise for the wedding,' he said. 'You can choose anything you want. I thought you might just want a suit, but you can have a dress. There's no reason why it couldn't be a dress.'

'The *wedding*?'

'You want new clothes, don't you?' he said. 'For the day.'

Kate gazed at him.

'I want to do this for you. It's my present,' he said.

She shook her head. 'You can't be serious.'

'Why not?' he said.

Kate looked at the designer. 'We haven't even discussed this.'

'You do need to plan a little in advance,' Miss Kelberman said. 'It would take me at least three weeks.'

'There you are,' Jonathan said. 'You see? This has to be done first.'

'But—'

'Anything you want. You see?'

Kate gazed at him. The thought crossed her mind that he had gone temporarily mad. She lowered her voice.

'Could we just talk?' she asked. She glanced at the designer. 'If you wouldn't mind?'

'As you wish.' The woman retreated into the hall.

'Jonathan,' Kate said, as soon as she felt that they were out of ear-shot. 'I don't want a new dress.'

'Why?'

'I just—' Baffled, she ran her hand through her hair. 'It just never occurred to me. I mean—'

Jonathan had stepped in front of her. He put his hands firmly on her arms, just above the elbow. 'Listen to me, Kate,' he said. 'We *are* getting married?'

'Well, yes . . .'

He smiled. 'And if we're getting married, you don't want it to be a hole-and-corner thing, surely?'

'I don't want a big fuss, Jon.'

'But you weren't envisaging just dodging out to a registry office in a pair of jeans?'

'I wouldn't mind.'

He stared a second, then laughed. 'Oh, no,' he said. 'Oh no, no, no.'

'That would be perfectly legal.'

'No, no. I want you to do this the right way. I know what I want.'

'Oh, really?'

'Yes,' he told her. 'I know exactly what will suit you. I've got it,' he tapped his forehead, at the temple, 'fixed right here.'

Kate looked at him, staggered.

'Please,' Jonathan said. He lifted one hand, and stroked the side of her face. 'Just let me organise this, will you? You don't have to do anything. Not a single thing. I know exactly what I want. And it will be perfect. Not showy. Just perfect.'

She looked into his eyes.

'Please, Kate,' he said. 'Don't fight me about this. It isn't worth it, is it?'

Down the hall, they heard the designer returning, her high-heeled shoes tapping on the stone floor.

'Please just let me do this, Kate,' Jonathan said. 'It's my gift to you, Kate. Please accept it. Just let go for once. Let me do it for you.'

The woman reappeared. She had two files in her arms, bound folders six inches thick.

'Everything OK?' she asked.

Jonathan looked pointedly at Kate.

'Yes,' Kate agreed, slowly. 'OK . . . yes . . .'

THIRTY-SEVEN

$\mathcal{K}$ATE WAS VERY LATE FOR HER MEETING that evening with Jack
Seward. She had told Jonathan that she was going to the newspaper
to tie up loose ends. He had softly, but resolutely, objected. Out of the
house after an agonisingly prolonged discussion, she had been reflect-
ing wryly on her need to tell him the white lie, omitting Jack's name.

She parked on the seafront in the dark, and ran the hundred yards
back to the pub, a tiny bar on the corner of a street. She pushed open
the door to a warm, fugged atmosphere wreathed in smoke, and saw
Jack immediately, propping up the far end of the bar, his head resting
on his hand, a newspaper in front of him.

'I'm sorry,' she said, as she got up to him.

'I thought you'd forgotten.'

'No, no. Just . . . held up. Sorry.'

'Drink?'

'Oh . . . a whisky. It's so cold.'

He ordered it; they walked to a table and sat down. She took a sip
of her drink. 'Have you been in to see Ken?' she asked.

'Why should I?'

'To get your job back.'

He laughed. 'I'm not crawling to that smug bastard,' he said. 'What about you?'

'I resigned.'

'I know that. I meant why.'

She looked down at her glass, ringing its rim with her fingertip. 'I was tired,' she said.

He watched her for a second, then changed the subject. 'Want to hear what I know?'

'Yes.'

He told her what he had been doing, while the games machine rang and stuttered in the opposite corner and conversation at the bar, between the barmaid and the handful of locals, threatened to drown them out. Kate leaned forward towards Jack, to catch every detail. At the end, she looked at him without speaking, her eyes large and unseeing, gazing past his face for a second before focusing on him again.

'Did you ring the adoption agency?' she asked.

'Yes. They won't discuss anything over the phone.'

'You have to go and see them?'

'That's right.'

'Where are they?'

He told her. It was an address in central London, off Holborn.

'What do you want to do?' he asked.

Her eyes ranged over him. 'What made you chase after this?'

'The letters.'

She considered. 'You think that he's alive?'

'Yes . . . I do. I think I do.'

'They will talk to you if you turn up in person?'

He smiled. 'I don't know if they'll talk to me. But they might talk to you.'

She sighed, finishing the drink and replacing the glass on the scratched table. 'Oh, Jack,' she said, 'what a mess this all is. I think . . .' She paused, trying to find words. 'I think maybe I ought to just leave it.'

'*Leave* it?' he said. 'Leave finding him?'

'No. Leave the looking.'

'Why?'

'I might spend the rest of my life turning up dead ends; finding one tantalising detail after another that never lead anywhere.' She shivered. 'I don't think I could stand it. Especially now. After Maggie. After Isabelle.'

'That's nothing to do with Jamie.'

'No. But it's to do with me.'

'Kate . . . it's a sick coincidence.'

'Whatever it is, I can't stand it.'

'You can stand it.'

'I can't, Jack. I just want . . . to crawl away.'

He started to laugh. The sound of it, rich and throaty, made her look up. 'No.'

'What?' she said.

'Crawl away. You've never crawled away from anything.'

She frowned. 'Oh yes, I have.'

'Not recently.'

'Yes, yes, I have . . .'

He rested both elbows on the table between them. 'I've known for five years that you lost Jamie,' he said. 'I never saw you slow up.'

'You didn't know me after Jamie.'

'No. But you put your life together again.'

'In a fashion.'

'That's right. A fashion. Not perfect like before. Different.'

She looked away. 'I just patched it. It looked sewn together. But I wasn't functioning.'

'Who told you that?'

'It doesn't matter.'

'You really think you can walk away from a possible lead like this?'

'I don't *want* to. I want to find him,' she said hotly. 'But leaving it alone is what I *ought* to do. I'll never start living if I don't leave it behind.'

Jack frowned. He thought he detected someone else's tone; the sentences were too pat, too stylised, too practised. It sounded like a lesson she had learned by rote.

'I'll have to think about it,' she murmured. 'Discuss it.'

'Who with?'

She glanced at him. 'Someone called Reeve. Jonathan Reeve.'

'Who's he?'

'A psychotherapist.'

This time Jack really did break into a broad grin. 'Come off it.'

'I'm serious,' she protested.

'You don't need your bloody head shrunk.'

'Don't be stupid.'

'Is that where you've disappeared to?'

'What do you mean?'

'Disappeared to this last week or so. You're telling me you've had your brain scraped?'

She smiled coldly. 'You really have a sympathetic way about you, don't you?'

'Tell me it's done you good.'

'It's . . .'

'You can't.'

'Of course it has. What the hell do you know about it?'

'Actions speak louder than words.'

'*Now* what are you talking about?'

'Doing something. Not talking about it. If some head-case is sending you letters, find out where they're coming from. Tell the police. Stick two fingers up to them. Who are they, anyway? Some piece of shit.'

'Oh, I see. Stick two fingers up to any psychopath that happens to come along?'

He leaned forward to within an inch of her face. 'That's it,' he said. 'That's exactly it. Crawl away and hide? Patched up? I *don't* think so. And neither do you.'

She sat back from him. Her face was red, her lips parted. He looked to her like the illustration from a child's fairy tale—the ogre waiting in the forest wings, all dark hair and eyes. He looked fiercely outraged. Something in her abruptly clicked. She started to laugh, and, once started, found she could not stop. She bent her head and grasped her sides, gasping like an asthmatic for a while until she straightened and wiped her eyes. 'Oh, Jack,' she said, at last.

'I'm glad I'm good for a joke,' he said. She took a handkerchief from her pocket, and blew her nose.

He put his head on one side, watching her. 'Tell me about this Reeve.'

She folded the handkerchief, and put it away. 'He's . . .' She tucked her hair behind her ears. 'He has a practice down the coast. I met him a year ago, doing an interview.'

'And met him again since?'

'I went to him about ten days ago.' She looked Jack squarely in the eye. 'The letters . . . I felt I was going crazy.'

'Uh-uh,' he said, unimpressed. 'And were you?'

She pinched back a smile. 'Maybe a bit.'

'And now?'

'Now, I . . .'

She thought. She had become used to treading carefully the last week or so, picking her words, examining every inflection of her own voice. Listening, she realised, for weakness. Jack was motionless, unmoving, his gaze fixed on her intently.

'I'm getting married,' she said.

The change in Jack's expression was quite amazing. Disbelief, then a kind of wounded surprise, chased each other across his face, then disappeared as rapidly as they had come.

'Well . . . congratulations,' he said. 'Oh, don't tell me, don't tell me. Let me *guess* the lucky man.'

She gave him a wry look. 'He's really—'

'Very nice,' Jack finished for her. 'I'm sure. I'm sure.'

'You must meet him.'

'Right.'

'I'm serious.'

'Yes, right. Fine,' Jack said. 'As long as he doesn't show me his ink blots.'

She laughed, shaking her head. He got up and returned a few seconds later with two more drinks.

'I shouldn't,' Kate said.

'Neither should I,' he responded. 'Here's to the happy couple. Many long years, et cetera.' He took a long draught, then put the glass down. 'So?'

'So what?'

'Are you coming to London with me to see this agency?'

'I—'

He held up his hand. There was a moment of silence during which his gaze bored into her.

'I don't want to hear what Doctor Jonathan has to say about it,' he said.

'You weren't going to.'

'Oh yes, I was. You've started to talk like him. I bet. And I've never even met him.'

'Jack . . .'

'Got a lot of clients, has he?'

'Yes. Yes, he has.'

'Lot of women?'

'I don't know.'

'Lot of dependent women. I'll put a tenner on it.'

'That's not very kind, Jack.'

'No,' he admitted. 'No. I'm not a very kind and caring person, am I?'

She took the reprimand, cocking her head on one side.

'I want you to find Jamie,' he said.

She didn't reply.

'What does Jonathan say about the letters?'

'He says . . .' She glanced away from him. 'He says that . . .' But she didn't know what Jonathan thought, exactly. He had pointed out the unlikelihood of Jamie's survival. He had told her that she attracted loss. She had lost the image of herself, or, rather, given it away, a barely wrapped parcel, and allowed him to peel away folds of skin, memory, tissue. She bled with him. And then he mended the wound. And then he opened another.

Pain is the route to healing. He had said that one night in Spain.

She looked up. Jack was waiting to hear what Jonathan said.

'Let me think,' she said.

'Either you want to follow it up or you don't. It's that simple.'

'It's not that simple. Be patient.'

Jack lifted his glass and swallowed the last third of the drink.

'I'm not Mr Patient,' he said. 'Remember?' He stood up, and plucked his jacket from the back of the chair. 'You're getting me mixed up with someone else.'

THIRTY-EIGHT

*I*T WAS THE OLD DREAM.

But it was not the same.

She was in the house, at the very top of the stairway, with the steps falling away behind her, tread after tread into darkness. She could feel her heart beating heavily with the exertion of the climb, but not with fear.

There was a room ahead of her, its door slightly open. Beyond it, light glimmered. When she walked, her feet were light. There was none of the old dragging sensation. She pushed open the door, and saw, in the far corner of the room, a low couch.

On the rug in front of it, toys were scattered haphazardly. It might have been any playroom. The couch was upholstered in soft, creamy linen. Its cushions were piled high. At its side was an empty cot, and empty highchair. Discarded shoes. A tricycle. A football. Toys that counted the years.

In the centre of the couch was a child of about ten years old.

It was a boy, fair-haired, slim. He held a book open on his knees and was reading it with his body bent forward, his finger on the page. Somewhere in the room, in its undisclosed other corners, music was playing. It was a violin, and she felt the sound in her hands, the long smooth tubes of columnar softness passing between her fingers.

'Jamie,' she said.

He looked up. He put the book down, smiled and stood up.

He was tall, like her.

'Oh, Jamie,' she repeated, holding out her arms. 'Jamie . . .'

She woke up, staring into the darkness where she had been looking into his face. There seemed to be no end, no edge to the dream; there was no startling sensation of breaking back into consciousness. The illusion neatly folded into itself, and was instantly replaced with the contours of Jonathan Reeve's room.

Kate sat up in bed, her hand to her throat. She felt an extraordinary, piercing mixture of sadness and joy. Joy from seeing her son. Grief that he was lost to her. For a moment—and it was only the most fleeting of moments—she smelled his skin.

At any other time, she would have immediately got up, brushing the feeling away, obscuring it with movement. But this time she savoured his proximity, reaching forward through the image to keep every detail.

Only after three or four minutes did she look across at Jonathan.

He was asleep, and breathing deeply and evenly. The bed was large—very wide—and he lay with his back to her, at the very edge of the sheet, the pillow pulled tightly around him. Strangely, he didn't lie curled, but straight. She had never seen anyone lie straight when asleep on their side. Between the place where she had been lying and where he was now, there was a cold and uncrossed space. Although they had made love, he had freed himself from her arms before he slept.

Her hand ran over the bed linen, wondering if she should wake him and tell him what she had dreamed. But she thought better of it. She got up quietly, and pulled on her dressing gown.

The house was still quite warm. She went downstairs and into the kitchen, where she poured herself a glass of water. She drank it with the light off, looking out into a garden made starkly monochrome by a full moon. Going back, she glanced in at the sitting room to make sure that the last embers of the open fire had burned down.

At the side of the fire, something metallic caught her eye. She went over, and saw that it was her own car keys, next to her handbag on the coffee table. She put them back in, and carried the bag upstairs, and put it inside the door of the bedroom.

Jonathan was snoring slightly. She smiled, realising that this was an imperfection, one of the very few that he could not control. He could lie neat and straight, but he couldn't help snoring. He is human after all, she thought wryly.

She glanced along the landing. She felt wide awake.

There was a set of steps at the furthest end of the house that led up to the loft. Jonathan had taken her up there, and shown her the partial conversion, the room with its sloping ceiling. 'This is where I store my patients' records,' he had said, his arm around her shoulder. 'All very boring.'

It had been, too. Just a boarded-over floor, an unpainted partition wall with a low door in one side, and a single four-drawer steel filing cabinet.

'I bet you would win a prize for Britain's cleanest loft,' Kate had joked. They had laughed, coming downstairs again while he continued the guided tour of the house.

There had been something about the space, though. Something she had rather taken a liking to. Like her flat at the Gallery, because it was at the very top of the building, it had a wonderful view. Kilcot Down House, standing as it did at the edge of downland, had an unhindered view right to the sea two miles away.

She wondered, now, what it was like at night. In moonlight.

She went back up the stairs. There was an ordinary door, matching those on the landing below. She crossed the smooth chipboard floor barefooted, and leaned on the sill of the Velux window, pressing her face almost to the glass.

In the eerie half-light the land looked almost like water, the short turf grass scattered by shadow. There was a hedge a few hundred yards away, now a black line. Beyond that, a rippled slope. On the horizon, the sea showed as a line of white.

She looked for a long time, wiping a circle in the condensation on the glass. She rested her hand on the top of the cabinet. Miles, she thought . . . miles from anywhere.

When she looked around, she stopped, and let her fingers drift down over the front of the drawers of the filing cabinet.

Patients' records, he had said.

She wondered how many people he saw. How long he had been in practice. He always dealt with those questions, when she asked them, with a kind of modest deference, invariably changing the subject.

Got a lot of clients, has he?

Lot of women?

Lot of dependent women.

Alongside the cabinet was a long, broad shelf. It started at the wall and ran right to the opposite right angle, and the second door in the ten-by-ten-foot square.

'Nothing behind there but empty packing cases,' Jonathan had said. 'Oh . . . and a very sad little plastic Christmas tree.'

Nothing in there.

And nothing on this shelf.

She wondered why he had built the shelf and then put nothing on it. There wasn't even a chair. Perhaps, she considered, he used it to put files on when he wanted to refer to something he had taken out of the cabinet.

But nothing to sit down on.

She looked again at the cabinet. They were private records, of course. She knew that. Confidential records. As private as any ordinary doctor's correspondence. Patient confidentiality . . .

Her hand touched the metal handle of the first drawer.

Got a lot of clients, has he?

Lot of women?

Strictly against the rules, of course, even to consider looking at those files. Strictly against Jonathan's rules.

And Jonathan had a lot of rules.

She pulled on the drawer.

It was locked. And so was the one below. And the two below that.

Standing alone in the darkness, Kate shook her head. She turned and walked out of the room, closing the door quietly behind her.

THIRTY-NINE

'WHAT TIME IS IT?' George Dale asked.

The WPC sighed as she glanced at her watch, then back at George through the narrow aperture of the holding cell. 'It's ten thirty,' she told him.

'I want to see my solicitor.'

She smiled wanly. The old man had lost weight visibly in the short time since he had been arrested. She had disliked that florid face of his the moment she had set eyes on it, but she could still pity him. Whenever she had looked in on him in the cell, he had been sitting in the same position, upright and anxious at the very edge of the bed, his hands always mobile, clutching at his clothes from time to time as if he were suffocating.

He was always very polite. He thanked her when she brought him a meal. He never raised his voice. He did not complain. The doctor had prescribed a sedative twice, but Dale's high colour had not diminished. Nor, she thought, had he slept.

'I'm sorry,' he said, seeing her expression.

'I can't call anyone out now.'

'I must see him. Or the policeman. The detective. Harris. Or Rossiter.'

'They've gone home.'

'I have to see them. It's important.'

'You'll see them in the morning when you go to court.'

'I can't go,' George murmured, distressed now. 'I can't go.'

She looked carefully at him. His whole personality had crumbled, disintegrated. He was the most unlikely murderer she had ever seen.

'Listen, I'll bring you a cup of tea,' she told him.

'No, please . . .'

He had stood and reached one hand up to the small grille. She touched his fingertips. 'Mr Dale, there's no way you can avoid going to court, is there?' she asked. 'It won't take long. It won't be as bad as you think. It's not a trial.'

'But I didn't do it,' he said.

She smiled. 'Righto.'

'I mean it.'

'You confessed, remember?'

'Yes,' he said.

'Well, then . . .'

George stepped back from the door. He leaned against the wall and closed his eyes.

'He wouldn't give me the bandsmen,' he muttered.

'What?' she asked, standing nearer to the door.

'He wouldn't give me the bandsmen. I had worked all year. He gave me threepence, or sixpence, sometimes. I got up every morning in the winter to make up his fire. I sorted deliveries. I helped him at house clearances . . .'

'Who?' she asked.

George was no longer talking to her, but to himself, behind his tightly closed eyes.

'I liked the man with the bugle best,' he was saying. 'I always thought it looked a bit too big for his body. It was like a drinking cup. You couldn't really tell if he was drinking something or playing something . . .'

'Who?' the WPC repeated.

'Of course, lots of boys had Britains figures. There was a lad in our class had the horse artillery, with the gun carriage and all the horses . . .'

The WPC leaned backwards slightly to see if she could attract the attention of anyone else on the shift. 'Harry . . . ?' she called.

'He wouldn't give me those bandsmen. That's what it was all about,' George said, unassuaged grief in his voice. 'Stupid old man made a joke about it, pretended to give the box to me, but then he took it back. I maybe still wouldn't have done anything, just gone home, accepted he was a tight old devil, mean old devil, if he hadn't just held that box out and then taken it back . . . You couldn't properly tell that it was a joke, even. He didn't laugh. He just raised his eyebrows, looking down on me because I hadn't got his meaning. "Maybe next year, if you're a good boy," he said.'

George sighed and lifted a hand to his eyes.

'What is it?' asked the other constable on duty, who had come along the corridor.

'I don't know,' the WPC said. 'Listen to him. What do you think?'

George's body sagged, though he remained standing.

'I wanted them,' he whispered. 'You don't know what that's like unless you've had it. Eats at you, to have things. Not to do anything with them. Not to sell them. Just to touch them and have them . . .' A sigh shook his body. 'The bandsmen were hung on the tree. It was January. He was taking down the tree and all the decorations. At Christmas, he had only given me the cigarette card. He started telling me how every one had been painted and cast. Salt in the wound, you see? Rub the salt in a little bit more. He was standing with his back to me, and I picked up a bronze. Heavy, it was. Horse and rider . . .'

'George,' said the WPC.

He opened his eyes, and looked at her.

'I didn't kill Isabelle Browning,' he told her. 'You understand? Not Isabelle Browning . . .'

FORTY

THE FOLLOWING MORNING, Kate came back to the house via the garden. Seeing Jonathan through the glass, she knocked on the kitchen window. He came to the door and let her in.

'Hello,' she said. 'It's cooler than it looks out there.'

'Where have you been?' he said.

She stepped inside and went to kiss him, but he moved backwards. He leaned on the worktop, hand on one hip.

'What's the matter?' she asked. She had gone to the fridge and now stood with the door half open.

'I asked where you had been.'

'For a walk. Why?'

'I couldn't find you.'

She was so surprised that she began to laugh. 'Jon, I've only been gone fifteen minutes. You were in the shower. It was a lovely morning. I just walked to the field to see if there was a footpath.' She looked at the table. It was laid meticulously with crockery, cutlery, coffeepot, toast.

'I've been waiting for you,' he said.

'Oh . . . well, thank you. But you shouldn't have. I know you've got a nine o'clock appointment. I don't want to hold you up.' She took out the milk, put it on the table. Feeling awkward now in his continuing silence, she waved her hand over it. 'Well, look at this! This is nice.'

'Why did you go out?' he asked.

Her heart dropped like a stone. 'Because it was—Jon, this is silly. I just went down the garden, and then I saw the field fence, and—'

'I'm not talking about that.'

'Well, what? What are you talking about?'

'You could easily have told me what you were doing.'

'It was only five minutes.'

'Fifteen. It was *fifteen* minutes, Kate.'

'All right. Fifteen.'

'Or more.'

'Yes, maybe twenty. I'm sorry.'

He laughed shortly. 'No, you're not.'

'Oh, Jon! Honestly.' She ran her hand through her hair in exasperation. 'You're picking a fight.'

'No, I'm not fighting.'

'Does it matter that much?'

'Yes—yes, it matters *that much*.' The tone of his voice—implacable, unruffled, with exaggerated patience—irritated her intensely.

'I had no idea I had booked into a prison.'

There was no reaction at all. She looked at him, then shrugged her shoulders. 'Sorry,' she said. 'I didn't mean that.'

'It's our home, Kate.'

'Yes, I know.'

'Where is the prison?'

'Oh, God!'

'How am I inhibiting you?'

'You're not. You're not inhibiting me. OK?'

'Evidently I must be.'

She bit her lip. 'It's just this constant surveillance—' She realised what she had said immediately, and held up both hands. 'No, no. I just meant I'm not used to—' She had almost said *clocking in*, but managed to stop herself in time. Nevertheless, the realisation that she was falling into the use of the same sort of words underscored Jon's point. 'I'm just used to being alone,' she said.

'Now we come to it,' he remarked.

'What?'

He pushed himself away from the worktop, came over to her with a sigh, and kissed her on the cheek. 'Sit down.'

She did so. He sat down opposite her, slowly poured the coffee and gave her a cup.

'Thank you,' she murmured.

'Kate,' he said, 'I don't want you being subservient.'

'Was I being?'

'Or defensive.'

'I'm—'

'Don't apologise. Just listen.'

She sipped her drink, put it down, and looked into her lap. It was only a bloody walk, she thought.

'Kate, darling, are you listening?'

'Yes.'

'I want you to be yourself. But neither walking out without a word nor acting in the way you *think* I want you to be will do. Do you understand?'

'I . . .'

'Just listen. How would you describe your last ten years?'

She tried to think. 'I don't know.'

'All right. Use colours. What colour would they be?'

'Nothing . . . I mean, oh . . . grey, white. Red.'

'Red? Why red?'

She put her head in her hands. 'Can't we leave this until later?'

'Why do you want to that?'

'It's nearly nine. Your client.'

'There's ten minutes before my client,' he told her equably. 'Why did you choose red?'

'I don't know.'

'Can you see the contrast between grey and red?'

She looked at him. At the tip of his tongue resting on his lower lip. 'Of course.'

'Can you see the absolute *difference* between grey and red?'

'Yes.'

'No shades between?'

'No.'

'And the drama of the colours themselves?'

'Well, yes, I suppose . . .'

'Red and white. Grey and red. Extremes.'

He had lost her. She gazed at him, wondering—as with most of their conversations—how they had reached this point. She took a deep breath. 'Couldn't you . . . please . . . just drop your profession for five minutes?' she asked quietly. 'Every conversation is like a session on the couch.'

'Are you trying to understand?' he asked.

'Of course!'

'Then don't evade the subject. You describe your life in extremes. It has *been* a life of extremes. Is that accurate?'

'Yes.'

'Is it comfortable to live a life of such extremes?'

'No.'

'And you want to change?'

'Yes.'

'You want to live a life of colours, Kate, is that right? Greens and blues, shades and tones. Is that right?'

'Yes.'

'And when things were at their worst, you trusted my judgement?'

'Yes, that's true. I came to see you.'

He smiled. She sat watching his face, seeing the kind expression, trying to reach behind that expression, and find him.

'Do you still trust me, Kate?'

'Of course.'

'There's no *of course* about it. You can stop trusting me at any time.'

'I do trust you.'

'Good.'

He drank his coffee, replaced the cup softly, carefully, in the saucer.

'Aren't you eating?' she asked.

'I've had mine.'

She looked at him obliquely. She had thought that half of today's problem had been that he had been waiting for her so that he could begin breakfast.

'Will you think over what I've said?' he asked.

'I'll try.'

He placed his hand over hers on the cloth. 'It's quite natural to resist, you know,' he said. 'It happens in all sorts of physical illnesses too. People stop taking antibiotics after a couple of days because the immediate problem is resolved. But the underlying problem remains. They want instant results. But there is no instant cure for anything. It must be worked at, sometimes for years.'

She looked away. She didn't want to work at this for years. She just wanted to talk about it for a while, then put it to one side. Looking down into the past was like looking into a formless abyss.

'You won't resist me, will you?' he said.

'No,' she murmured. But her throat closed around the word.

He stroked her hand on the table top. He moved his chair a little closer and put her hand on to his thigh. 'What are you going to do today?' he asked.

'I hadn't really thought. There is the flat to clear . . .'

'Why don't you leave that until the weekend, when I can help you?'

She didn't want to leave it until the weekend, but saw another argument if she said so. 'OK,' she murmured.

'Would you like to go into town?'

She looked up. 'Is there something you need?'

'I'd like you to see an estate agent about Isabelle's house. Just to test the market. You can ask him to value this one too. Then we know exactly where we stand.'

'All right,' she said.

He stood up. 'Do you think that's a reasonable plan?'

'Yes.'

Along the hall, the doorbell rang.

'You're quite sure,' Jonathan continued, 'that you agree? If you have another opinion, tell me.'

'No,' she replied. She began to clear the remaining dishes from the table. 'No, I don't have another opinion, Jonathan.'

The estate agent almost fell over himself in an effort to be accommodating. When Kate had first arrived, coming in off the busy morning street, wrapped against the bright cold day, a girl had shown her to a desk and begun to take details; but it seemed that after the size of each property was mentioned, the man in the pinstripe suit was far more interested in talking to her.

She was ushered into the holy of holies, a partitioned glass office.

'Coffee?' he asked.

'No, thank you.'

'Right. Let's see—the house in Lovatt, that would be yours?'

'It's a legacy. The keys are still with the solicitor.' She gave Manners' name.

'And the other property . . .'

'Belongs to my husband. My husband-to-be. Mr Reeve.'

'I see, I see. And you want to sell both and buy another house between you?'

'No. Yes. Well, I don't know . . . it would depend on the valuations, the logistics . . .'

'Quite, quite. I would think, just off the top off my head, that the Lovatt house might be the more popular. One of those terribly sought-after areas, conservation village, and so on.'

'It's a lovely place.'

'I'm sure.' He was writing furiously on a very long form.

'My friend owned it,' Kate said. 'She died last week. I had no idea that she had left it to me . . .' The man glanced up. 'She had lived there for fifty years; she was very fond of the garden . . .'

Isabelle came back to her, on a summer morning, bending over the roses. Isabelle came back, making tea in the narrow kitchen with its painted brick walls.

Jonathan would undoubtedly want to change the outdated range, Kate thought; the pantry with its green paint door and slack hinge, and wooden shelves warped by time. Jonathan would want to change the kitchen. Jonathan would change the cracked stone floors, and the doors that never shut exactly right. He would want to take down those paintings and curtains. Isabelle even had a wooden draining board, bleached almost white with use, as smooth as polished stone. She could see Jonathan now, pursing his lips critically as he looked them over. He liked everything neat. She could visualise him, his eyes running over Isabelle's stack of mismatched cups lined up on the sill with herbs in them. The windows had a fretted engraved design along the edge. They all let in the draught . . .

'. . . suitable?'

'I'm sorry?' Kate said.

'Would tomorrow afternoon be suitable?'

'Oh . . . yes.'

'At Lovatt? Two o'clock?'

'Yes . . .'

'And perhaps we might follow on then to Kilcot Down?'

'I'd have to check with Mr Reeve. He runs a business, a medical practice, from the house.'

'Would you like to ring him to check?'

'No. He'd be occupied at the moment. I can ring you back at lunchtime.'

'Fine. Now, if I could just confirm exactly where the house is in Lovatt . . .'

I wanted to be here.

A house kept you from your husband?

Not just the house . . .

What then?

This area . . .

'It's on the corner near the stone cross. You can park outside . . .'

This was your home?

Yes, our home.

Oh, Isabelle, she thought. Where are you? What the hell happened with you? Come and tell me what to do.

'Excuse me,' she said.

The estate agent looked on in horror as she rummaged for a handkerchief in her bag. 'I'm sorry,' she said. 'This is . . . but . . .'

He got to his feet rapidly and closed the door. The two girls in the outer office stretched in their seats to see what was happening.

'Oh dear,' he was saying. 'Oh dear, oh dear.' She half expected him to start running round in small circles; evidently dealing with weeping women was not quite his thing.

'I'm all right,' she said.

'Let me get you a drink of water.'

She waved her hand. 'No. I'm fine.' She blew her nose. 'It's just that . . . it was only last week . . .'

'I can see how upset you are. Are you sure you want to go into all this just yet?'

'Yes. My husband thinks we should.'

She realised at once how shamefully lame that sounded. She would not have believed, a month or so ago, that she could have been capable of saying it. 'At least,' she continued, 'we discussed it, and we thought . . .'

'It's very soon after her death, isn't it?'

'Yes.'

'Perhaps if you waited a month or two, things would be clearer. A little calmer.'

She looked up at him gratefully. 'Actually, I don't think I want to sell the house in Lovatt at all,' she said.

The man smiled. 'You have made a decision, you see,' he said. 'Just now.'

She smiled back. 'My husband did say he could easily move his practice there.'

'Well, perhaps the appointment should just be for Kilcot Down after all?'

'Yes.' She stood up, collecting her coat and bag together. 'Thank you for being so patient.'

'No problem.' He opened the door for her. 'You'll ring me?'

'Yes. Thanks again.'

She walked out of the office, stopping in the street to put her bag over her shoulder. She thought fondly of the Clarice Cliff on the wall, and the book-lined sitting room, and all the proportions so small and crowded, and she tried to think of a way she could tell Jonathan— without causing another scene—that he could not change Isabelle's house at all . . .

And then, and only then, trying to place Jonathan in that cramped, dark front room, did she remember exactly what he had said yesterday after they had seen Manners.

They had been walking up the street, when he had said . . .

. . . *that* front room.

Jonathan had never seen The Linen House. And yet he said . . .

Lighten it.

Lighten *that* front room . . .

She got back to Kilcot Down House at midday.

There were no cars in the driveway, but the door to the consulting room was closed, and Kate could hear Jonathan's voice as he spoke on the phone.

She went into the sitting room, looking around herself. She felt profoundly uneasy; she wanted to talk to Jonathan, but couldn't imagine holding a conversation with him in which she felt equal.

She stood for a long time by the window, staring out at the green view in an agony of indecision. She was lost in a rapidly changing landscape. She had forfeited all her usual routines. She had left the paper, her flat, her single life, all in the space of a fortnight. It really was, she thought wryly, a case of burning your boats behind you. And she had clung to the nearest life raft, only to have it smother her—smother her with Jonathan's unremitting, probing concern.

On the coffee table was a pile of letters. She sat down and leafed through them; they were all addressed to Jonathan. One, she saw, was from a hotel in Tresco. She wondered, without any frisson of excitement or interest, if this was where Jonathan intended that they should take their honeymoon. She felt that she had regressed twenty years, to a point where every aspect of her life was lovingly but firmly controlled by someone else. It was one of the reasons that she had left her aunt and uncle without so much as a backward glance when her mother reappeared on the scene. She could not bear to be restricted.

I ought not to get married, she thought. It sent a charge of apprehension through her.

She let the envelope drop, staring into space. Then she got up. She walked along the hall and stopped outside his door, her hand raised to knock.

She could hear his raised voice; his side of the telephone conversation. She listened, her hand still raised, her ear to the door.

'You are angry with the question.'

It struck an immediate chord with her. She frowned, holding her breath.

'No,' she heard him saying. 'Are you listening?. . . Are you listening to me?'

There was a silence while he waited for the reply.

'Why do people always leave you?' he asked.

Kate sprang back from the door as if it were alive with electricity. It was the same question, the same tone of voice. She heard him continuing to cajole, to beat down, with that same even, smoothly flowing tone. The words were indistinct now as she stood three or four paces back from the door; but she could hear the inflection in his voice.

That gently superior, destructive insistence.

She turned and ran up the stairs to the bedroom.

FORTY-ONE

*G*EORGE GOT OUT OF HIS CAR IN SLOW MOTION.
He felt as if he had been away from the house for weeks, not days. His body complained as though he had been put through torture; the accumulation of hours of sitting rigidly in interview rooms, or the cell. His clothes stuck to him, smelling of that same anxiety. He would take them off and burn them, he thought, as he locked the car door. He longed for a bath, and for sleep in his own bed.

He went into the house, threw off his coat, and lay down on the sitting room couch. The silence swelled around him. He missed China. He ought to go and fetch her from the neighbours Kate had left her with along the lane, he thought. After a while, he put his hands to his eyes and cried soundlessly. It was twenty minutes before it occurred to him that it was stupid—pathetic, stupid—to sit crying by himself in the dark. He sat up and gazed around him. What was done now could not be undone. And there was some relief in having told them.

Forty-seven years is a long time to keep a secret.

He turned on the table lamp. Immediately, the image of Mr Angel sprang up, as it had done many times in the last few hours. The worst

222

of it . . . his eyes ran away from his own distant reflection in the mirror on the far wall . . . the worst of it was that Angel, without family and with few friends, had left his entire shop to George. Angel was the source of everything George had: this shop, the house, his reputation, all his wealth, and the undoubted luxuries he enjoyed.

The old man had already made his will in George's favour when, so many years ago, smiling at his own private undisclosed joke, he had given George only the cigarette card from the Christmas tree.

Not long after, the boy had killed him for the bandsmen. Not that George had actually formed the idea in his head that he would kill. He had only meant to stop Angel for a moment. Surprise him or shock him, perhaps. It was done in a fit of teenage pique, petulance. He had been horrified at the sudden ease with which Angel succumbed to the blow. In his innocence, George had supposed that it took a man to kill a man. Never for a moment had he realised that one touch of the bronze could accomplish it.

One irrational act in his life, committed at the age of thirteen. A kindly, sardonic old man killed for a set of lead toys.

The will stood.

After all, the police proved nothing against him. It was finally accepted that there had been a burglary in the night, and what George said—that he had found Angel like this early in the morning—was the truth.

Some truth, he thought now. Some lie, more like.

A skinny little boy who could not properly inherit until he was twenty-one. By the time he had done his National Service, and come back to his home town, the legacy had matured to eleven thousand pounds. He had cashed in the money, and moved away.

He had been bailed by the police this morning, after pleading guilty to a forty-seven-year-old murder committed as a juvenile. The police did not think he would go to prison.

In addition, they had told him that fingerprints found on the bracelet belonged to some criminal from London, a fact which evidently they found as mystifying as he did. The DNA print from Maggie Spence did not match him either, and nor did the hair that they had found still grasped in Isabelle Browning's hand.

Small mercies, he thought, as he stood up now. A small mercy for an overdue guilt.

He went through into the kitchen, where he opened the fridge. Taking out the makings of a sandwich, he reflected dully on those other, more minor idiocies. Paying ridiculous amounts of money to satisfy a whim, for instance. Chasing a woman who was half his age. Another utter foolishness. What Kate McCaulay must have thought of him he did not like to consider. She had been remarkably patient with him. He must have made her life, recently, something of a misery. It was a miracle that that man of hers, Jonathan Reeve, hadn't felled him for what he had done.

He put down the knife which he had been using to butter the bread, abruptly turned, and picked up his doorkey.

He would go and get China now, he resolved.

And when he came back, he would stay with her in the house. No shop, no sales, no people to face. Until the horror at himself burned down to something bearable.

FORTY-TWO

*T*HE LIGHTS OF THE FLYOVER, barring the windscreen in orange and black, woke her up.

Kate opened her eyes and looked on a once-familiar landscape: London in the encroaching dark, roofs and streets passing beneath her; lit windows of houses providing drifting tableaux.

She sat up in the car seat, rubbing her hands over her face. The car began to slow as it approached a set of traffic lights. She glanced across at Jack Seward.

'Feeling better?' he asked.

'What time is it?'

'Nearly five.'

She sat up. 'How long do you think it'll take us?'

He shrugged, changing gears as the lights turned to green again. 'Rush hour now. Maybe half an hour.'

'Where are we?'

'Hammersmith.'

Once into Earls Court, they felt the full impact of the traffic; they slowed to snail's pace crossing up through back doubles. They reached the Embankment and turned up through Blackfriars, Kate glancing at the clock on the dashboard. As they got close to Lincoln's Inn Fields, she asked, 'Where will you park?'

'Here,' Jack said, swinging in to the last in a row of meters.

'Jack,' Kate warned, 'there's a woman in a BMW reversing into this space.'

'Not now there isn't,' he muttered.

They got out, and began running at a slow trot along the narrow lanes round the pavements of Lincoln's Inn, skirting lawns and benches and the persistent oncoming flow of commuters making for the underground. They came out into Chancery Lane, and ran across it.

Kate had taken the scribbled note from her bag and held it in one hand.

'Which one?'

'It's one of the little streets . . . here,' she said, glancing up at the sign of the building above them. They turned down into a darker courtyard.

'What number?' Jack asked.

'It's 4A.'

They looked along the line of the terrace, bounded by black iron railings.

'This is 16 . . . it's further along.'

On the final building, narrow and redbrick, was a set of callboxes for the offices inside. Some names on the narrow white strips of paper were obscured by damp, others were handwritten. The name of the agency, however, was typed on a piece of card.

'Here it is,' Kate said, after running her finger down the board. She pressed the bell.

They looked at each other, smiling and out of breath.

'Let's not do this again,' Jack said. 'I'm not built for speed.'

She pressed the bell again. 'Come on,' she whispered. Then, to Jack, 'What time is it?'

'Five forty.'

'They said they'd be here until six.' She stepped back and looked up again at the building. There were lights in various rooms in the five floors above them. She pressed again, twice, leaning on the buzzer.

The door opened. A woman started to come out; in her late fifties, she was drawing a coat around her. Seeing them, she let them pass without comment.

They went up the stairs two at a time. Four floors. Eighty uneven steps. The doors on the fourth landing were bolted. They stared for a second at the agency's name.

'Oh shit,' Kate murmured. All energy suddenly flooding from her, she sat down on the top step, screwing the piece of paper into a ball. 'They said six. I specifically asked, and they said six.'

Jack sat down beside her. There were a few seconds of silence. They could hear subdued noises from the floor above—the sounds of cupboards being closed and machines unplugged. Someone was talking, and laughing: one side of a telephone conversation.

'Want to tell me?' Jack asked.

She glanced at him. 'Tell you what?'

'What this is all about.'

She looked away again, turning the ball of paper over and over in her hands. She had arrived at Jack's house in a taxi, carrying a small suitcase, at two o'clock that afternoon, and asked him if he would drive to the agency in London. He had asked no questions; he had simply said yes.

'I suppose I owe you an explanation,' Kate said.

'No,' he replied. 'You don't owe me anything. But if you feel like telling me, I have to say I'm dying to hear it.'

She smiled, and stood up. 'Let's go and get something to eat,' she said.

'I'm broke.'

She had already started to walk down the stairs, and glanced back at him. 'That's all right,' she said. 'I'm not.'

They ended up in a sandwich bar close to the Strand. Taking the last of the day's dried-out rolls, they sat down at a table near the window, while the crowds surged past outside.

'I used to work near here,' Kate said. She was watching the faces of the pedestrians. 'Always busy . . . like this.' With her sandwich half-finished, she pushed the food to the side of her plate, and put the plastic cup on to it, linking both hands around the rim. 'Where we were just now, in Lincoln's Inn . . . I used to play netball there. Did you see, in the centre, where the benches were? The paper had a team.' She smiled down at the cup. 'We were useless. We were kicked off the league after one season.'

Jack had been watching the nostalgia in her face. 'Why don't you come back here?' he asked. 'You could get another job.'

'No, I couldn't. I'm too rusty.'

'You—'

'And it's another life. I don't want to rehash it. It wouldn't work.'

The sandwich bar staff had finished cleaning the display cabinets and worktops, and were waiting for Kate and Jack to leave.

'Let's walk,' she said.

They went out, and, after a minute or two, Jack realised that when she said walk, she meant *walk*. He wondered how long it was going to be before she admitted to her exhaustion: a weariness not just from today but, it seemed to him, of a great deal longer than that. They reached St James's Park, then Green Park, crossed Hyde Park Corner, and on into Hyde Park. Eventually, to Jack's immense relief, Kate's relentless pace slowed, and, at the Serpentine, she stopped and sat down on a bench, looking across the water.

They watched a couple hurrying past. Kate followed their progress for some time along the pathway. Then, just when Jack thought that she was not going to say anything at all, she murmured quietly, 'I've done something very stupid.'

He turned towards her to listen. She sat hunched forward, her arms crossed over her. 'I've promised to marry him, and I don't know who he is.'

'Jonathan?'

'Yes.'

He took a deep breath. 'Sometimes these whirlwind things are right. Meant to be.' It wasn't what he thought at all. But he thought she wanted reassurance.

'I should think that, mostly, they're disasters,' she responded.

'Why did you say yes to him, then?'

She shook her head. 'I didn't actually *say* yes. He wants to marry me. And he tells me that's what I want.'

Jack smiled crookedly. 'He *tells* you?'

'He's arranging it all. Even the dress.'

Jack was aware that he was treading through something of a mine-field. He chose his words carefully. 'Maybe he just likes to be in charge.'

'Yes, but . . .'

'But what?'

She leaned her elbows on her knees, and lowered her chin into her cupped hands, staring at the ground. 'He picked me up. He looked after me. While we were away, it was so easy to let him take over. It was comfortable . . . it was a relief.'

'And now?'

She turned her gaze obliquely on Jack. 'Now he seems intent on unpicking me, like a piece of sewing that has gone wrong. Stitch by stitch, line by line.'

'Can't you just take time out from it for a while?'

She laughed softly. 'You don't know Jonathan.'

'I don't want to.' He touched her arm, very gently. 'If he's that manipulative, step back. Why not?'

She seemed to be thinking aloud. 'I heard him doing the same thing to someone else today. This is therapy . . . supposedly . . . taking down to build up again.' She glanced up. 'Have you ever seen one of these therapists?'

'No,' he told her. 'They'd lock me up.'

She smiled, but did not laugh. 'They don't do that any more,' she said. 'They listen to every thought. Every thought is valid. Every word is valid. Every dream, every idea, every experience, every picture in your head.' She passed a hand over her face. 'When I first met him to interview him for the paper last year, he told me that he cured people of phobias. Flying, spiders . . . of obsessions. He told me how fragile a personality was, a set of ethics; how we were underpinned by our childhood. He told me how important all that was. Yet everything he's said in the last few days contradicts that.'

'How, exactly?'

'Telling me my mother didn't love me . . . Jamie, Richard.'

'What!'

She paused for a long time, her eyes ranging over Jack's face. 'I can't do right. I can't do anything right.' She held his look, one corner of her mouth pinched in as she chewed on her lip.

Jack sat forward. 'What is he, a psychiatrist? A counsellor? What?'

'A psychotherapist.'

'What qualifications has he got?'

'I don't know.'

'You know that anyone can set themselves up in that business? Anyone, right off the street. There are no laws governing it.'

'Yes, I know.'

'There was a TV programme on it not long ago. There's no regulations. They can put letters after their name . . . it means nothing. Of course, most of them are fine. Do the whole training bit. Fine. But there's nothing to stop the loose cannon.'

'I know. But he's been in practice for a long time.'

'How long?'

'Well . . . I'm not sure. Several years, at least.'

'In the same place?'

'No. I think he said that he moved here a couple of years ago.'

'He could have a trail of complaints and you wouldn't know about it. How many clients has he got?'

'A lot. There's a filing cabinet in the attic. A four-drawer, full of files.'

'You've seen the files?'

'It's locked.'

Jack considered this in silence for a moment. 'Have you seen anyone coming to the house?'

'Four, so far.'

'What were they like?'

'Female . . .' She paused. 'Upset.'

'*Every* one?'

'At some point during the hour, yes.'

'You listened?'

'I can hear them . . . but then they wouldn't come if they didn't have a problem, would they?'

'Crying so loudly that you can hear them?'

She sighed. 'I know.'

'Does he make you cry?'

The pause was longer and more tense. 'Yes,' she admitted.

Jack was unable to say anything. The thought of Jonathan Reeve browbeating Kate—after all that had happened lately—made his blood boil. His right hand itched with a swift desire to punch the bastard smack in the face. Suddenly, Kate got up. She walked forward a pace or two, looking steadily at the water ahead. Then, she turned.

'I haven't had any letters for ten days.' He questioned her, silently, with a raised eyebrow. 'I expected there to be something waiting when I went back to the flat the other day, but there was nothing.'

He stood up too. 'And . . . so?'

She stared at him, not answering. Then, to his surprise and pleasure, she linked her arm inside his.

'I'll have to go back to the agency in the morning,' she told him, rapidly changing the subject. 'But don't feel that you have to stay.'

'Of course I'll stay,' he said. 'How else will you get back home afterwards?'

'I can catch the train.'

'Well, I like that! I traipse over half the countryside, and you want to jettison me just when it gets interesting.'

'I'm thinking of you!' she protested. 'If you want to get back, I don't want to hold you up.'

'What would I need to get back for?'

'Oh, I don't know—'

'Of course, if you'd rather go ahead on your own . . .'

'No,' she said quickly. They had halted in the centre of the pavement, looking at each other. 'No,' she repeated. 'I didn't say that.'

FORTY-THREE

*K*ILCOT DOWN HOUSE WAS IN DARKNESS.

It was almost midnight, and every contour in the garden and in the fields beyond was picked out in the last quarter of the moon, a waning light. Frost had already formed on the glass of the window, in the unheated attic.

Jonathan Reeve was alone in the top room of the house, in the space he had stripped to make ready for Kate's arrival. He was sitting on the floor, staring without seeing.

Next to him, on the floor, was a letter he had read a dozen times.

Just give me a little time. I will ring you.
Kate.

He had heard her go out. Heard her come downstairs. Heard the front door open and close. For a moment, the danger hadn't registered with him. Because he had insisted that she tell him exactly where she was going every day, he had been confident that she would have only been walking in the front garden; perhaps getting something from her car. He had listened to his telephone caller with only half a mind on what she was saying, impatient with the usual litany of pain; he was listening to make sure that the engine did not start on Kate's car. If he had heard that, he would have dropped the phone and run.

But she hadn't got into her car.

He heard her footsteps fade down the drive.

Another unpermitted walk. He had gritted his teeth at her ability to resist him, at her perseverance.

But then, that had been the attraction, hadn't it? Beside the obvious, more practical reason why he had to marry her. Leave that aside for a moment.

No, it was her refusal to bend, to weaken, that had been the unique appeal of this game. Kate McCaulay, tempered by ten years of fluctuating agony and recovery—Kate McCaulay, with her strictly repressed longing—could not be cracked even in a fortnight. Delicious, the idea of spinning it out for weeks, maybe even for months once they were married. Perhaps even a year . . . or two. She might provide enormous amusement as she capitulated. Show him depths of despair he had never really taken such time to explore. That was the lure of it. That had been the key, the appeal.

Still, he had been surprised. So much thrown at her, directed at her. And she still held her head that way . . . *I'm all right*. It made him laugh, when he was alone. Sometimes he had to go into another room in the house and laugh with his face pressed into his hand. The way she glanced at him, hanging on to her bloody-mindedness. As if she could ever win.

But in the last couple of days he had detected a fracture in that control. Just a little fracture. She took a long time to go to sleep, for instance. Her hand shook a little doing small tasks.

Just give me a little time. I will ring you.

He fought down the temptation of fury. After all, anger had not achieved anything. Slow, remorseless, persistent, time-strung patience had brought him to the threshold of his reward.

Although the chase was almost as good. He had to admit that. Much, much better with Kate than with anyone else.

ELIZABETH COOKE

Now, in the dark, he looked down at the letter, although it was impossible to read the words. He did not know exactly how long he had been sitting here, trying to work out what to do. It must have been six, seven hours . . . even eight hours, since the light faded.

That afternoon, after another few seconds of listening to the caller, he had put down the phone, off the hook, still hearing that soprano whine on the other end of the line, thin and brittle . . . and he had looked out of the window to check where Kate was.

Just in time to catch the colour of the receding car along the lane. A flash of white.

The bitch had called a taxi.

Immediately, he had run from the house to his car; then, cursing, found that his keys were not in his pocket. By the time that he had gone back into the house, got them, and returned to the car, he knew that he would never catch her up. Though he had still got in the car and tried to manoeuvre it past hers—parked askew in the drive, where she had—purposefully, he could appreciate now—left it.

He had come back inside, gone up to the bedroom, seen the open wardrobe, the open drawers, and the hastily scribbled note flung down on the bed.

Just give me a little time.

Oh no, Kate, he thought.
He picked up the letter, and began to tear it, slowly, into pieces.
Oh no.
There was no more time left.

FORTY-FOUR

*J*ACK AND KATE WERE BACK ON THE DOORSTEP of the agency at nine the next morning. The street door was open, and, four floors up, so was the office.

'Hello?' Kate called, knocking.

There was no response, so they walked in. The room that greeted them was untidy and dirty; desk tops covered with papers, a stack of unanswered mail, used coffee cups. A computer monitor in the corner was tacked with Post-It notes. The waste baskets overflowed. Even the windows were filthy.

Kate turned to Jack, raising her eyebrows in silent criticism.

The far door opened, and a woman emerged.

She was in complete contrast to the office, large and well groomed. She caught sight of them and stopped, surprised. Then she came forward, a smile pasting itself automatically to her face. She was dressed in a loudly checked red suit, with a heavy string of pearls at her neck.

'Good morning,' she said. 'I'm Anne Michaels. You must be . . .'

'Kate McCaulay,' Kate told her. 'Jack Seward.'

They shook hands.

'Are you early?'

'I'm sorry?'

Anne Michaels had turned around a ledger on the nearest desk, and was running her finger down the page. 'For your appointment?'

'No. We haven't got an appointment. But I rang yesterday.'

'Really?' Anne Michaels' expression had frozen rather. 'We don't see anyone without an appointment.'

'I understand,' Kate replied, 'but this is a rather special request. It won't take long. I did ring yesterday, and explained we would be arriving at about six . . .'

'Oh?' Anne Michaels said. 'I wonder why we said that. We close at five.'

Kate didn't argue with her. She felt the going would be tough enough as it was. 'Could we have a brief word?' she asked.

Mrs Michaels had been quietly eyeing Jack's rumpled appearance. 'Can you tell me what it's about?'

'It's about a friend of mine,' Kate lied, resisting the temptation to cross her fingers behind her back. 'She was registered with you ten years ago. I've lost touch with her, and—'

'We don't give out clients' addresses,' Anne Michaels said.

'No, I appreciate that,' Kate told her. 'But this is terribly important, a family matter. It's a . . . a medical thing. She must be traced.'

'Well, we couldn't help. I'm sorry. Have you tried the police?'

Kate hesitated for a second. 'This is about a child,' she said.

Anne Michaels considered her. Then she turned. 'Come into my office.'

There could not have been more of a contrast between the Reception area and Anne Michaels' own room. Seeing Jack and Kate's brief look of surprise, she smiled and pointed them to chairs facing her desk. 'We have lost two filing girls in the last fortnight,' she said. 'I have another lady, but once the phones begin ringing in here, believe me . . . it's absolute murder.'

Kate smiled. Personally, she couldn't have walked through the visual pandemonium outside every day without attacking it resolutely with a bucket of water and a large rubbish sack. But that was none of her business. And certainly not relevant just now.

Anne Michaels had sat down gracefully opposite them, crossing her legs and folding her hands in her lap. She was waiting.

'Ten years ago,' Kate began, 'you had a woman registered here. She had a very unusual name. It was Meresamun . . . it was her Christian name. She was married to an American.'

'Yes?'

'You remember her?'

Anne Michaels smiled. 'We have a great number of clients. My memory isn't *that* good.'

'We really need to contact her. Someone told us that she was registered here, and that you would know her address.'

'I doubt that we still have her records.'

'But you could look for us?'

Mrs Michaels retained her icy, mirthless smile. 'No. It's against all our rules of confidentiality.'

'But—'

In the outer office, they heard someone come in, and the door close.

'Is that you, Mrs Collett?'

'Yes,' came the subdued reply.

Anne Michaels looked back at Kate and Jack. 'Ours is a very sensitive business,' she said. 'We deal with people's lives here. Infertility is a distressing subject.'

'Yes, I see that—'

'And you haven't told me who you are—or rather, *what* you are.'

'Well,' Kate glanced at Jack. 'Actually, we aren't anything. I mean, we have no job—we aren't employed by anyone.'

'We had a newspaper enquiry here last year that lost us a considerable amount of business. A so-called investigation, founded on absurd, baseless gossip. It was a couple posing as childless. It turned out they weren't even married. They were reporters.'

'How much do you charge?' Jack asked.

Mrs Michaels turned a glacial look of recognition on him. 'You work for a paper, do you?'

'No.'

'Media of some kind. I know the voice, the attitude.' She stood up. 'I can't help you,' she said.

Kate stood up too. 'We don't work for a paper, or the television,' she protested. 'We're trying to trace a child called Jamie Lydiatt.'

'Jamie . . . ?' A faint recall in the other woman's look.

'He was stolen, as an eight-week baby,' Kate said. 'This woman—this Meresamun—knew where the Lydiatts lived. She knew about the birth of Jamie. She was registered with you at that time, seeking a baby to adopt. She disappeared at the same time that Jamie disappeared.'

Mrs Michaels rewarded Kate merely with a stony stare. 'And you obviously have concluded that she stole this child. On rather shaky evidence.'

'It's all we have. She may be innocent, yes. Probably is, in fact. But we need to speak to her. You can understand that, surely?'

Anne Michaels walked around the side of her desk. She was looking at Kate intently. 'Who are you, really?' she asked.

'I'm Kate Lydiatt.'

The two women stared at each other for some seconds. Kate took a tentative step forward. 'I never found my baby,' she said. 'Would you please help me?'

Mrs Michaels said nothing for perhaps twenty or thirty seconds. Once, just once, she glanced across at Jack. Then, abruptly, she walked to the door, and, though it was already ajar a little, she opened it wide.

'I'm afraid that I can't help you,' she said.

Kate looked desperately at Jack. 'We've come a long way,' she said. 'This could be our only chance . . .'

Jack walked up to Kate and took her arm gently. 'Kate has had letters saying that he could be alive.'

Not a flicker of emotion crossed Anne Michaels' face. 'I'm very sorry that you have had such an experience,' she said. 'But—even if I decided to show you our records—there's no guarantee that we would still have anything relating to ten years ago. As you can see, we have very little space for storage here. And we only put new cases on the computer.'

Kate glanced into the outer office, where the same middle-aged woman that she and Jack had passed on the steps yesterday evening was sitting at a desk, looking at the group in the doorway of Anne Michaels' office. Her hands were inert on the pile of mail.

'I don't mind searching through the files,' Kate said. 'If you just show me the right ones, I won't take up any of your time.'

Anne Michaels gave a breathy little laugh. 'I couldn't *possibly* allow you to look through the records of our clients,' she said. 'Now, please, if you don't mind . . .'

'But, a name like that—so unusual—'

'But no *sur*name. We file everything according to surname,' Anne Michaels said. And then, more pointedly, with some sarcasm, 'Everyone does.'

'Look—' Jack began.

Anne Michaels cut him short. 'No, *you* look, Mr Seward,' she said. 'I have never seen you before in my life. You come with no proof of your identity, and you practically demand that I show you personal records that have nothing whatsoever to do with you. I simply haven't the time to stand bandying words with you. I have people arriving in—' she glanced at her watch, 'precisely four minutes.'

'Well,' Jack said coldly. 'You heartless bitch.'

'Jack!' Kate said. She pulled on his arm. 'Let's go. Come *on*.'

'You heartless bloody bitch,' he continued. 'Kate has been looking for her child for ten years, and *you*—'

'Jack, please,' Kate repeated.

'All you're interested in is taking whacking great fees off desperate people, aren't you?' he said. 'That's all that motivates *you*.'

Anne Michaels remained silent, but her mouth set in a dangerously thin line.

'I wouldn't be surprised if you weren't in one of these baby smuggling operations,' Jack said.

Kate hauled on his arm just as Mrs Michaels reached for the nearest telephone. 'If you won't go, I shall ask the police to remove you,' she said.

'Jack,' Kate hissed. '*Now*.'

She almost bundled him out on to the stairs, and down the first flight. He kept looking back at the green painted door of the agency that had been slammed behind them. On the second flight, they met a young couple coming up. They were holding an agency card, their faces tight with a last-ditch despondency.

Kate and Jack stood aside to let them go, and watched them in silence until they disappeared from view.

'I need some fresh air,' Jack muttered.

Kate followed him out slowly into the street.

They sat down on the step of a closed shop opposite.

'Well,' Kate said, at last, 'you handled that very well. Remind me to nominate you for the Diplomatic Service.'

Jack winced. 'I'm sorry. I can't stand that sort of woman. All hair-spray and charm bracelets. I'll bet you any money she's working a scam in that place. Enormous registration fees for zero results.'

Kate shrugged. 'What does it matter? Short of breaking in, and even then . . .'

At that moment, the street door of the agency opened, and the middle-aged woman who had been working in the agency's outer office came hurrying down the steps. She saw them at once, and walked quickly across.

Kate stood up.

The woman was breathing heavily with the exertion of rushing down so many steps. Her face was flushed. 'I'm so sorry about all that,' she said. She glanced up at the windows above them.

'I expect we caught her on a bad day,' Kate said.

'Oh no!' Mrs Collett grimaced. 'She's *always* like that. If I didn't need the money, I'd walk out. The others do. But then they're young. They've got nothing to lose.'

Jack smiled. 'Thanks for coming down, anyway.'

'It was the papers last year. They made her life hell. I haven't had a civil word out of her ever since. Not that she didn't deserve it—the investigation, I mean.'

'Oh?'

'She's lost interest in actually doing any work. Even keeping the office cleaned. She just wants the money.'

Jack shot Kate a meaningful look.

'I'm sorry,' Kate said. 'It can't be very nice for you.'

'Never mind,' Mrs Collett said. 'I didn't come down to moan about her. I came down to tell you about the other woman. The one with the Egyptian name.'

Both Kate and Jack spoke at the same time. 'You remember her?'

'Oh, yes. I don't forget names. And I keep the records properly, despite what *she* says.'

'You worked here then?'

'Yes, though it wasn't run by Mrs Michaels then. She bought into the business three years ago. It was very respectable, and we *cared* about our clients.'

'And you really remember this Meresamun?'

'Absolutely. She was only twenty; a lovely girl. Very cheerful and polite, with one of those nice Southern American accents. I always think of *Gone With the Wind*, don't you? And yet, the poor girl couldn't have children. So tragic for her. I recall her distinctly; she would have made a wonderful mother. Her husband worked for the American Air Force; they were based in England. I even remember registering her. We had a little laugh about her name; it was such a mouthful, and I couldn't fit it all on the card for the index. That peculiar first name, and then two such ordinary ones! She was called Meresamun Jane Charles.'

'What!' Jack looked at Kate, laughed, and did a little impromptu dance of triumph on the pavement. 'You know her surname!'

After her long speech, Mrs Collett had paused for breath, and was now beaming broadly at both of them. 'And I remember where they lived,' she added triumphantly. 'On the base near Greenham.'

Kate stared for a few seconds at the unremarkable, bespectacled face in front of her. Then, she reached out and hugged the woman tightly. 'Oh, you miracle,' she exclaimed. 'You are a miracle.'

Mrs Collett had blushed a deep shade of self-conscious red as Kate released her. 'Oh, I'm only too pleased to help, too pleased,' she replied. She dug her hand into the pocket of her skirt, and brought out a slip of paper. 'I scribbled it down for you. The name and the address.'

Kate couldn't frame a reply as she took the paper. It was left to Jack to shake Mrs Collett's hand in his bear-like grip and to thank her.

'It's nothing,' said the woman. 'I'm glad to have my uses.'

'I can't tell you what this means,' Kate told her.

But at this, Mrs Collett's face showed the first shadow of concern. She put one hand softly on Kate's arm. 'The only thing is, she was a very nice girl. A *very* nice girl. You see . . . I just can't imagine Mrs Charles stealing a baby.'

Kate nodded. 'I understand. Well, thank you anyway . . .'

'I do hope you find him,' Mrs Collett said fervently. 'You'll tell me, if you do?'

'Of course.'

The older woman nodded once or twice, looked at her feet. 'Yes, good. Good, that's fine . . . Well, I ought to go back up. I expect the old monster will have been bawling for tea for the last five minutes.'

Jack laughed. She turned to go.

'Thank you,' Kate said to her retreating back. 'Thank you so very much.'

FORTY-FIVE

I T WASN'T THE SETTING HE WOULD HAVE CHOSEN.

Jonathan sat on a bench outside the municipal building, in a small and threadbare garden, looking at the road. Just beyond the boundary wall, the traffic streamed past, a four-lane approach to the junction. On the opposite side, there was a large, fifties-built pub, strung with a banner advertising a cheap Sunday lunch. The garden at his feet was grass, with a border of rosebeds where the soil was so grey that it was almost white.

Still, the location didn't matter. Not really. He looked down again at the form on his knee.

He had Kate's passport open, and her face smiled up at him. It was a good likeness; the slightly strained expression that masked so much, the emphatic smile that denied it. He would have liked to see her hair longer. He was sure that she bleached it to get it to remain that colour. Older women never retained the bright blonde of their youth.

He would get her to grow her hair, and stop colouring it. He would like to see her fade a little more. He raised his hand, and with a thumb and forefinger, squeezed her image, as one would extinguish the light of a flame.

When he picked up the pen again, his hand was trembling. He began to write, and then realised that he had filled in the wrong parts of the form; he had transposed their details, putting Kate where he should be. Putting himself where she should be.

He got up, and went back into the building.

'All finished?' asked the woman behind the desk.

'I've made a mess of it,' he told her. 'I need another.'

She smiled at him. 'Never mind,' she said. 'Nerves.'

This time, he sat inside, writing quickly. His hand did not shake so much if he did not think. He took it to the desk again and paid the money, watching while the form was checked.

'That's all in order,' the woman said. She picked up a ledger from her side, and flicked the pages. 'What day?'

'Tomorrow.'

She raised her eyebrows. 'That isn't possible. You have to allow one clear waiting day.'

'The day after, then.'

'Any particular time?'

'The first appointment.'

She wrote it down.

She gave him the slip of paper and returned the passports. 'All our little rules are printed on the back, about photographs, confetti, that sort of thing,' she said.

Jonathan took it without a word, and walked out.

FORTY-SIX

*I*T WAS EARLY EVENING when Jack and Kate arrived in Lovatt.

Jack had given a slow whistle as they had drawn up outside The Linen House in the quiet village street. There was no one about, and, above the roof of the house, the church spire was outlined against the darkening hills. There could not have been more of a contrast to the city they had left behind.

'What a place,' Jack murmured.

They let themselves in using the keys they had picked up from Isabelle's solicitor. Once inside, Kate shuddered; the house was cold, and—more poignantly—Isabelle was everywhere. Andrew Manners had told them that two of the ladies from the church had come in to clean after the police had left; but nevertheless, Isabelle's presence enveloped them.

Jack had checked in the utility room, switching on the electricity and the central heating.

'You look shattered,' he told Kate, scrutinising her face.

'I'm fine.'

'Tea?'

She glanced around the kitchen. 'I feel I'm trespassing.'

'Well, let me take you back to the flat, then.'

'No . . .'

'Do you want to go to Jonathan?'

'No.' This time her refusal was adamant.

'*You* make the tea,' he said. 'I'll bring in the groceries.'

They had stopped at the village shop to get a few basics; and, after the drinks were made, they sat down at the kitchen table with a spartan meal of soup and bread.

'Where do we go now, do you think?' Kate asked, when they had finished supper. Their attempts to get through to Personnel in the USAF had, quite properly, met with polite stonewalling. Information about staff did not come easily, especially with the complicating factor of a transient workforce.

'The Charleses could be anywhere in the world,' Kate said. 'Her husband may even have left the Air Force.'

Jack had been turning the subject over in his mind on the journey home. 'I've got a couple of contacts in the police,' he told her. 'They might be able to help. But—' he looked up at her, putting down the spoon that he had been twirling between his fingers—'I think it'd be a hell of lot quicker if you put this with the professionals. I've got this far on a wing and a prayer—and a couple of strokes of good luck. But I'm no expert. And I certainly can't chase them across any number of continents.'

'You mean, an investigation agency?'

'That's right. One specialising in missing persons.'

'I see . . .'

'Although it wouldn't be cheap.'

'No.' Kate indicated the house with a turn of her head. 'Well, things have changed lately.'

'Shall I try a few names?'

'Yes, all right.' She touched his hand across the table. 'You've been very good to me, Jack.'

'I know.'

She sat back, and laughed. 'Such modesty.'

He held her gaze. 'Kate . . . what are you going to do about Jonathan?'

She pursed her lips, looking at the empty plates in front of them. 'Tell him, I suppose.'

'What, exactly?'

'That I don't want to be married.'

Jack said nothing for a while, then, after one or two false starts in which he opened his mouth to say something, then evidently tried to rephrase his thoughts before he spoke, he asked her, 'What about telling the police?'

'Tell them what?'

'What you've told me. That the letters have stopped since you've been with Jonathan. Then there's all that badgering and bullying . . .'

She sighed, smoothing frown lines across her forehead. 'But what am I accusing him of? Writing the letters?'

'They could at least look into it.'

She sighed, crossing her arms and staring out at the garden beyond the window. 'I can't really believe he would write them.' She nodded once or twice to herself, as if confirming this decision. 'No, he wouldn't write them. He couldn't.'

'Who did, then?'

'I just don't know. Maybe George. Maybe someone I've never even met. Someone who reads the paper, some crank. Maybe someone from ten years ago that I worked with and upset.'

'*Did* you upset anyone?'

'No. Not that I know of.'

'Or, it could be Jonathan.'

'But why? That's what I keep tripping up on. Why would he do such a thing? What could he possibly gain?'

'What does any headcase gain? Maybe he knew it would drive you into seeing him. As a patient.'

She gave an incredulous laugh. 'A bit of a long shot,' she said. 'I could have consulted dozens of others.'

'Perhaps he likes domination. From what you've told me, he gets a kick out of handling women a certain way . . .' He gave a short laugh. 'It's certainly one novel way to drum up business. Drive someone out of their tree, and then charge them for treatment.'

'But he doesn't charge me! You see, it's crazy. It doesn't fit. I mean . . .' She searched for the words. 'I think he's got a problem of his own, yes. What you call the badgering and bullying. But *handling* people is his job; I think it's a case of letting that side of him—the guiding, the persuading—get out of hand. Become too controlling. When it comes down to the letters, I can't see what he could possibly gain from it. Whereas George . . .'

They considered the subject silently for some time.

'Do you think that George killed Maggie Spence?' Jack asked.

Kate was genuinely shocked. 'Maggie? No! He didn't even know her.'

'But *you* did. Isabelle and Maggie were people you knew.'

She frowned. 'I don't think I've got anything to do with that. George probably argued with Isabelle over an old grudge over one of her purchases. She bought a lot of stuff from him. Maybe she discovered a fault. George is crazy about his stuff. Possessive, greedy. That's much more his style.'

'But the bracelet—'

'Well, maybe I *did* figure in it in some inexplicable way . . . But not Maggie.'

'Did Jonathan kill Maggie?' Jack asked.

'What!'

They stared at each other, then Jack began to laugh to himself. 'No, all right, I can see that's getting a bit far-fetched.'

'You actually think—'

'No, no, forget it. Like you say, what would he gain?'

'In any case, Maggie's lover was a married man. She told me herself.'

'Yes, OK. Just a wild thought.'

'He's not a *killer*, Jack. Don't you think I'd sense it, if he were?'

'Yes. You're right. Forget it. Just a brainstorm.' He got up slowly, pushing back his chair. 'I'd better go. It's late. Will you be OK?'

'Yes.'

'Sleeping here?'

'Yes. I'll be fine.'

He stood up, his height and bulk seeming to fill the room. 'I'll get on to the agencies in the morning.'

'Well, tell me who they are, and I'll do it.'

'No,' he said. 'I want to do it for you. It's only a few phone calls.' Kate stood up too. 'How will you get your car back?' he asked.

'Phone Jonathan, I suppose. I owe him an apology, I think. Haring out of there like a scalded cat.'

Jack's expression showed obvious disagreement, but he did not voice it. 'When you want to go over, let me know. I'll drive you.'

'OK.'

At the door, which she held open for him, she suddenly kissed him lightly on the cheek. He paused, searching her face.

'Be careful,' he said.

'I'm in no danger,' she told him.

He did not answer. Without looking back at her, he walked down the path to the street.

After she had washed the plates from the supper, Kate went out into the garden.

It was pitch-dark and cold, with a frost already forming on the grass. She walked up the path to the gate through to the church, and turned to look back at the house with its silhouette of uneven roof, and the spoked bare branches of the trees.

After a while, she came back into the house, carefully locking the door, and climbing the stairs. She found clean sheets in the airing cupboard, and made up the single bed in the spare room, not able to bring herself to sleep in Isabelle's bed, even though it had been stripped, and the eiderdown and blankets piled neatly on the mattress.

She went back to the cupboard for an extra cover, and saw that Isabelle's summer shoes—sandals, and deck shoes—were in a haphazard row on the floor. She kneeled down, and gently paired them one on top of the other. Behind them were a stack of shoeboxes, and she pulled out the first, thinking sadly of the brutal task ahead of her of packing away all of Isabelle's clothes and possessions. As she opened the lid, however, she saw that the first shoebox wasn't empty.

On the very top were receipts, guarantees, and a notebook. Opening it with an uncomfortable sense of intrusion, Kate saw that it was a household reminder, of dates for servicing and insurances, kept in neat columns. As she put the book back, she noticed that, underneath, were a few photographs.

They were black-and-white. In the first, a very much younger Isabelle stood in a shorn, early version of the luxuriant garden outside; Isabelle at thirty or thirty-five, shading her eyes from the sun, a garden fork in one hand.

The next was a woman that Kate didn't recognise, sitting at a table, reading a newspaper, with a rather dour expression. There was something of Isabelle, Kate thought, in the squarish shoulders, and in her colouring. Next to the woman, half cut off in the photograph, sat a small boy. His hand could be glimpsed on the table top, stretched, as if trying to catch the woman's attention.

Kate brought out the half-dozen photographs, and, sitting down on the floor of the landing, she spread them out.

Here was Isabelle in another, strange garden, one cropped suicidally neat with a few thirsty plants in undug borders. The house behind was very small. A high wood fence separated it from its neighbours. Isabelle's hands were clasped in front of her. Again, it was from the same period: perhaps late 1950s. This time, the sun did not shine in the photograph. It was an overcast day, and Isabelle, her face bare of any expression at all, stood rigidly in a dark suit.

Kate looked at the very last picture.

It was one of those taken on a seafront, by a photographer touting for business. Isabelle and the other woman—who looked several years older than her—were walking along a promenade. It was nowhere local; behind them were steep cliffs. Isabelle and the woman were talking—an animated, even angry, conversation. Holding the other woman's hand was the little boy; older now, about eleven or twelve. He looked miserable, his face turned in profile towards the sea.

Kate turned the pictures over. There was nothing on the back of any of them. She wondered who the woman was. Stacking them together, with the last on the top, she looked again closely at the trio.

There was something familiar about the boy.

His hair was fairish. He was untidy—almost uncared for. She noticed that one of his shoelaces was undone. He looked thoroughly miserable, and was pulling on the hand that gripped him as if he wanted to get away.

'Who are you?' Kate wondered aloud.

She stood up, edging the boxes and paired shoes back into the cupboard before she closed it.

FORTY-SEVEN

*I*T WAS HALF-PAST SIX when Andrew Manners made his way down-stairs from his sitting room into the ground-floor room that he used as his office.

He switched on the light and began searching the top of his desk, untidy and littered with unread mail, now that he had been away from it for only two days.

'Bloody place,' he said to himself, as he sifted the files. 'Can't function if I get behind. Can't function.'

He continued muttering furiously to himself until the light on the stairway went on, and his wife's strident voice echoed down the steps.

'What on earth are you doing?' she demanded.

'Looking for something,' he said.

He heard her come down, tut-tutting under her breath. 'Really!' she exclaimed, coming in the door. 'I leave you for two seconds . . .'

'I have to find this file.'

'You have to find nothing. You ought to be in bed. Your tempera-ture was 101.'

He waved his hand dismissively. 'It's a cold, Martha, not the Black Death. I *must* find this. I ought to have sent it out.'

She regarded him resignedly. 'Your cold became pneumonia last winter, but I don't suppose you need reminding of that,' she said. She gave an enormous sigh. 'What are you looking for?'

'Browning. Isabelle Browning.'

'Let *me* look.' She pushed him into the chair while she sorted methodically. 'Here it is,' she said, holding up a brown envelope folder. 'Right under your nose.'

'Is there a letter inside?' he asked.

She looked. 'Yes.'

'Addressed to Kate McCaulay?'

'Yes.'

'I want to post it. I should have done it days ago. It was tucked in the back and I forgot to give it to her.' He made a move to get up; his wife, coming swiftly across the room, promptly pushed him down again. 'No, you don't!'

'I'm going out to post it.'

'*I'll* post it.'

'I want it in the Sheldrake Lane box. It's got a seven o'clock collection.'

She pursed her lips. 'If I post it, will you get back in bed?' she demanded.

He looked from the envelope to her face, then admitted defeat. 'Oh, all right,' he muttered.

She put the folder into an envelope, wrote on the address that he dictated, and, giving him a last warning look, went out into the hall.

FORTY-EIGHT

*I*T WAS VERY EARLY THE NEXT MORNING, before seven, when the phone rang in The Linen House.

Kate, fast asleep, woke with a jolt and a sense of complete disorientation. The old phone in the downstairs hallway had a shrill, rattling tone. She listened to it, head back, staring at the ceiling, for a second, before she scrambled out of bed, and, pulling on her dressing gown, ran downstairs barefoot.

'Hello . . . yes?'

There was a pause, an intake of breath.

'Yes . . . who is it?'

'Hello, Kate.' It was Jonathan's voice. 'I thought I might find you there.'

'Oh . . . hello,' she murmured.

'How are you?'

'OK . . . I'm OK.'

'Thank goodness for that. I've been worried.'

She heard his solicitous tone, and blushed. 'Yes . . . I'm sorry, Jonathan. Sorry for rushing out like that. Did you get my note?'

'Yes,' he said. And then he laughed, very low. It was a kindly sound. 'What was the hurry?'

'Well . . .' She ran her fingers over the carved banister ahead of her, embarrassed. 'I went to London with Jack Seward. We had some news about Jamie.'

There was another fractional silence. 'Really? What kind of news?'

'A girl who might know where he is.'

'But that's wonderful, Kate.'

'Yes. It's a shot in the dark, but . . .'

'Can I come and see you? You can tell me all about it.'

She paused, making a face of extreme self-consciousness into the receiver.

'Wouldn't you like to see me, Kate?'

'Of course, but—'

'You want some time to yourself?'

'Yes,' she answered at once. 'I want a bit of time to myself.'

'All too much, too soon?'

'Yes.'

'I understand.'

He said nothing else. She raised her eyes to the ceiling, helpless. 'Look, Jonathan, I truly am sorry. I'm a bit overwhelmed.'

'I understand.'

'It was getting very rushed, and—'

'Darling, I *understand*.'

She smiled. 'I know.'

'Look, could I buy you a coffee?'

'Pardon?'

'I've got to come over your way today. I have to see a client in Wolverham at ten. Let me come over early, and I'll buy you a coffee in that horrible old tea room in the village. They're still there, I take it?'

'Yes,' she said. 'But—'

'About half nine?' His voice came down the line, low and soothing. 'Neutral territory. All right?'

'Yes,' she said. 'All right.'

'Marvellous,' he said. 'See you soon, then.' And he hung up.

She put down the phone, and looked at it anxiously. 'Oh, bloody, bloody hell,' she muttered.

FORTY-NINE

As JACK PUT THE PHONE DOWN after speaking to the agency early that morning, it immediately rang again.

'Jack? It's Eddie Bates.'

Eddie worked at the *Journal*.

'Hello, Eddie. How's it going?'

'I've been trying to get in touch with you for days.'

'I've been away. What's the problem?'

'No problem. Just want to pick your brains. Did you hear about Bartlett?'

'No. What?'

'Sacked for incompetence. We've got a new boy now. More your style, Jack.'

'Oh?'

'You ought to come in and see him. Off chance. You never know.'

Jack pursed his lips. 'I'll think about it. What can I do for you?'

'It's this George Dale. I wondered if you knew anything about him. Would he do an interview?'

'Shouldn't think so. How would you get to him?'

'That's what I want to ask you. He won't come to the door.'

256

'Come to the—' Jack did a double take. 'You mean he's out?'

'Yeah . . .'

'On bail? For murder?'

'Forty-seven years, mate.'

Jack pressed his fingers to his forehead. 'Just a minute. What forty-seven years? He's out on bail for the murder of Isabelle Browning.'

Eddie Bates laughed. 'Behind the times, Jack. George Dale is out on bail for the murder of some old bloke he walloped forty-seven years ago, when he was a kid.'

Jack took this in open-mouthed for a second. 'And Isabelle Browning?'

'They're still looking.'

'What about Maggie Spence?'

'Still looking . . . though the word is there's some sort of new forensic evidence. Helped free George Dale. DNA, and fingerprinting. The fingerprint stuff is interesting, apparently; my little bird tells me it's the same prints at Maggie Spence's flat and at Isabelle Browning's house. And there was some hair—not Dale's—in Mrs Browning's fist. They're still following it up.'

Jack stared at the opposite wall, his mind drifting, circulating around the image of Kate. Eddie's voice again broke into his train of thought.

'I wanted to ask Dale if he'd give us his story after he's come to trial. After all, it'd probably be a probation job, after all this time . . . Jack? You still there?'

'Yes,' Jack replied. 'Look, I don't know him. Sorry.'

'I thought he was Kate's landlord. Can't raise *her* either.'

'No,' Jack said absent-mindedly.

'Going for a drink in the Crown on Friday?'

'Probably.'

'See you there, then.'

'OK. See you there . . .'

Jack put the phone down slowly. He got up, walked to the kitchen, filled the kettle, and stood next to it, his hand on the switch, unmoving.

How did the bracelet get to Isabelle's house? he was thinking.

Who took it from Kate's car?

FIFTY

*I*T WAS HALF-PAST EIGHT when the front doorbell rang in The Linen House.

Kate went to the door, wiping her hands on a tea towel. She had already begun cleaning the kitchen. Going into the front room first, she saw the post van parked outside, and the postman standing on the step.

She went back to the front door, and opened it.

'Morning,' he said. 'Can't get this through the box.' He handed her a large, thick brown envelope.

'Oh, thanks,' she said, taking it. She looked at the letter box in Isabelle's front door. 'It isn't very wide, is it?'

'I always have to knock,' he said. He was a large man of about sixty, with a friendly and very florid face. 'You're Miss—' He tipped his head, and looked again at the envelope. 'Miss McCaulay?'

'That's right.'

'Taken it over after Miss Browning?'

'Yes—'

Kate, smiling as she talked to him, glanced over his shoulder. She was standing on the step, at an angle, and she had a view of the street and the small square with its memorial cross. A movement there caught her attention.

Her own car had emerged from a side turning, and was drifting to a stop at the end of the pavement beyond the house. As she watched in amazement, Jonathan got out, and waved to her. He held up the keys, and jangled them in his hand, as if to show her that he had brought her a present. Then, he walked quickly towards her.

'You've filled out the form?' the postman was saying.

'Form?' Jonathan was smiling at her.

'There's a form for a change of address, so that all your mail gets redirected.'

Jonathan stepped up on to the pavement outside the house. His smile was absolutely fixed, broader than ever. Behind him, the village street lay silent, blocks of highlighted colour in the early morning sun.

'Yes,' she replied, not taking her eyes off him. 'I know, I—'

'Hello, darling.' Jonathan stepped up beside her, putting both hands on her shoulders, and kissing her, lingeringly, on the lips.

She stepped back.

'I'll be getting on,' the postman said, grinning.

Jonathan had walked into the house, brushing past her, almost pushing her off balance. The postman crossed the road. Kate stood with the door still open, looking back at Jonathan in the hallway.

'Well, it *is* a lovely place,' he said.

She didn't move from the step. 'I thought you said half-past nine,' she replied.

'Come in,' he said. 'You'll catch cold.'

She hesitated. There was something different about him, and she tried to think what it was as he stood there with his hands in his pockets and that old disarming look on his face. Her eyes wandered over him, and came to rest on his feet, and shoes with a border of mud.

'Who's your letter from?' he asked.

Distracted, she glanced away. There was no franking mark on the plain envelope, but it was intriguingly heavy. Glancing momentarily again at the street, she closed the door.

'I don't know.'

'Why don't you open it?'

She began to, and, taking out the blue file inside, saw that there was a short, hastily written note pinned to the cover. It was from Manners, Isabelle's solicitor. Or rather, from his wife.

Andrew wanted you to see this straight away. Miss Browning has left a letter for you.

Kate stopped, looking up. 'Why did you come so early?' she asked. 'Who's your letter from?'

'Mr Manners.' She put the file back into the envelope. 'Why did you come so early? Why did you come in my car?'

'I've got something for you,' he said.

'Jonathan—'

'You wanted it back, didn't you?'

'What?'

'The car.'

'But how will you get to your client?'

'I've got something for you,' he insisted, and took a piece of paper out of his pocket, and held it out to her.

She frowned; then, grudgingly, walked to him, and took it. It was folded, and opening it, she saw the coat of arms of the local County Council, and the address of the registry office. Under her name and Jonathan's, was tomorrow's date and a time, nine a.m.

'What's this?'

'Can't you guess?'

Something sank inside her. She felt a weight, a dead weight, the freezing grip of something solid and intractable, turn her blood sluggish, slow her heart. She closed her eyes for a second, then looked up.

'Tell me what it means,' she said.

He didn't reply. Instead, he began shaking his head sawingly from side to side, with that *well, I can't believe you haven't the wit to work it out* look.

'Tell me,' she repeated.

He astonished her by remaining motionless and silent, with the smile fastened in place. Staring at him, she realised in one flash of recognition what was wrong, what was different about him. He wore a shirt whose collar was dirty, and a sweater that, now she was close to it, smelled damp.

She stepped back instinctively, towards the door.

'You don't mind about the dress?' he said.

'Sorry?'

'The dress,' he said. 'Your dress won't be ready.'

She held out her hand, palm outwards, in a refusing, retreating gesture. In two steps, he was upon her, and had gripped her wrist.

'Let go,' she said. But the words were swallowed in a gasp for breath.

'Are you going to marry me?' he asked.

She looked into his face, her pulse rising rapidly. There was no escaping the truth now. 'No,' she said.

He brought his thumbs to the base of her throat, his fingers circling the back of her neck, and his thumbs instantly pressing inwards.

She dropped the envelope, and brought both hands to his, but, as she tried to wrench the thumbs away, he squeezed hard. She snatched at breath for a second, then tore at his grip. The air was gone, replaced with a burning sensation. She slammed back against the door and thrashed from side to side, losing her footing and slipping to the floor. He stood over her, never releasing his hold, as she kicked at him.

Then, as suddenly as he had started, he stopped. Both hands flexed open at once, and Kate slumped on the inner stone step, gasping and retching.

She thought he had quit—regretted his anger, was moving back to help her up, his mouth framing an apology. Instead, he picked up the brown envelope, turned it upside down, and let the pieces fall to the floor. He opened the file, and took out a long white envelope addressed to Kate in Isabelle's looping, stylised hand. Jonathan dropped the folder, wrenched open the letter, taking out two sheets of paper, running his eye quickly over them both.

For a while, there was no reaction at all.

Then, he began to laugh.

It never progressed beyond a small, hitched snigger, but rolled on and on as he continued to read. He turned the page. The amused sound in his throat was that of a small boy smirking at something smutty. At one or two points, he shook his head.

Kate lay staring at him, feeling the cold draught under the door at her back. She wondered if she had shut it completely; if she could reach behind her and prise it open.

Jonathan looked up. 'A nice little history,' he said. 'Want to see it?'

'No,' she said.

'No? Why not?'

Kate's voice emerged as a broken, breathy note. 'Not now.'

'I think you should.'

'No, I—'

'You should.' He crumpled the letter into a ball, and threw it at her. It hit her in the face. She was too astounded, too shocked, even to raise her hand.

I must get out, she thought. I must . . .

'Get up,' he said.

She looked at him, her mind racing around her best option. She had heard somewhere that any attacker relished resistance. She started to lever herself from the floor, but she had not been quick enough.

He grabbed her hair at the back of her head. She let out a cry—her hair was short, and his nails dug into her scalp, and she could feel the hair pulling out at the roots. He took hold of the front of her head with his other hand, and pulled her.

She screamed. The pain was blinding, white. Her hands fluttered over his, the muscles in the back of her neck stretched to tearing point. He pulled her, by the hair, up the first few steps of the stairs, as her feet scrambled for purchase on each tread. She felt for the stairs, the wall—anything to relieve the pressure on her scalp. All the way up, he walked at a near-normal speed, but backwards, as if performing some ordinary, if rather awkward task. She thought she heard him make a tut-tutting sound: impatience, disgust. He threw her along the landing.

She lay for a second, eyes squeezed shut in agony, unable to believe the searing pain in her head.

'You must marry me,' he said. She opened her eyes. He was standing over her, his arms crossed. She had a foreshortened view of his body, his downturned face.

She pushed herself back, into the corner.

He was on her in a flash, picking her up by the same torturing method.

'No!' she screamed.

He kicked open the door to the bathroom, and kicked it closed behind them. Still holding her hair with one hand, he began to run water into the deep sink.

'No—no,' she said. She squirmed, feeling the hair tear with a prickling like hot needles. Her eyes streamed. He lost his hold, and she punched him, as hard as she could, missing her aim slightly, in the stomach. It didn't look as if he felt it. She launched herself at the door and succeeded in opening it halfway before he held her from behind, swung her round, and plunged her head into the water.

It was hot.

Not scalding, but hot.

She was submerged perhaps only four or five seconds, while he pinned her against the sink with his body. He pulled up her head, and she gasped for breath, her face burning. He pushed her down again and she swallowed water, propelling it straight into her lungs as she tried to shout.

Sound buzzed in her ears, high notes swarming with colours. Her hands tingled. She coughed underwater, and liquid poured into her throat.

Jamie sprang into her mind. Jamie in her arms, in one of his rare moments of peace, looking up into her face. No imprint of knowledge or opinion in that searching look. Just for a second, she felt herself detached from her body, drifting loose, all sensation fixed on the lost picture of her child gazing soundlessly into her face, the blue of his eyes becoming tinged with hazel at the rim. She felt him in her hands, as part of her.

The scourge of the hot water was gone, the constriction in her throat and chest. The floor was dreamily moving in a wave to meet her. A voice rolled in.

'You must *listen*,' he was saying. 'You resist all the time, you don't listen . . .'

He stepped backwards. She looked up at him.

Then he slid down the opposite wall and put his face in his hands.

She watched him. There was no way out unless it was past him. She coughed; her chest was on fire. Huddled in the corner with the sink above her, she waited, trying to see anything in the room that she could use against him.

'You have to be different,' he murmured. 'You think you know best.' He looked up, wiping his face with the back of one hand. 'All of them listen. But not you.'

She stiffened. His gaze was focused beyond her.

She thought of the locked cabinet in his attic. *All of them. All of them.*

Quite suddenly, he glanced up. The absence had vanished from his expression; his eyes bored into her.

'You have to listen,' he said, evenly. 'I don't want to start over.'

'Start . . . ?'

'You're pushing me back. Because you don't do what I tell you. You push me back, I don't want to repeat. I want to do it the other way. I don't want to . . . Do you remember Peter Doherty?' he asked suddenly.

'Who?'

'Do you *remember*?' he insisted. His fist slammed the floor. 'You're the journalist, you're the journalist. Think. Peter Doherty.'

'No, I don't remember.'

'The woman in the park. The Italian tourist. The park off Caversham Square.'

'No . . . no, I . . .'

'When you worked in London.'

She said nothing; he laughed in disgust. 'Too many to remember,' he said.

'You knew her?' Kate asked.

'She had a chance, if they had got to her quickly enough. The man ought to have seen it.' He shook his head. 'He just walked past.'

He was shaking, very slightly, but completely—his hands, legs, head. Even his feet on the sodden carpet. Shaking. Incredibly, as she stared at him, fear now inching through her, colder with every second, he reached into his pocket and took out a neatly folded handkerchief.

'You are Peter Doherty?' she asked.

Fragments. Fragments of recall.

Just before Jamie went missing. The photofit picture on the front page of the *Evening Standard*. The description from an office worker who had seen a man leave the covered bench, and who had looked him straight in the face as he walked away.

He smiled.

That's how the office worker remembered him.

Jonathan wiped his face; and then blew his nose, as precisely and slowly and carefully as always, though his fingers bunched the material, his fingertips dancing in their own uncontrollable rhythm.

'You are Peter Doherty,' she repeated.

Not a question this time.

'I was in Brixton for a while,' he said. 'And then an open prison, after six years. In there, I had . . .' This time, the pause was very long. He froze, looking at the floor, a small reflective smile on his trembling face. Small muscles at the corner of his eyes and over his forehead convulsed rapidly under the skin.

He began to speak in his smooth, featureless monotone. 'I read about you when I was on remand,' he said. 'I saw your photo in the paper. For weeks. They sucked that story dry. I was sick of seeing it . . .'

He shook himself, as if to rid himself of the thought.

'What . . . what did you have?' Kate asked.

'Have?'

'You said, in prison, you had . . .'

He nodded. 'Guess.'

A broken sound escaped her. 'No . . .'

'Psychotherapy. I had psychotherapy.'

She looked at his smile.

'Psychoanalysis. Therapy. Visualisation. All the techniques. All the techniques.' He sighed. 'I came out four years ago. I set up a practice in London. I had a lot of ladies, and some came to see me once or twice, and some came more often, and those that came more often . . .'

'You killed,' Kate said.

He raised an eyebrow, then laughed. This time, it was a note of pure amusement and humour. The sound rose in a high crescendo. She had really delighted him.

'Killed?' he said, putting his hand on his chest. 'I don't kill anyone,

265

Kate. You see, I don't want to go back to Doherty. Too messy, too short, too obvious. My other way is so much easier, so much more interesting . . . you see? I don't need to kill them outright.' His eyes glittered with a frozen light. 'They kill themselves.'

He recovered only slowly, repeating to himself, 'Kill themselves . . . kill themselves . . .'

Then, he laid his arms across his drawn-up knees, folding each hand neatly on to the opposite arm.

'It's very unsatisfying,' he continued. 'A minute or so to murder someone, and eight years in prison. Ridiculous. Don't you think?' She could not reply. 'Better to disable them, send them out with a permanent weakness.'

'A destruction you can't see.'

'Well, there's pleasure in knowing that all those little time bombs are ticking somewhere out there . . .' He lifted his head and looked at her.

'But you would be linked—if your patients all destroyed themselves—'

'Well, I move around. Every couple of years or so. And they don't . . . not all. Just the few who have scope. A capacity to self-destruct. That fatal, entertaining weakness.'

She returned his look, and his silence, for some time. Then, she asked, 'Did you write the letters about Jamie?'

He raised his hand and pointed at her. 'Now, here's an interesting thing,' he said. 'Can you imagine what the effect would be if you sent a letter like that to every single person in one street?'

'No,' she said.

'Think about it. Perhaps not those words. They were for you personally. But not even a sentence. Let's say, something like . . . *I know.* Just that. *I know.* Put a letter through a hundred doors, unsigned, with just that one sentence.'

She felt sorrow pushing hard at her throat, tightening and constricting her breath: the weight of unwept tears. 'You wrote them,' she murmured.

'But you see my point?' he replied. 'Why was the first letter about Jamie? You leaped to the worst conclusion straight away. Just as those people in those hundred houses would leap to the worst conclusion. "My God!" they would say. "I've been found out! Someone *knows!*"' He shrugged contempt. 'If you think about it—think about the first letter—Jamie wasn't mentioned. You just assumed the worst. You *assumed* they were about Jamie.'

'But you—'

'Oh yes, I sent them. I sent the phrase that would disturb you most. But you—*you* did the most damage with your own reaction.'

She stared at him, horror possessing her in every particle. 'Is he alive?' she whispered. 'Where is he?'

He smiled. 'Oh, I don't know where he is. I never did. It was simply the phrase most likely to hurt you.'

Rage stung her, obscured her vision for a moment.

'Aren't you going to say, "Why me?"' he asked. 'Or—let's see— "How could you?"'

She said nothing.

He leaned forward and crawled to her, across the six feet of floor, on his hands and knees.

'That's what I do love about you, Kate,' he said. 'Despite you resisting me the way you do, I love you for that same resistance.'

She recoiled from him.

He stroked her thigh.

'Do you realise that I first heard your name in this house two years ago?' he asked.

'In . . . this house?'

'That's right. When I came to see Isabelle.'

'You knew Isabelle?'

'Of course. She was my aunt.'

The boy in the picture.

'I knew his face,' she murmured.

'In all the nice photos?' he asked. 'Isabelle and my mother didn't really get on. We met up for the occasional day or two, but my mother didn't approve of Isabelle's affair, and . . . well, being Mother, never let her forget it. But the fact remains—' his face clouded visibly, 'I was her only living relative.'

Kate sat forward abruptly. 'The letter downstairs—'

'Tells you all this. She cut me off, you see. After I was convicted. A house like this, an estate worth all this money, and suddenly I wasn't fit to inherit it. Her only living relative. Such a good boy I was, too. All my life I had been nice to Isabelle. And then she dismisses me. She wants to give it to a . . . *friend*.'

'The bracelet . . .' Kate murmured. Her thoughts were racing ahead to George's arrest.

'I took it from your car, that first afternoon you came to see me, when you were asleep,' Jonathan said. 'I thought it would get Dale off my back. Off *your* back, Kate. I'd done my research, you see.'

'But—' Kate shook her head in disbelief. 'Why do you want this house? You've got money. Kilcot Down is worth—'

'That's not the point! I've earned Kilcot. I earned it listening to women, hours and hours at a time. But this—this house is my right. Not yours.'

Kate stared hard at him. 'That's why you wanted me? Why you wanted to marry me? To get the *house*?'

'The estate. Don't forget the house in London, and the investment accounts. That, combined with the ultimate lure of you, Kate. Taking you to little pieces, Kate. What could be better? More lovely?'

'But—' She could hardly comprehend it.

He patted her knee. 'I couldn't believe my luck when you actually came to the door. I was all ready to come to you—walk in at the height of your grief over Maggie and the letters—*and you came to me.*' He shook his head, laughing. 'A stroke of luck.'

She thought aloud. 'You tried to engineer a breakdown, to—'

'Make myself indispensable, at exactly the right psychological moment.' He nodded. 'You have to admit, I was right. Absolutely one hundred per cent right, in my estimate of how you would react.'

'But . . . Maggie . . .'

He turned his face away from her, showing the first sign of real disturbance and irritation. 'She was a mistake. Too needy,' he said.

Kate heard herself take two long, deep breaths; but the racing and pounding in her head did not slow for a second. 'Maggie was murdered by a married man,' she whispered. 'She told me he was married . . .'

He made a brushing-away movement, in the air. 'She would *cling*,' he said. 'Not even that would make her back off.'

'You murdered Maggie,' Kate whispered. 'And Isabelle. To make me depend on you. To break me?' Appalled disbelief filled her voice.

His expression changed.

He stood up. She, too, scrambled to her feet. She glanced at the closed opaque glass window over the bath. Much too narrow to get through, even if she could break the pane. He stepped forward. Her glance fell rapidly through the narrow room, finding nothing to pick up, to use against him.

He looked her over, contempt and confusion distorting his features. 'Why don't you break?' he asked. 'You should break . . . you should *break*. That's the game.' She saw the ultimate detachment, the dislocation from any human feeling, in his face. A look that she had seen, in parts, in brief moments, before and taken for calmness and control, now revealed itself as an unfathomable vacancy.

'That was the point, the *appeal*,' he continued. Lightly. Smoothly. 'Because you were special, I was prepared to go back to that whole—' he fought for a second for the exact words—'that whole *inaccurate art* of murder. I didn't want that. It was for you. You ought to have been spectacular. A longer fall than most. More suffering to uncover. You ought . . .' He walked forward, frowning. 'Why *don't* you break?'

Kate flattened herself against the wall, her fists balled behind her back, watching him.

'Tell me!' he demanded.

She flinched, gasping in her effort to breathe. 'Because I got to the bottom,' she told him at last, 'where there was nowhere else to go. Where there was no one else. Long before you met me.'

He pulled a face. 'That makes you more vulnerable.'

'It doesn't.'

'It should, it—'

'No,' she cried. 'You don't see it yet, do you? You couldn't see it before. You—' And this time it was she who advanced on him, making him retreat a step. They were within an inch of each other. 'You can't touch me, Jonathan,' she told him. 'Because I've had the worst. No matter what you do to me, you can't make a deeper mark.'

He remained perfectly still.

She felt the time slowly ticking into minutes, totalling against him and the impulse that had dragged her by the hair and tried to drown her.

'I went to visit someone one day,' she said. 'A friend I had known in college. They lived in Sussex. I went by train. It was February, and when I got off the train it was dark.'

In her mind's eye, she saw the platform again, a deserted strip under a single yellow light. Enamel signs on an old station. A flight of steps up to the ticket office.

'I had been in the last carriage,' she said. 'The platform was slippery with ice. By the time I got close to the steps, the train had pulled out. I looked ahead, and I could see the line, curving under a bridge, and off towards the right, out of sight, with high embankments on each side . . .'

She lifted her head, as if drawing breath through that remembered cold.

'There was a slope from the platform down on to the line. I looked up the stairs, and there was no one waiting for my ticket.'

She began to shake.

'I walked forward, under the bridge. Down the slope. On to the stones at the side of the line. Along a little way, around the bend. Into the dark.'

She gave a brief, empty smile. 'I thought that any second someone would call me back. But no one did. I walked on for about two hundred yards, past the lights. Looking for a point where the train would have picked up speed. Where there was absolutely no light to let the driver see me. I looked at the line . . . very smooth. Very smooth and clean, sitting on top of the sleepers. As smooth as a knife. I sat down. And then I kneeled. And I thought of Richard, and my mother, and of the friend whose house I was supposed to be walking to.'

But they didn't matter.

She closed her eyes.

'And I thought . . .'

Of Jamie.

She had thought of him lying in another woman's arms. Thought of him growing in another woman's house. Thought of him on the day he began school. The day he learned to cycle, or tie his laces, or count, or play football. Thought of him, in ever-expanding pictures, stretching ahead on the smooth blade of rail, at thirteen, fourteen. Thought of him as an unknown adult . . .

'I got up, and walked back,' she said.

She opened her eyes.

'You can't break me,' she said slowly. 'Because I want to see Jamie again. Because I hope to see him. There . . . that is your truth you asked for.' Her eyes ranged over his face. 'Whatever you intended, you've given me something,' she said softly. 'I don't dream about the house or those steps any more. I dream about Jamie. As he would be now. You've done the opposite from what you intended, Jonathan. That's the irony,' she told him. 'You've brought us back from the dead.'

They looked at each other.

'And the reason that you can't break me,' she added, 'is because there is nowhere that you can send me that is worse than where I've been.'

He remained absolutely still for a second, then a change came over him. His mouth parted, and his tongue rested lightly on his lips. To her amazement and disgust, she saw lust in his expression.

'Tell me again,' he murmured. And the smile—the terrible, masking smile stretched across his face, the very embodiment of fathomless cold—hit her, contaminated her with its unconscionable cruelty. He extended his hand, the hand that had touched her so often. 'I want to know how it feels,' he said. 'That's what I want from all of you . . . that's what I want . . .'

She hit him, with her fist, between those empty eyes.

He staggered back a pace, making a small grunting sound of surprise.

She pushed him, wrenching open the bathroom door, running out on to the landing. The walls around her seemed to balloon and waver; the stairs rocked. She put her foot on the first and slipped, getting her balance only halfway down. She heard him open the door above her, shouting her name.

At the bottom of the stairs, she saw the keys of the car where he had left them, next to the phone.

All she could think of was that, if she ran along the quiet street, he might catch up with her, and bring her back.

She snatched up the keys, flung open the front door, and ran. He had locked the car door, and, as she fumbled with the keys in the lock, he came out of the house.

'Kate!' he shouted.

She got into the car, slammed the door, locked it, and started the engine. It roared into life; she engaged reverse, leaning with one arm on the seat and looking behind her. As the car leaped backwards, another vehicle appeared around the corner, heading straight for her.

'Jesus!' she whispered.

The oncoming car swerved and bounced as it hit the opposite pavement. In her panic, she had not taken her foot off the accelerator, and she had a momentary image of the other driver as she catapulted backwards. Her own car slewed in the road, and stalled.

'Oh, please, please, God . . .' she begged. She looked down at the dashboard, turning the key, pumping the gas. It restarted and she put it into first, releasing the clutch.

It was the work of two or three seconds.

The car raced forward, she stood on the accelerator . . . and Jonathan walked out into the road, holding up his hands.

On the opposite side of the street, Jack Seward jumped out of the other car.

He saw Kate, white-faced, look up only at the last moment. And Jonathan Reeve stock-still in the car's path, his face perfectly calm, the attitude of his body relaxed, as if confident that she could be commanded.

That, even now, she could be stopped.

Kate's car hit Jonathan at speed, pushing his body over the bonnet, and dragging it for a moment. Just for a split second, she caught sight of his face in front of her, through the windscreen. Caught the last look of his life—a smile of implacable arrogance.

Before the impact dragged his body down, crushing him under the wheels.

POSTSCRIPT

*F*OUR MONTHS LATER, in another car, in another country, Kate McCaulay sat waiting.

She stared at the houses, each set in its own perfect square of lawn; blinds were pulled against the day. A breeze blew down the street, scented faintly with oranges. Salt. Dust.

Four months since Jonathan had died; three months since the inquest verdict of accidental death, where Jack had supported her as a vital witness. A month since Kilcot Down House had been sold. She could still see, in her mind's eye, the chilling scene behind that small locked door in the attic; the typewriters, arranged in rows.

She closed her eyes.

Occasionally, the image of Jonathan, typing those letters to her on the machine that the police had matched, caught her unawares. At such times, she could only wait—wait, as she waited now—for the agony to pass.

Jack Seward, sitting beside her, suddenly put his hand on her arm to get her attention. 'She's coming into the drive now,' he said.

Kate opened her eyes.

In the bright sunlight, the station wagon bumped up the

entrance of the house opposite them on the corner, and came to a stop.

Meresamun Charles got out, sweeping her long dark hair back with one hand. She was laughing; talking. She opened the back door, reached in, and lifted out a toddler, a boy of about three. On the other side of the car, an older girl stepped out, and ran forward, with the keys of the house swinging from her fingers.

Jack and Kate, too, got out of their car, from the cool of air-conditioning into the heat of the Florida morning. Jack came round the car, and held out his hand.

Kate took it.

'Don't let Deo out,' the woman was calling. Her voice was mellow, relaxed. 'Abby—don't you let him out now, honey. You hear? Keep your foot in that door.'

They could hear a dog barking wildly inside the house. Jack and Kate turned off the sidewalk, into the driveway. At the side of the house, the lawn was littered with bikes, footballs. A volleyball net was strung inexpertly between two trees.

The woman let the toddler down, watching him as he ran towards the door.

Then she turned back to the car.

They were about ten feet from each other. For a moment, Meresamun raised her eyebrows questioningly. Then, the smile froze on her face. She went completely white. Her hand felt along the car for support.

'Mrs Charles?' Jack asked.

'Yes,' she said.

'My name is Jack Seward.' He turned, indicating Kate with his hand. 'And this is—'

The woman shook her head, her eyes fixed on Kate's face.

'That's all right,' she told Kate. 'I know who you are.'

They sat, an hour later, in the deep shadow on the back porch. Between them, untouched glasses of iced tea. In the yard, the youngest boy lay in a pushchair, asleep under the trees. From the house came the sound of a television.

'I knew you would come,' Merry was saying. She cried softly, unremittingly, without sound or contortion of her face, the tears spilling and streaming down. 'I waited for someone to come from the first day. We both did.'

She looked up. Kate was sitting silent, on the edge of the wicker seat, listening.

'I watched you. I watched the house for days. I can't excuse it by saying it was spur of the moment. It wasn't. I planned it. I had my passport. That morning, I saw you put Mark—I mean, James—into the car, and I saw you drive away . . . And I followed you.'

Her words were disjointed. She looked agonised. Guilty, terrified.

'I shouldn't have done it. I know . . . I've always known. I've thought of you, believe me . . . all the pain I've put you through . . .'

She put her hands to her face, pressed them there a moment.

'Everyone around me had babies. I needed a child. It was a sickness . . .' She shuddered, looking out at the boy in the shade of the tree. Then she turned her gaze to Kate. 'You won't understand . . . but this is a relief.'

Kate didn't comment. Jack, instead, asked the question.

'How did you hide him?'

Merry bit her lip. Her hands wrung unconsciously in her lap. 'I went straight from the motorway services to the port. We were only ten miles from Dover. There was a ferry right there, waiting to leave. I was incredibly lucky—'

She looked at them both, made a self-deprecatory grimace at her choice of words, then carried on. 'I put him in a holdall. I was so lucky that he didn't cry. Movement calmed him, I think. Just a half-hour later, and I'm sure I'd have been stopped. But I got into France, and drove to Germany. We had friends in Garmisch.'

'But surely they knew it wasn't your child.'

'Yes, they knew. I told them I had bought him.'

Jack and Kate looked at each other.

'I told them it was an East German deal. Strictly illegal, done through agents in Hungary. They never questioned it. Dealing with the East was a court-martial offence for our husbands. They kept everything quiet for six months. In that time, Michael bought a birth certificate. On Mark's . . . Jamie's . . . passport, it says he was born to me in Turkey, while we were on holiday.'

'My God,' Kate breathed.

'You sick, stupid people,' Jack said. To her surprise, Kate heard real emotion—sadness, not anger—in his voice.

Merry looked away from them. 'This has been a weight on our backs for ten years,' she murmured. 'You can never know . . .'

'Oh yes,' Kate said, heated, her restraint threatening to crack. 'I *know*.'

Merry nodded. She wiped her face. 'I realise that you can never forgive me,' she whispered. 'But, if it consoles you at all . . . I have loved your son. We both have. We have loved him so much.'

There was a moment of utter silence before she spoke again. 'You've told the police?'

'No,' Kate said.

'Over here, I mean. The State.'

'No.'

Merry's gaze flickered from Kate to Jack, and back again. 'But—when will you? Today?'

'No,' Kate said. 'We're not going to.'

The news hit the other woman like a blow. She rocked back in her seat, one hand clenched at her throat.

'We came here a week ago,' Kate said slowly. Her attitude in her own seat was still rigidly tense. 'We have all the documented proof from the agencies. The first thing we intended to do was to go to the police, the first morning.'

She thought back seven days, to her sleepless anxiety. Closer now to her child than ever, the old griefs stormed to the fore; she had felt numbed and lost, here, at the very edge of discovery. It was as if Jamie had only been taken yesterday.

She and Jack had not slept that first night. Their plane had landed at nine a.m., and their body clocks still insisted that it was the afternoon. They sat in a coffee shop, untouched food in front of them, until midday.

She had been going to come to this door. Knock on the door and demand her son. Scream for him until she woke the world. Jack had persuaded her that nothing ought to be done until they felt calmer. He had wanted to contact the police the next morning. At six, however, Kate had got up, and driven back alone, without him, conscious that she was rejecting his calming influence. Drawn by the same overpowering blind desire.

She had wanted to see Jamie alone.

The husband left for work at a few minutes before half-past seven. She had seen Merry come to the doorstep and pick up the paper.

It was an hour before Jamie had wheeled his bike from the back, just before eight. Kate had sat forward in the car, fingers white on the steering wheel. She had turned, to open her door.

And then, the little girl had run from the back porch, leaping towards Jamie with her arms outstretched. She had squealed with delight as he caught her, and he had whirled her around, swinging her upside down.

Kate wound down her window, to hear what they were saying.

'Around, around!'

Jamie had been laughing. He pitched her upright, cuffed her loosely on the chin. 'Want to throw up again? Over yuh new dress?'

It was a strong Southern American accent. That one thing stopped her hand depressing the handle of the door. Jamie spoke in the same tone as his Texan father.

She had watched, need knotting with painful desperation. She needed to run to him, touch him. She *needed*, she *wanted* to take him away. Just as he had been taken from her; soundlessly, without leaving a trace. Until that very moment, she had believed that was possible. In her subconscious mind, he was still someone who could be moved or carried as she wished—not a tall American boy with a mind of his own.

What would he say if she rushed up to him? Tried to hold him? Told him that she was his mother?

He would think she was insane.

So she watched him leave the house, bundle his sister back inside, wave to her all the way down the street.

She had gone back to Jack, found him in the hotel restaurant, and told him that she couldn't take Jamie away.

'Are you mad?' he had said. 'That's what we came here for!'

'I can't do it,' she said. 'I can't take him to England, uproot him from everything he knows. I can't make him suffer like that. I can't do it to his brother and sister.'

'Why do you think I looked for him from the start? To give him back to you.'

'I know. I know, Jack.'

'You told me, that first day, that Jamie was dead.'

'I know—'

He grabbed her hand. 'I knew you believed he was alive—somewhere. That's why I looked.'

She raised his hand to her cheek, rested her face on it. 'I can't repay you for everything you've done,' she said.

'I don't want repaying. I want you happy,' he said.

She looked at him with that old, direct, unwavering gaze. 'There isn't an all-happy way out of this,' she told him. 'If I'm happy, he won't be. And, in the end, that would make me miserable too. Back to the beginning. A different sort of pain.'

They had argued not for the day, but for the six days since. In that time, they had passed Jamie's school a dozen times; they had watched him, from a distance, play baseball. She had driven past this house, fighting with herself, with her divided instinct both to have him back, and to protect him against pain.

'She's a criminal,' Jack had said. 'She ought to be prosecuted.'

'Why?' Kate had asked. 'What's to gain from it?'

'Your child!'

'Yes . . . *my* child. And that's what it would all be about—me. Only me. Nobody would gain from it but me. I'd be happy—and everyone else's life would be destroyed. But this isn't about Meresamun Charles. If it were just her and me, I would strangle her with my bare hands. But it isn't just that. I don't care about her. It's *him*. Can't you see?'

'She's a danger. She could do it again.'

Kate had shaken her head forcibly. 'No. Not now. She has her other children now. We know they were through IVF, not abducted. She's no threat to society. She's a mother—*his* mother.'

'She can never be that.'

'Not biologically. But in every other way. And you've seen—*I've* seen—the way she looks at him, talks to him. She loves him. So does his father.'

'I can't believe I'm hearing this,' Jack had said.

She had bowed her head. 'Neither can I,' she admitted. And, that night—last night—she had cried for the first and only time. The tears were unstoppable. Jack had helped her from the bar, and they had stood on the dark sidewalk, his arms around her, while people in passing cars stared.

But, this morning, she had woken up with the decision formed in her mind. She had talked to Jack again, and explained what she intended.

She looked at Meresamun now, her hands folded calmly in her lap.

'I want you to tell Mark that I'm a friend of yours from Germany. Someone you met while you lived there.' She gave the merest ghost of a pitiful smile. 'I want you to tell him that I looked after him when he was very small. I want him to realise that I will be familiar in his life from now on. You will introduce me as a family friend—a kind of honorary aunt, if you like. Explain we are close. I want us to agree that you will never deny me access to him, and that I will never lose contact with him. He will never be out of reach. And, for my part of the bargain, I'll agree never to tell the police what really happened.'

Merry stared at her for some time. 'But what about his father? His real father?'

'I'll talk to Richard,' Kate said. 'And nothing will be final until he's been told where Jamie is. But . . .' she considered her words carefully, 'he has his own family now. Other considerations. I think he will want to see Jamie on the same basis as me. I can't imagine that he will want to tear Jamie away from everything he knows.'

Merry's face was still deathly white. 'You think . . . it's really the right thing to do?'

'No,' Kate replied coldly. 'But then, there isn't a right way out of this.'

Merry began to speak again, but she was interrupted.

They heard the sound of shouts in the street; a group of voices, one raised higher than the others in a chorus of goodbyes.

Merry Charles jumped up. 'He's home,' she said. Her gaze flitted anxiously to Kate. Fear was etched on her face.

The boy came around the side of the house, the bike skidding to a halt. He walked up to the porch, smiling, and threw his schoolbag along the floor.

'Mark,' Merry said. 'This is Kate Lydiatt . . . from England . . .'

'Hi,' he said.

He was very suntanned. She would remember what he wore: the grass-stained T-shirt, the jeans with the snake-shaped buckle, the Nike trainers threaded on one side with a green lace.

'She's a special friend . . .' Merry was saying.

None of the four had moved an inch. Kate saw puzzlement momentarily cross the boy's face as he glanced at his mother, heard her unusual tone, her trepidation.

'On holiday,' Kate said.

'Yeah? Great. Like Florida?'

'Yes . . .'

'Seen Universal?'

'Not yet,' Jack said.

Kate looked him over, shading her eyes against the sun.

Was it really him?

He looked too dark to be her son. His face too broad, now he was really close and she could see, to be related either to her or to Richard. Although he looked a little like a photograph she had once seen of Richard's father. The tracing by the agency had been meticulously thorough, but, even so . . .

Through the house, they heard the volume on the TV rise. Some programme was ending. Kate stood up, taking a step in Jamie's direction.

'Kate used to live in Garmisch, where we lived . . .' She could hear terror in Merry's voice.

She could say it now.

Now.

Fracture a dozen lives for ever.

I am your mother . . .

The musical pitch behind them leaped. Louisiana blues on fiddles and horn.

Mark Charles immediately stretched the fingers of his hands, then folded both under his armpits as if to shield them. 'Ouch, ouch,' he said, under his breath. He turned away, walking down the garden towards the pushchair. 'Hey, Brendon . . .' he called.

On the way, he lifted one hand, stroked the palm, wriggled the tips of his fingers. Kate stood watching him, the corresponding sensation of the synaesthesia tingling down her own wrists.

'Hello,' she whispered. 'Oh Jamie . . . hello.'

Jack came alongside her, stood with her.

Merry sat down, unable to speak, on the reed chair.

But Kate didn't see, or hear her. Every ounce of her attention was fixed on the figure of the boy lifting the sleeping child into his arms down the shadow-barred lawn.

Before she left, she thought, she would allow herself the luxury of touching her son.

Just one touch, as lightly as she was able, on his shoulder. As Jack was touching her now.